ROGUE FORTRESS

By John R. Monteith

Stealth Books

Table of Contents

CHAPTER 1

Jake Slate stood beside the Philippine naval commander, his arm shielding his face from the pelting rain. As he watched the fantail of the *Gregorio del Pilar* jerk and shake the helicopter, he balanced himself by extending his free hand towards a handrail welded to the converted frigate's superstructure.

"Let's do this," he said.

"This is the limit of safety for helicopter operations," the commander said in accented English.

"That doesn't bother me," Jake said. "I'm sort of an adrenaline junkie."

The commander remained silent, and as Jake glanced at him, he shrugged his shoulders.

"That means I like adventure."

"Every man likes adventure. Your plans appear to be of an entirely different category."

"Let's just say I'm fearless, as long as I don't think about what I'm doing."

"I was warned about your demeanor," the commander said. "From what I understand, you rarely think about what you're doing."

"You have a point."

"Your safety is not my concern since it is apparently none of yours. However, the safety of my helicopter crew concerns me."

"Come on! The weather isn't that bad. We're running out of time. We may not get another shot at this."

As the commander turned and opened a door into the ship, he snapped a response over his shoulder.

"I will order the flight crew to take off before my better judgment makes me change my mind."

Jake knelt and hoisted his Kevlar fabric equipment bag over his shoulder, and its straps pinched his wetsuit. He shifted the weight to his other arm, stooped, and yelled to the helicopter crew huddling in rain gear behind him.

Part of him, the invincible SEAL he had wanted to become

two decades earlier at the United States Naval Academy, compelled him to scream out something audacious.

But dignity curtailed his bravado as he recalled that he might again kill, despite any merciful intent, and he choked out a stark command to the Filipino men flanking him.

"Follow me, gentlemen" he said. "It's time."

He trotted, fighting the rolling of the fantail to reach the AgustaWestland AW109 helicopter. A man in a flight suit that he recognized as the crew chief opened the door, and Jake ducked into the aircraft. The remaining team boarded, and the flight crew won the battle with the elements to lift the vehicle skyward.

As the helicopter gained altitude, the frigate's slow rocking yielded to faster wind-whipped oscillations. The Philippine frigate, a revamped American *Hamilton*-class Coast Guard cutter, became a tiny toy tossed on wave tops as it receded over the horizon.

The aircraft reached ten thousand feet and cruised at one hundred miles an hour. Time advanced in quantum slices as a Filipino jumpmaster helped him don his gear.

Night vision goggles squeezed his wetsuit's hood, and a parachute clipped to a rebreather strained a strap across his back. A reserve chute at his chest balanced him, and a belt and torso harness connected him to a nylon rope coiled beside him. Under the weight of the equipment, he labored to breathe at altitude in the unpressurized cabin.

"Raise arms high," the jumpmaster said.

Jake reached for the overhead, and the straps pinched his shoulder. The jumpmaster, a full head shorter than him, buzzed around him adjusting fastenings and redistributing the equipment's mass. He reached under Jake's chin and wrapped a Velcro strip from his wetsuit's neck through the dangling face mask.

"To hold it when you jump," he said. "Raise arms again."

Jake felt tugging, releasing, and tightening as the man gave his ensemble a final adjustment.

"That's better," he said. "Thanks."

"Here," the jumpmaster said as he handed Jake a carbon dioxide canister.

In his arms, the cylindrical container surprised him with its softness.

"It's charged with the fentanyl-derived gas," the jumpmaster said. "Wrapped in foam with industrial tape, to prevent banging against metal."

Jake rolled the canister and saw the hose jutting outward and curving back into the wrapping where gray tape outlined the form of a conical nozzle.

"Looks great," he said.

The jumpmaster pointed his gloved finger at an inflection point in the tape's form.

"When you are ready, cut here with your knife."

Jake slapped his left thigh to verify it held his blade.

"Got it," he said.

"I am hooking it into your harness to assure that you do not drop it, but hold it while you descend. Make sure you hold it tightly when you enter the water, or else it will act like an anchor."

The jumpmaster slipped behind him and probed his back. A click filled the cabin, and Jake glanced up at his parachute's hook clinging to a static line.

Expecting his mouthpiece to render human speech useless, he relied upon a waterproof liquid crystal display wrapped around his forearm for communications with his jump partner. Shifting the canister under his arm and twisting his free wrist, he saw the green characters counting down the time remaining until his jump. It showed three minutes.

"The pilot has visual contact," the jumpmaster said.

"Where is it?" Jake asked.

"On the horizon."

Jake flipped his night vision optics into his view, looked through the open door, and scanned the green-hued seas.

"I don't see anything," he said.

"The helicopter's system sees it. It's right where it's supposed to be."

Jake glanced at his forearm display. Less than a minute.

"When do I jump?" he asked. "I mean how accurate is this countdown?"

"It's time now," the jumpmaster said. "Open."

He lifted a mouthpiece, and Jake bit down to clamp it in place.

"Stand at the edge."

His flippers dangling in the void outside the aircraft, Jake balanced at the door's lip as his heart pounded.

"Ready?" the jumpmaster asked.

Jake nodded.

"Go!"

A slap on the back accompanied the order, and Jake leapt into rain that had receded to a trickle. The free fall ended with the whipping sound of unfurling canvas as his chute wrenched him upward.

The instant heaviness of the repurposed fire extinguisher surprised him, and it slid from his arm. He spat out his rebreather mouthpiece.

"Shit," he said.

Cold droplets stinging his face, he bent forward and lowered his arms to the canister's cord. Hand over hand, he lifted the cylinder to his arm and pinned it against his ribs.

"I hope nobody saw that," he said.

His comment reminded him to scan the sky for his colleague. He flipped down his night vision, looked to his left, and saw a commando's body trace a green outline that the anti-thermal coating on his partner's wetsuit weakened.

Nylon at his belly yanked on his harness and pulled him towards the commando. A voice buzzed in the earpiece under his wetsuit's hood.

"I am pulling you left," the commando said.

Jake pressed a speaker under his hood against his throat.

"Can you see it yet?" he asked.

"No. But the helicopter crew is guiding us in. Don't worry. I could land on a postage stamp."

The view through Jake's goggles remained uninspiring until the liquid crystal display showed an altitude of three thousand feet. He looked up from his forearm display and saw the dark vertical shaft.

"I see it," he said.

"Can you see the feather?" the commando asked.

The tiny wake behind the submerged vessel's snorkel mast shimmered in the night vision-enhanced moonlight.

"I think so," Jake said. "Coming at us."

"Very good. Test your rebreather."

Jake flipped his night vision atop his head, lifted his mouthpiece to his teeth, and inhaled. He contorted himself to position his forearm under his canister and tap a button on his display indicating that his status was okay.

"I received your 'status okay' message," the commando said. "Prepare to disengage from your parachute on my mark. You will enter the water first."

Again, Jake tapped his 'status okay' button to acknowledge the order. His survival instinct compelled him to look down, but the black seas held no clue to his pending impact's timing. He trusted his colleague's guidance.

"You are at ten meters," the commando said. "Grab your disconnect."

Behind his ears, Jake interlaced the fingers of his free hand into a master ring.

"Five meters, four, three. Release your parachute. Pull now!"

Jake yanked the ring, freeing the chute. As he accelerated into free fall, he hugged his canister, pressing it against the reserve chute at his stomach. His fins smacked the water, and buoyancy tried to squirt the container from his arms. But he held as he submerged and then shot back to the surface.

When floating, he let the canister go, and it drifted by his head as he released his reserve chute and abandoned it to the swells. He then ripped his face mask from his neck, elevated it, and dumped water from it.

Tightening it to his face, he looked through it at his forearm. He tapped his 'status okay' button and waited to read a response from his colleague. Scant seconds passed, and his partner confirmed his safe immersion into the water.

Then came the command at his forearm to swim course three-three-zero.

Jake flipped onto his belly, studied the compass on his forearm display, and began kicking. The rebreather's air tasted stale as his breathing rate accelerated. As he gained speed, he tapped the 'three' button twice, the 'zero' button once, and then the 'acknowledged' button.

The nylon line connecting him to his swim partner rubbed against his ribs as he alternated kicks. The line to his trailing canister cut into his crotch.

Then came the lurch.

The nylon line snapped and pulled at the hook at his gut. Water flowed diagonally over his body, and he grabbed the nylon to right himself as it dragged him.

He reached for his forearm display and tapped the 'line engaged' button. Unwilling to become fodder for the submarine's propeller, he began climbing hand over hand up the line that dragged him, kicking to assist his movement.

Fear of the submarine, with its hazardous propulsion system and water intake valves, spurred him up the line. Grasping its first hard rubber grapnel signaled that he had climbed ten meters of its length. The distance to the submarine's snorkel mast remained a mystery as he pushed the grapnel aside and scurried up the moving rope.

Three grapnels later, the rope seemed more rigid. As he progressed forward, stronger water pressure pushing his face mask suggested his presence within the laminar layers flowing around the mast, and an eerie sensation informed him that the entirety of a Malaysian *Scorpène*-class submarine prowled below him.

His glove found the next grapnel, which offered a rigid rail for him to grab. He traced its shaft with his finger and felt the firm form of the snorkel mast.

The mast protected him from the water flow, and it offered him leverage as he shimmied upward and wrapped his ankles around its cylindrical shape. Having achieved his destination, he unhooked the nylon line from his harness. Feeling his thigh, he touched the hilt, withdrew his knife, and severed the now-needless section of rope that had dragged him.

His knife sheathed, he probed the far side of the mast and verified that the remaining rope held taut and dragged his commando accomplice.

He climbed, and flowing water yielded to a gentle breeze as his head broached. Running his fingers down the line attached to his harness, he pulled the trailing canister towards him. The motion became awkward as he hugged the mast with his right arm and yanked the line with his left to his immobilized right hand, length by length.

As the canister came within reach, a tug at his ankle startled him. Then he felt the Filipino climb up his back. Counting body parts, he felt two legs and one arm probing his body for leverage, and he figured that his accomplice dedicated his final limb to another canister.

He turned his head and saw a hooded head broach behind him in the moonlight. The commando spat his mouthpiece to talk, and Jake did the same.

"I told you I would land us perfectly."

"You're a stud," Jake said.

"Hold my canister."

Before Jake could respond, the commando wedged the second container under his arm. A knife appeared over his ear and began slicing through masking tape, exposing nozzles and handles.

Jake had planned for success if either man reached the mast, but he welcomed the company and the second canister. Teamwork would simplify the task and double the impact.

"You climb," Jake said.

"Okay. Hold tight."

The commando mounted Jake's back and locked his arms atop his shoulders. He then reached for the exposed mast and placed his knee beside Jake's neck. With graceful ease, the slim warrior slid up the cylinder and steadied his fins on either side of Jake's head.

"Canister please!" the commando said.

Jake fumbled with his hugging arm to hold his extinguisher underwater while gaining a firm grasp of the second container. He hoisted it high, and the commando grabbed it.

"I cannot reach," the commando said.

The weight on Jake's shoulders lifted, and he looked up to see his accomplice climbing with one arm up the mast. The sick feeling that the submarine's crew could decide to lower the mast and crush him under its fairing passed through his mind as he scaled higher to offer his partner secure footing.

"I'm high enough," the commando said. "Come support me."

Jake inched higher until he felt the fins resting on him again. He contorted his head and watched his partner hold the canister by its handle with his hugging arm. With his free arm, the warrior aimed the nozzle into the induction intake. He then squeezed the handle, and Jake heard the compressed fentanyl-based gas hiss into the submarine's thirsty intake.

As the hissing died, the commando dropped the expended container into the flowing water, and Jake handed him the other one. Again, incapacitating gases hissed into the submarine, and the warrior dropped the used extinguisher.

Silent steel concealed the crew's status, but Jake knew that the ventilation system channeled his gases throughout the submarine en route to the hungry diesel engines.

He assumed that nobody below him could reach emergency air in time to remain conscious, but if a handful of men had succeeded, they were likely tucked away in a remote corner of the ship, confused and frightened as their shipmates collapsed.

His accomplice returned to his back and spoke into his ear.

"Would you like to claim our success to the *Pilar*?"

"Sure."

The waterproof radio appeared in front of him. He grabbed it, moved it to his lips, and keyed its microphone.

"Home Base, this is Angel Team. Over."

He welcomed the familiar accent of his French friend and crewmate, Henri Lanier, who waited aboard the Philippine frigate.

"Angel Team, this is Home Base. Go ahead. Over."

"Home Base, Angel Team. It's good to hear your voice."

"Angel Team, Home Base. Agreed. What's your status?"

Jake smirked.

"Home Base, Angel Team. The package is wrapped. Come pick it up. I have a present for you."

CHAPTER 2

Jake recognized the gas attack's success as the Malaysian warship sank, slipping deeper into the oceanic abyss with undisturbed grace. A meter above him, the smooth fairing, designed to create a flush seal with the submarine when retracted, slid closer to his head as he and his partner crawled up the sinking induction mast.

"The frigate isn't going to get here before we go under," he said.

"I agree. It's still seventy minutes away."

The creepy concept of riding a sinking submarine spooked him.

"Do we have enough air?" he asked. "I mean, if the helicopter doesn't find us before we go under?"

"No," the commando said. "But the helicopter is close."

"How close?"

Sprinkling droplets, the commando's forearm broke the surface, and he glanced at the display.

"Ten nautical miles."

"We should be okay," Jake said.

Silent patience rewarded him with the chop of helicopter blades. With the incapacitated submarine crew, the aircraft had no need to stay high to separate its noise from the water, and the looming chopper became a hovering hurricane.

Violent wind and spray hit Jake's mask, and he welcomed his accomplice's skill in the hostile environment.

"Hold tight!" the commando said.

He hooked a rope to Jake's harness, bit his mouthpiece, and swam. Before Jake could assess the sanity of his partner's tethered swim in the tempest, he felt the commando's rope pulling at his chest, signaling his return swim to the mast.

A fresh canister from the helicopter under his arm, the commando appeared next to Jake and wrapped his free arm around the mast.

"Knife please!"

Jake reached to his thigh and obliged. The commando took the blade and sliced it through masking tape, revealing the handle and nozzle. After returning the weapon to Jake, he balanced the handle in his hand and discharged the canister into the intake. He then released the extinguisher to the seas and pulled a floating line to drag another one to him.

The commando discharged the next container, tossed it aside, and wiggled closer to Jake. He screamed in his ear over the whipped air.

"That should take care of any man who escaped the original gassing or who may have regained consciousness."

Jake leaned into his partner's hooded ear.

"No man regained consciousness," he said. "Not unless he's superhuman or a freak of nature."

"Must be prepared for superhuman freaks."

"Good point."

Jake tilted his head and nodded towards the head valve.

"When that thing hits the water, it's going to sense wetness and shut. It'll open again if it rises. We'll probably hear it cycle a few times on the way down."

On cue, the ocean obliged his prophecy, and a series of waves dragged the diesel intake into the water. Jake held his breath, trusting that he'd rise again, and the valve clinked shut above him.

Swells swept the inlet upward, and air rushed back into the submarine. The diesel engines' subtle, sound-insulated rumble remained audible through Jake's gloves.

"Perfect timing," he said. "This thing's going under, and the diesels will die soon."

"I agree."

The commando raised a radio to his mouth and yelled commands in a language foreign to Jake.

"I just ordered the helicopter to drop the buoy."

Jake felt the tug at his belt as his accomplice checked their connection, turned, and kicked away.

The ocean dragged him under, and he popped his rebreather's

mouthpiece between his teeth. He needed several breaths as the head valve labored to rise again.

Surfaced, he removed his mouthpiece and gulped fresh air before the water reclaimed him. Inhaling from his rebreather, he heard the valve shut and felt the rumbling recede as the diesels died. He glanced at his display to note the time as the submarine's battery cells bore the strain of propelling the submarine.

In a darkness reverberating with the penetrating thump of chopper blades, Jake felt his partner tugging at the line joining them. With a probing glove, the commando tapped his arm and returned to his side.

A bright light cast a conical beam into the aqua, outlining the snorkel mast's silvery form. The commando pushed the light into Jake's hand and then worked in the newfound illumination.

Pinching the smooth steel between his knees, the commando wrapped a nylon line around the mast and secured it with a hitch knot.

He then made eye contact through his mask and pointed upward. Jake nodded.

The commando departed again, kicking out of sight. When he returned, Jake noticed a steel line hooked to him. His accomplice removed the buddy line between the swimmers and replaced it with the hook from his own harness. He then whipped his finger in a circle, awaiting Jake's confirmation.

Jake nodded, and the commando swam to the surface before slipping into the trailing blackness.

Then the line yanked Jake upward. He released the mast that had represented safety from the ocean's abandoning vastness, squeezed the flashlight under his arm, and grabbed the steadying steel cable with both hands.

The helicopter's belly grew larger, and hands reached from the cabin to drag him inside. He turned to watch the scene below.

An orange pulsating light cut the blackness that concealed a buoy tied to the sinking submarine. As the aircraft maneuvered to pluck his partner from the water, Jake addressed the familiar jumpmaster.

"How long now until the *Pilar* can get here?"

"Thirty minutes. Maybe sooner. Look."

The man pointed, and Jake stared out a window at darkness. Remembering his night vision, he lowered his facemask, flipped down his goggles, and saw the light green image of the frigate.

He did the math aloud.

"Best I can guess, that submarine's sinking one meter every ten minutes," he said. "The bottom grates will be almost thirty meters deep when the divers get to them."

"The dive team is ready. They will move quickly."

"Okay," Jake said. "Let's get my buddy and get back to the ship."

Hoisted by the winch, his accomplice reached the cabin. The door closed, tennis shoes replaced swim fins, and Jake thanked his partner, who retained the unreadable smirk that accompanied a commando's confidence. Through the window, the pulsating light shrank as the helicopter climbed and accelerated towards the frigate.

In calmer seas, the landing proved simpler than the takeoff, and Jake stepped onto the steady fantail. A junior officer greeted him and showed him the dive team.

Two men in wetsuits stood beside tanks that Jake suspected contained pressurized oxygen, nitrogen, and helium. An air compressor rested on the nonskid surface next to a long length of coiled rubber hose.

"They look ready," Jake said. "Take me to the captain."

The young officer escorted him to the bridge, where the deck plates and bulkheads smelled old, like the training vessels he had tinkered with as a midshipman at the Naval Academy.

The commanding officer stood beside the helm, and through the front windows, Jake saw that he pointed the bow towards the flashing orange beacon.

"I don't know why I doubted you," the commander said.

"No offense taken. I surprise myself sometimes, and this took a little luck."

"Really? How so?"

"No, not really," Jake said. "I was just trying to be modest."

"It doesn't become you."

"You're right, but I need to at least make the effort. Nobody likes an arrogant jackass."

"Apparently, you have accomplished enough notable feats to warrant being arrogant."

Jake shot him a sideways glance.

"I didn't know that you'd seen my dossier."

"I've never seen your dossier," the commander said. "But the intelligence that allowed you to find that submarine is proof that you've impressed many people. Such knowledge requires resources that money alone can't buy."

"Good point."

"I don't suppose you'll share how you found the submarine."

Jake remained ignorant of the events that had allowed him timely proximity to the Malaysian target. Had an American submarine trailed it? An Australian submarine or possibly Japanese? Or could it have been pure satellite surveillance or some technology he had yet to consider?

He accepted that he wouldn't know, but he trusted the CIA officer who had orchestrated the capturing and sharing of the information—Olivia McDonald.

Olivia—the CIA officer who had ended his vagabond fugitive life. The one who had become his lover, his captor, his confidant, his battle partner, his friend, and then his memory.

He had wanted her to stay a memory as she rocketed up the CIA's career ladder and became arrogant—even hedonistic in her success. But she had resurfaced in Argentina, driving regime change while he once again advanced her career by commanding his friend's personal *Scorpène* submarine in the 2017 Falkland Islands conflict.

Then, three months ago, he had found himself talking to her about stealing a Malaysian *Scorpène* submarine. The theft would double his friend's mercenary submarine fleet's abilities, earn him and his colleagues hundreds of millions of dollars, and redeploy the ownership of land and resources within the oil-rich Spratly Islands.

She had used her growing, darkening power within the intelligence community to place him atop the targeted warship.

"If I knew how the information flowed to me about that submarine's location," Jake said, "I'd be fearing for my life. That's the sort of clandestine shit I try to avoid."

"Maybe you are wiser than you behave."

"Thanks, I think. Anyway, you have the hard part now, getting us close enough."

"It's not that hard. It just needs a little skill and patience."

"But you don't have all day," Jake said.

"How fast is it sinking?"

"I figure a meter every ten minutes," Jake said. "But there are variable factors that can make it accelerate the wrong way. No need to delay."

"It's difficult to take station on a moving vessel, but it can be done."

"How close do you need to get?" Jake asked.

"Thirty meters," the commander said. "The dive team can handle it from there. But I intend to get within fifteen to simplify their work."

In unnerving silence, Jake watched the frigate's bow barrel down on the orange light. He clenched his jaw to stifle the urge to usurp the giving of engine and rudder commands.

As the prow dipped into a wave, the ship rolled, and Jake feared the frigate and the submerged treasure before it would collide.

"Right full rudder," the commander said. "Starboard engine stop."

Jake agreed with the instruction, but as a young Filipino rotated a wheeled helm and slid an engine order telegraph from its 'flank' to its 'stop' setting, the actions seemed incomplete.

As if hearing his mental protestations, the commander issued his next order.

"Starboard engine back two-thirds," he said.

The *Gregorio del Pilar* shook with a violence that threatened its ancient hull. It twisted and drifted sideways, its forward advance and lateral transfer setting it parallel to the undulating orange aura.

"All engines ahead one third," the commander said.

"Nice," Jake said.

"I don't know why you ever doubted me."

After a minute, the commander slowed the frigate to four and a half knots, matching the pace of the pulsating light and the cubic buoy that appeared under it with each flash.

"Do you see any reason to wait?" the commander asked.

"No," Jake said. "Send them."

"I need to keep the ship on station and avoid colliding with the submarine," the commander said. "But you need to observe the action from the monitor as you give commands. One of my lieutenants is already on the line, waiting for you."

Jake turned to a closed-circuit television feed that showed men on the fantail through night vision. Two emerald-hued forms slipped over the side, out of sight, and into the water.

He lifted a sound-powered headset from its cradle and slid it over his ears.

"Jake here," he said.

Olivia McDonald and the CIA security experts at her disposal had agreed to let him use his first name with the Philippine crew. Since he had officially died ten years ago stealing an American Trident missile submarine, all trails of evidence leading to his identity hit dead ends.

"Switching to diver camera," the lieutenant said, the circuit deepening his voice as it clipped its higher tones.

The monitor before Jake glowed with the empty white sphere of LED lighting probing the oceanic void beneath the waves. Then the lead diver swam into view, his fins whipping swirling vortexes. The thin opaqueness of the buoy's tethering line appeared in the distance as the diver's gloved hand groped it for guidance.

"Yeah, I see them now," Jake said. "That's the buoy line, right?"

"That's correct, sir," the lieutenant said.

On the back of the diver's hand, Jake saw a round disk with a thick edge running its circumference.

"What's that on his hand?" he asked.

"It's a suction cup, sir. He will rotate it to his palm to hold himself to the submarine. Both divers have them."

The first swimmer reached the mast and began to crawl down its length. The image became a white light swallowed by surrounding nothingness as the second diver reached the mast and allowed the camera to point in a random direction.

When the camera steadied, a bird's eye view showed suction cups helping the lead swimmer walk hand over hand along the submarine's deck. Then the image pointed into random nothingness again as the second diver crawled down the conning tower to join his partner.

Upon reaching the deck, the second diver aimed the camera at his comrade who propped a level tool on the straight steel. The bubble steadied off center.

"That looks like about half a degree down," Jake said.

"I agree," the lieutenant said.

"That's tending to drive the ship downward and explains part of our problem about why it's sinking."

"It possibly explains the entire problem, sir."

"Maybe. Let's solve it. Send the divers to the forward vents."

"Yes, sir."

After a minute without visual insight, Jake saw the image steady again. It showed the lead diver running a gloved finger over the smooth fairing between the vent and the deck.

"Confirmed," he said. "The forward ballast tank vents are shut."

Although caution made submarines operate with closed ballast tank vents to allow emergency surfacing, Jake welcomed the confirmation.

"The team will proceed to the grating," the lieutenant said.

The camera flopped as the diving duo progressed along the side of the submarine. For the first time, the image showed the hose trailing behind the second swimmer.

"The team is inserting the air feed now," the lieutenant said.

"Got it. Don't run it until I tell you."

"No, sir."

Underneath the vessel, the image steadied again with a close-up of the lead diver's hand. With the suction cup returned to the back of his hand, he grasped a horizontal bar of the ballast tank's underside grating. The water flowing under the submarine dragged the swimmer on an upward angle.

Beside his hand, a grapnel held an air hose that ran between bars and into the tank.

"That's good," Jake said. "Run the air."

"The air is running," the lieutenant said.

The undersea image lacked insight into the physics of the operation, but Jake trusted that air pushed itself into the tank with a pressure of one hundred pounds per square inch. The gas rose to the top of the tank, settling under the closed vents and expelling water through the bottom grating.

Jake expected the air to make the submarine lighter and elevate its nose. With the grapnel holding the feed, he watched the divers combine their free hands to press the level tool against the vessel's underbelly and film its tilting as his hopes became reality.

Minutes passed, and the bubble started to budge. When it showed two degrees up, the lieutenant betrayed his impatience.

"Should we stop now?" he asked.

"No," Jake said. "Keep going to four degrees. That submarine is moving slow, and we need more upward driving force."

"I understand, sir. Four degrees," the lieutenant said.

"What's happened to the submarine's depth?" Jake asked.

"It's gone up half a meter since we started."

"Good, but not good enough," Jake said. "After you get the submarine to four degrees of up angle, send the dive team to the middle ballast tank."

While waiting, Jake turned his attention to the commander.

"How's the navigation going?"

"This is tedious. You may not have noticed, but I've given a dozen engine and rudder commands to keep a constant distance to that vessel."

"I heard you," Jake said. "But I wasn't paying attention. Can you keep it up all night?"

The commander looked at a clock.

"Night is about to end. Sunrise is in three hours."

"I'm hurrying," Jake said.

The lieutenant's voice from the headset startled him, and he looked to the monitor showing the undersea image.

"The submarine is at four degrees of up angle."

"I agree," Jake said. "Send them to the middle tank."

He watched as the divers repositioned themselves amidships and forced air into another ballast tank with the grapnel and air hose.

Minutes later, lookouts reported the head valve's broaching, and then they announced the induction mast's rise.

"It's coming up fast," the lieutenant said. "It's going to be surfaced soon."

"Twenty more minutes, per my estimate," Jake said.

He turned to the commander.

"Is the infiltration team ready?" he asked.

"They're aboard the helicopter already. We'll cut through the hull and gain access within minutes of it surfacing."

Confident that the fentanyl-derived gas remained potent in the vessel's submerged, unchanging atmosphere, Jake expected no resistance. But he couldn't be sure.

"Are you using stun grenades and tear gas?"

"Of course," the commander said. "The men are professional warriors and have trained for this mission. They will carry side arms to neutralize any resistance as they see fit, but I've ordered the most humane entry possible."

"Thank you. I don't know how many more deaths my conscience can take."

Through a side bridge window, Jake watched the helpless submarine push aside cascading sheets of water to reveal its conning tower and then, minutes later, its forward deck. As the helicopter hovered overhead, a commando wearing a rebreather and mask rappelled to its deck, followed by a second man.

With impressive speed, the warriors shaped military explosive plastic into a circle atop a hatch. They stepped away, trailing a detonation cord, and then wisps of gray smoke wafted over the freshly cut steel.

Positive pressure within the submarine shot the disk of severed metal upward, and as it crashed against the deck, the men lobbed stun grenades and teargas canisters into the hole.

As reinforcements rappelled onto the prize, the lead pair aimed rifles into the exposed compartment. Then the submarine swallowed the commando team, and the helicopter veered away.

"You'd better get ready," the commander said. "You're in the third wave."

"The second wave is medics, right?"

"Correct," the commander said. "To anesthetize the Malaysian crew in case they wake up."

"And to offer medical attention as necessary."

"Yes, if necessary. If it eases your conscience."

Jake left the bridge, turned corners, and descended stairs towards the wardroom. Despite cleaning efforts to keep the ship sanitary, the passageways betrayed the frigate's age with a lingering damp mustiness. The wardroom door creaked open with the lethargy of a centenarian who wished for its time on earth to end.

The first face that greeted him from a seat at the room's dining table warmed him. He welcomed the sight of his right-hand man, the retired French submarine mechanic, Henri Lanier.

"What news?" Henri asked.

"The commandos are in the submarine. Medics go next. Then us. Are you guys ready?"

Seated near Henri, his engineer, the wiry Claude LaFontaine, and his sonar expert, the squatty Antoine Remy, nodded.

"Good. I take off in ten minutes. You guys will be going in about thirty."

"You should change, Jake," Henri said.

The beige khaki pants and white collared dress shirt that his French companions wore had become their mercenary navy's de facto uniform.

"No, not me," he said. "I'm going in first with self-contained air. But thanks for reminding me to get a new rebreather. I'll see you guys on our new submarine."

Alone in the helicopter with its flight crew, Jake watched the surfaced submarine bobbing next to the frigate, proving that the commandos had remembered to flip the high-pressure air switches to blow all the ballast tanks dry.

Once above the vessel, he rappelled to its deck. He then knelt and placed his fingers on the cut metal to descend between the jagged edges before he slipped into the submarine.

The familiar confines of a *Scorpène*-class control room became a cramped myopia through the blinders of his facemask. Rifles remaining behind the backs of the Philippine commandos confirmed his expectations that the Malaysian crew had succumbed to the gas and had offered no resistance.

As medics administered intravenous anesthetics to the incapacitated crewmen, the slow breathing of the unmoving men reminded Jake of a morgue for half-dead zombies.

He stepped to the panel that controlled the ship's ventilation and waited for a signal from a medic. Sucking from a rebreather, a medic crouching beside an unconscious Malaysian sailor shook his head and raised his palm.

Jake lowered his hands to his sides to signal agreement to wait. He watched the medics creep to the last four men in the room who had fallen beside seats facing the liquid crystal displays of the Subtics tactical system. After the final injection entered the last vein, the nearest medic nodded and gave Jake a thumbs up.

Twisting a knob to start an intake fan, Jake heard air flowing into the ship from the induction mast. He then leaned and reached for a second knob, turned it, and felt the deck rumble through his feet as a low-pressure blower stirred to life in the engineering space.

Jake needed the blower to inhale clean air into the submarine and push gasified toxins out an exhaust plenum atop the conning tower. Wind swishing through the plastic-cut ingress hole helped clean the atmosphere, and he risked a breath.

He inhaled, and the room started to spin. Dropping to a knee, he popped his mouthpiece against his tongue and drew in deep breaths. A commando shook his head and laughed with his eyes while he attached a ladder to the escape hatch.

As he gathered his senses, Jake watched another commando assist with the ladder, climb it, and disappear into the late morning darkness. Helicopter blades became audible, and then the commandos returned into the ship with a body harness. They dragged the closest Malaysian sailor to it, wrapped its belts around him, and wiggled their comatose captive through the ingress hole as a wire pulled him up.

While the commandos reached for the next subdued sailor, Jake stood and tried another breath. Feeling fine, he faced the control panel and flipped a switch to raise a radio mast. He then walked around the central navigation table and stepped up to the elevated conning platform. He adjusted dials to line up a high-frequency voice transmission at its lowest power.

While the medics drew courage from him and risked unaided breaths, he lifted a radio handset to his lips to give the formerly Malaysian submarine *Razak* its new name.

"*Pilar*," he said. "This is the *Wraith*. Over."

He waited for the frigate commander's voice over the loudspeaker.

"*Wraith*, this is the *Pilar*," the commander said. "I assume the atmosphere is clean. Over."

"Clean enough," Jake said. "Send my team in."

"I will have them sent in."

"Thank you," Jake said. "How long until you can send the replacement hatch and get it installed? I don't like being on the surface with a big hole I can't close."

"Thirty minutes to get it to you. An hour for install. I first need to complete five round trips with the helicopter to evacuate the prior crew."

"I understand the priorities," Jake said. "We'll still be working in darkness by then, right? Over."

"Correct, but just barely. My best men are on it. Over."

"Thanks. Hurry. Over."

"I will," the commander said. "And on the last round trip, I'm sending you a bottle of champagne. No matter how long it takes to replace the hatch, you have your submarine, and you need to christen your new ship."

CHAPTER 3

Pierre Renard choked back doubt. Duplicity had caused his previous client's betrayal, but he blamed himself for having believed that he could master the Argentine president as his puppet. The South American leader had escaped his control, embarrassing him and placing his protégé, Jake Slate, within a whisker of death aboard Renard's personal French-designed, Taiwanese-built *Scorpène*-class submarine, the *Specter*.

Renard had precedent to believe he could manipulate regimes. He had developed his decades-entrenched intelligence network, defense community connections, and gifted wisdom in military planning by bending boundaries between nations. Assuming his few failures behind him, he had expected to impart his will in Argentina, but instead he now suffered nightmares of stumbling as he had tried to orchestrate the return of the Falkland Islands to South American ownership.

Failure had taken its psychological toll, but Renard had survived. As had his protégé. As had his crack crew of submarine operators pilfered from the French Navy, where he had learned his art as a submarine commander. As had the *Specter*, which rested atop the deck of its transport barge en route towards the Philippines.

Alive and with his arsenal of resources, he had distracted himself from his Argentine miscue by seeking his next opportunity. His intelligence sources had identified the Spratly Islands, a collection of islets, rocks, atolls, and reefs sprinkled atop the world's fourth largest oil reserve, as a hotbed of political activity. Of the half dozen nations vying for dominance in the region, the Philippines fit the mold of his ideal client.

As a Christian democracy standing against Islamic Malaysia and communist China, located adjacent to his favored clients in Taiwan, the Philippines offered him fertile soil for business. With the nation's weak leader and undersized navy, he had wedged himself into a lucrative military planning operation.

After Jake stole the Malaysian submarine, Renard had claimed success in the first phase of that operation, doubling his fleet and enabling him to use it against the neighbors of the Philippines. He inhaled from his Marlboro to calm himself.

After faltering in Argentina, he feared treachery, poor judgment of character, and outright bad luck. But Jake's theft of the Malaysian submarine–now his *Wraith*–inspired him, and he drew confidence from his protégé's success.

He crossed his leg over his knee and angled himself in the wooden chair to face the rosewood desk that spanned the floor of the Presidential Study. The Philippine president kept his face stern, but Renard noticed the flushness. He had impressed his newest client, and hope shone through the façade of indifference.

"President Andrada," Renard said, "I wish to thank you for the commitment and professionalism your military showed in the first phase of our operation. The report from my team contained immense praise for the effort of your nation's finest men."

Andrada abandoned his sham of coolness and flashed bleach-white teeth.

"I had my doubts that you could do it until I heard the report for myself. Very impressive, Mister Renard. I was happy to clear the latest installment of payment for your fees, and you have my confidence in moving forward with your plan."

"I do appreciate prompt payment," Renard said. "All is prepared on my end for the next phase. The Malaysians tended well to their submarine, and my staff has deemed it fit for use."

"It's your submarine now, Renard. Please–call it by its proper name."

"Of course. The *Wraith* is ready for the next phase of the operation. Other than replacing the hatch that was used to gain entry into the vessel, no repairs were required."

"Your team is familiar with all the ship's systems?"

"Yes. It's several years older than the *Specter*, but it's of the same design. The vessel is a gem, as expected."

"You've rid the waters of an adversarial submarine, you've

taken that submarine as your own, and now you have a dozen of my navy's men aboard with your team for training. You surely know how to demonstrate your abilities."

"My crew could handle the next phase by themselves, but your men will gain vital learning from experts in preparation for the arrival of your nation's first submarine of its own."

Andrada lit a thin cigarette and inhaled. His enthusiasm waned, and he furrowed his brow.

"Your intelligence gathering has been masterful," he said. "It has been a cornerstone of your success. But do you have the information you need to outfox the Chinese?"

"I do. In fact, I anticipate that within two days, the *Wraith* will be able to engage Chinese combatants."

"Two days? That hardly gives me time to mobilize my assets."

"You have ample time," Renard said. "The Chinese will believe that it was the Malaysians who wronged them. You will enjoy secrecy in erecting your defenses while your communist adversaries are focused elsewhere."

"You have not yet led me astray in delivering what I considered unthinkable. I see no reason to doubt you. How long do you think I have?"

"After the *Wraith* engages the Chinese, I expect at least five days before the Chinese will recognize it as a diversion and be able to react to your real movements. After the ruse I intend to inflict upon them, they will be blinded by rage and looking elsewhere for vengeance."

Renard suppressed a smile as he reflected upon the markup he had charged Andrada for the advanced weaponry he had sold him to defend his new island in the Spratly archipelago. The Philippine operation promised to be his most profitable.

"And the *Wraith* will keep Chinese surface ships from harassing my forces?" Andrada asked.

"Of course. The landmass will be yours, and it will serve as a base for controlling the air and sea around the reserves that will catapult your nation from a net importer to a net exporter of oil."

"Not to mention rich fishing havens. My economists say that the increased fishing revenue will be substantial."

"Agreed," Renard said. "And it will allow you to hide military surveillance assets within your expanded fishing fleet. But we are getting ahead of ourselves. Let's focus on establishing your stronghold before talking about preserving it."

Motion across the room irked him. He had ignored the president's trio of advisors, but he expected their protests.

After months of sales calls to Andrada's formal home of Malacañang Palace, the Frenchman considered the chief of staff and his two lackeys as token naysayers. Per his reckoning, they served the sole purpose of giving their passive leader a chance to exercise his presidential right to override somebody's opinions.

The beady-eyed smallish man with a shiny scalp voiced the requisite protest.

"This is too dangerous," the chief said. "The risk is too grave. We would be better poised to use diplomatic channels to secure ownership of the islands that are rightfully ours. Military action will only bring military retaliation."

Renard clenched his jaw to avoid laughing as the president hesitated and feigned a dramatic pause before assuming the strongest air of authority he could muster.

"No," Andrada said, "The diplomatic channels move too slowly, and they produce decisions which are regrettably unenforceable. The islands are controlled by military power only. We need to start standing our ground."

"We have no navy to speak of," the chief said. "And you can't rent the submarine of a mercenary forever. We can't hold whatever ground you hope to gain. This is folly. You've already spent too much money on this operation with Mister Renard."

"I will recoup the entirety of his entire fee in only six months of drilling," Andrada said.

"Only if you can keep the Chinese air and naval forces from demolishing our drilling operations. And what of the Malaysians or the Vietnamese? Even the Taiwanese may react violently against our expansion."

The Frenchman cleared his throat and slapped a neutral look on his face. Hiding the eagerness to profit from the collective manipulability of Andrada and his staff required effort.

"I have a longstanding relationship with the military leadership of Taiwan," he said. "In fact, they built the *Specter* for me. I have advanced much of my career with Taiwan's support, and I assure you that I can navigate any diplomatic channel to maintain them as benevolent partners to your cause."

"An excellent point, Mister Renard," Andrada said. "The Taiwanese are indeed our de facto allies. Their prime minister paid me the courtesy of informing me when they added a naval pier to their airfield on Taiping Island. Taiwan is standing up against our common enemies in the Spratly Islands, and we must establish our own stronghold to appear strong beside them."

"It's too dangerous," the chief said. "There's nothing you can do to stand against the full might of the Chinese. They have too many assets."

Renard glanced to the president and feigned deference.

"May I address this, President Andrada?" he asked.

"You may."

"I agree that the Philippines cannot withstand the full might of the Chinese. But your defenses will be sufficient to deter them from risking their full might. They will send ships and aircraft to challenge you, but I know what they will be willing to risk, and I have advised you how to survive this challenge. My expertise in working against them runs deep, and I speak from experience when I say that I can predict their response."

"Even if that is true," the chief said, "then the Malaysians may retaliate. Or the Vietnamese. Or the Taiwanese. You can claim that they will be allies if we spark war, but there is no proof of it. This is madness."

"War already is sparked," Renard said. "Your landmasses have been taken. The Chinese park fishing fleets atop shoals in your economic exclusive zone. They've even built permanent structures on reefs you rightfully own."

The chief met his glare, and Renard thought he noted a hint of intelligence as he continued.

"We're having this discussion because you've just stolen a naval submarine from your neighbor. That our agreement places the *Wraith* in my possession hardly absolves you of your key role in its theft."

"We could sink the *Wraith* and let the Malaysians speculate how they lost their submarine," the chief said. "That's a simple and clean resolution to the problem. But if you instead proceed with this plan of using the submarine against China, you invite exposure of our role in this."

"You consider the capturing of a world-class submarine to be a problem?"

"It's a danger we never should have allowed. We should have simply sunk it and been content to weaken an adversary."

Renard inhaled soothing nicotine to calm himself and continue the charade that he cared about the chief's opinion.

"A simple sinking, as you suggest, would have been loud and difficult to hide. The violence required to sink a submarine by military means would likely have been noticed by your adversaries."

"But we can sink it now. Quietly. And then we can return to the business of running the country without the risk of military retaliation from forces too great to counter."

"Your country needs the oil," Renard said. "The rewards of the world's fourth largest reserves hang in the balance. Your economic future depends upon acquiring your fair share."

"Not this way. There are other ways to strengthen an economy."

"Agreed," Renard said. "But if you had been able to find such a way, I would not be here. You need me. And worse, if you do not procure your share of the reserves, then your adversaries will take it—and then some."

Renard's hunting snout sensed that the chief's requisite protest had sputtered. A quick glance to the president revealed that his temporal joy in playing judge had yielded to impatience.

Andrada furrowed his brow and frowned.

"Enough debate," he said. "It's time to move forward."

In the months since Renard had revealed his idea of making a stronghold in the Spratly Islands, Andrada had been hooked. As the Frenchman reeled in his catch by guiding a rote conversation to its predictable terminus, he wondered if it came too easily. A doubting voice told him that deceit would undermine him again.

Then he noticed a change in the chief.

The man's demeanor shifted, and Renard sensed a subtle but distinct toggling from prey to predator. He appeared taller in his chair, and his eyes gleamed with a new fire. A nod to his underlings suggested that he had completed his charade as the president's lackey and had morphed into a creature of strength.

When he addressed Andrada, his voice carried a sharp edge, transforming his question into a veiled command.

"You'll have me move forward with the next phase of the operation."

"Yes," Andrada said. "You must see to it, and make haste given the timing that Mister Renard predicts."

"Since you have ordered it," the chief said, "I will see that it is done."

The president stood, his shirt's bulging buttons protruding from his suit jacket. His staff stood, and Renard reacted on cue, stretching the stiffness from his legs.

"That is all," Andrada said. "We will reconvene for an operational briefing after dinner at seven."

The chief marched across the wooden floor, his subordinates trailing him. His terse command carried an authority that Renard respected.

"Join me in my office," he said.

The Frenchman followed him out of the study, and an indiscernible movement in the chief's carriage sent his underlings in the opposite direction. A brief walk through a hallway lined with pictures of past presidents brought him to the chief's chamber.

The room seemed tight compared to the president's study, but meticulousness kept it orderly. Shelves lacking books and a sleek laptop workstation suggested that the chief embraced modern technology. A thin stack of outgoing papers cut a right angle atop the rosewood desk, and seeing no evidence of work in progress, Renard grasped the man's efficiency.

A placard displayed the chief's name, and after his demeanor shift, the Frenchman deemed it worthy of remembrance.

"Mister Navarro," he said, "you appear to have had a recent change of opinion in erecting defenses in the Spratly Islands. Have I won you over with my charm and wit?"

Navarro leveled probing eyes at Renard and seemed to dissect him. The Frenchman held his composure under tense scrutiny. When the chief had completed his exam, he leaned back in his chair and spoke with a tone that carried a surprising enthusiasm–checked by a businesslike efficacy.

"Of course, you won me over," he said. "Before I let you in front of the president, I pieced together enough of your history to know that I needed you. There's no better man for hire that can redefine a military strategy, navigate intelligence channels, and acquire weapons."

"Then your protestations have been a charade from the beginning."

"The president needed to hear me voice the countering opinion. It's part of the routine I must follow to manage him. If I had accepted you too eagerly, he would have hesitated."

"You speak of him like a child."

Navarro smiled.

"In a way, he is. I served as his father's chief of staff during his rise in the senate. If only the cancer hadn't taken him, I would now be serving the wiser of the two men."

Renard scanned his memory banks.

Five years ago, the elder Andrada had been a favorite to rule the country. Sympathy for his death and a cash influx from supporters who wanted to see the Andrada name carried to the presidency had lifted the son into the office.

"You're doing an admirable job tending to the president you inherited."

"He's not the politician his father was, but he has his gifts," Navarro said. "In front of a camera, he is magical. And from his corporate management experience, he understands how to value assets and liabilities, including favors."

"I appreciate your candor."

As the chief's back stiffened and his stare returned, Renard felt Navarro ascertaining his mettle.

"I brought you here for more than my candor," he said. "I need to share information with you that is highly sensitive. I need to trust you."

Renard broke the stare and reached for the ashtray on the desk. He doused his Marlboro in it, clasped his hands on his lap, and resubmitted his gaze to Navarro for inspection.

"I am a man of my word," he said. "My actions have earned me enough enemies that I can ill afford to compound my situation with lies and deceit. Honesty with my clients is a policy I must follow."

"I am not your client. My president is."

Renard wondered if Navarro established a separation with Andrada to protect the president, or if he meant for it to protect himself.

"My truthfulness extends from my clients to their agents. As long as you are true to Andrada, I will be true to you. If, however, you deviate from my agreements with him, my loyalty to him shall trump any agreements you and I may reach."

"Then I offer you a gentleman's agreement," Navarro said. "I will share information with you that I need you to keep secret from the president. If you determine that the information is in keeping of the spirit of your agreement with the president and that protecting him from such information is also necessary, then you will adjust your planning to account for the new information I share."

"Agreed. But if I determine otherwise?"

"Then I will have a difficult decision."

"As long as the burden of choice is upon you," Renard said, "you may as well tell me what you want me to hear."

Navarro leaned back in his chair.

"I want you to bring a second submarine into the operation."

Renard measured his response. He had just doubled his fleet with the theft of the *Wraith* from its prior Malaysian owners, and he would hesitate to risk both it and his *Specter* in a single operation.

"May I ask why?"

"Increased intelligence," Navarro said. "I know that the *Wraith* can defend a given location from the Chinese, but a second submarine allows insurance."

Renard was recruiting a new crew to staff the *Specter*, and the ship needed a year to be ready for action. He stretched the truth but made sure to avoid lies in this new, growing relationship.

"The *Specter* is in transport at the moment, but I could transport it here within a week. However, for the added risk of involving my other submarine, I would have to demand a very high premium."

"I didn't mean the *Specter*," Navarro said. "I meant the *Rankin*."

The Frenchman accessed his mental checklist of the world's submarine fleets.

"An Australian *Collins* class?" he asked. "Why? How?"

"Because I've identified my allies," Navarro said. "To my north, I have Taiwan. They are, as you say, de facto allies. And though I believe they are too far away to have any business in the Spraltys, they have a stronghold at Taiping Island, and they will continue to stand against the Chinese regardless of anything I do."

"Agreed. But the Australians?"

"My allies to the south. Getting their attention required reaching out them."

The news alarmed Renard. It felt like a betrayal.

"So you simply approached them? Depending on what you've shared, you may have overstepped the boundaries of my agreement with President Andrada."

"I did not approach the Australians. Olivia McDonald did. She arranged my first discussion with the Minister for Defence, and I shared nothing with the minister without clearing it first with her. I trust that you trust her, given that you called upon her to arrange for the tracking of the Malaysian submarine that is now in your possession."

Scenarios of duplicity ricocheted off the insides of Renard's skull. When he had met her a decade ago, Olivia was a young officer trying to nourish her budding career within the CIA by bringing him and Jake Slate to justice. She had found him, but he had proven that he and Slate could serve American interests better as mercenaries operating under CIA control than as trophies behind prison bars.

News of her working further behind his back than he could have imagined–involving the Australians–worried him. But it also clarified parts of a murky puzzle. It told him that the Australian submarine *Rankin* had tracked the Malaysian submarine, sharing its location and making possible its theft and conversion to the *Wraith*.

He tucked away a mental debt of gratitude for the Australians, filing it next to his reminder to watch for signs of growing, unchecked power from Olivia McDonald.

He forced a smile as he reached under his blazer for a fresh Marlboro.

"Miss McDonald and I have traded favors for eight years," he said. "I trust her implicitly. If she has approved the involvement of the Australians, then I shall make every effort to accommodate them into this operation."

"Good," Navarro said. "I assume you see the importance of joint operations between an Australian submarine and the *Wraith* with Philippine trainees aboard it."

Renard expected delivery of the first Philippine submarine within two years, and he had agreed with Andrada to train his sailors aboard the *Wraith*, following a pattern he had established with the Taiwanese on prior operations aboard the *Specter*. The arrangement allowed his client's nation to learn how to operate a submarine under his crew's instruction, and it gave him free labor.

"Of course," he said. "My concern is the command structure, given the involvement of a second nation's navy."

"Our navy commands the operation, just as you planned with President Andrada."

"That is logical. You're more familiar with the waters, and the territories and supporting assets are yours."

"There's more to it than that," Navarro said. "I must protect President Andrada from knowledge of the Australian participation. The only people who can know about the inclusion of the *Rankin* are you, me, and a small population of naval personnel."

"I see. Plausible denial in the event that this ends poorly."

"Yes. President Andrada will remain in ignorance of how we tracked the *Wraith* to its commandeering, and he will likely continue speculating that it was an American submarine."

"So be it," Renard said. "What then, would you have me do with the *Rankin*?"

Navarro looked at the ceiling for inspiration before returning his gaze to the Frenchman.

"Consider it a temporary gift," he said. "It's an asset at your disposal as long as you are defending Philippine interests."

"You are most gracious," Renard said. "I shall adjust my plan to secretly incorporate the *Rankin*. There is, however, one issue with which you must assist me."

"That is?"

"I will require that customized torpedoes from my inventory get loaded aboard the *Rankin*."

"I don't understand."

"In my campaign in Argentina, I developed a limpet torpedo designed for tracking submarines, creating a better option than simply destroying one's enemy. I have since created a third option, called the slow-kill torpedo."

"How did the limpet perform?"

"Splendidly, and more than once. As did the slow-kill in my recent tests. It's based upon the limpet design."

"What's a slow-kill torpedo?"

"Its warhead is divided into twenty-four submunitions like the limpet, but instead of attaching and chirping sonic frequencies, the slow-kill submunitions include small warheads that detonate in a delayed sequence. Depending on the size of the targeted vessel and how many submunitions attach, the ship will slowly sink or perhaps survive in a state varying from crippled to slightly hindered."

"I don't see the point."

Renard swallowed. He had created the limpet as a tactical necessity of tracking a British submarine near Argentina, but he had created the slow-kill weapon as a favor to Jake.

"My commanding officer wanted it. He claims to be growing weary of killing, and I must humor him. He wanted me to create a weapon that would disable a submarine but give time for its occupants to surface the ship and survive."

"Interesting," Navarro said. "But is it effective?"

"Yes. It's completely effective against submarines, given the water pressure at depth, their small sizes, and their small number of watertight compartments. However, the design is less robust against surface combatants."

"If you say the weapons are effective, I have no choice but to trust you. But will your weapons work with the *Rankin*?"

"Other than warhead modifications, they remain Italian Black Shark torpedoes, which are designed for global sale. So I expect little problem in integrating them with the *Rankin's* tactical systems. You will, however, have to recall the *Rankin* to Naval Base Cavite to load the weapons. I will have my torpedoes flown in from the *Specter's* transport barge."

"I will see to it," Navarro said.

"Will you excuse me then, so that I may adjust my plan?"

"Just one more thing."

"Of course."

"When you place a submarine at risk per your new planning, Mister Renard, be sure it is the *Wraith*. None of our adversaries are as humane in their armaments as your commanding officer, and as I strengthen my relations with the Australians, I cannot tolerate the loss of the *Rankin*."

CHAPTER 4

Jake Slate smelled grime.

After ventilating the *Wraith* clean of incapacitating gases, the submarine assumed its decade-old ground-in dirt stench that had survived the most meticulous cleanings. He expected his nose to adjust to the smell, but the visual oddities disoriented him.

As he stood behind the polished railing of the elevated conning platform, he surveyed the control room. Though written in the familiar Latin alphabet, every printed word came from an alien language. Numbers etched onto metal labels and printed onto wire-bound operation manuals appeared normal, but he'd have all remnants of Malaysian ownership replaced with English annotations before the *Wraith* would feel like home.

The metal casing that housed the consoles and monitors of the Subtics tactical system seemed brighter than that of the *Specter*, but he doubted his memory. Despite spending months aboard Renard's other *Scorpène-class* submarine, the subtle details distinguishing the two vessels escaped him.

Key faces made the *Wraith* familiar. To his left, before one of six dual-stacked Subtics panels, sat the toad-like figure of his sonar systems expert, Antoine Remy. Like all his ace veterans, Remy had honed his skills in the French Navy prior to recruitment to Pierre Renard's growing mercenary fleet.

Jake looked to the right and saw a handsome man wearing his mercenary crew's unofficial uniform of beige slacks with a white dress shirt. Seated in front of panels and gauges that controlled the vessel's skeletal and cardiovascular systems, the white-haired, sharp-featured Henri Lanier epitomized dignity in stature, appearance, and knowledge of any moving part of a submarine.

Younger French-trained mercenaries, some familiar from the Falkland Islands mission aboard the *Specter* and some with new faces, filled the room alongside uniformed Philippine sailors. The Asian riders struck Jake as eager and frightened newbies, trying to appear brave during their first dive. He pegged the senior Filipino, a lieutenant commander and former commanding officer of an offshore patrol vessel, to be in his late twenties.

"Lieutenant Commander Flores," he said. "Approach the conn."

Stooped beside Henri, learning from the French veteran, the officer craned his neck and gave Jake a quizzical look.

"That means 'come here'," Jake said. "Bring Henri with you."

Henri shot a knowing look that bordered on condescending, as if Jake had offended him by verbalizing his demand. The French mechanical systems expert appeared chafed that Jake forgot that he could predict his commands before they issued from his lips.

If the Frenchmen held a grudge for the faux pas, he buried it by the time he slid by the room's central navigation table and reached Jake. Flores, however, clenched his jaw to hide his nerves.

"You'll be fine, Flores," he said. "We do this all the time."

"Of course, sir. All of us from my fleet have undergone psychological evaluations and training to become submarine sailors. We're ready to deal with the stresses."

Jake shot a glance to Henri who looked away to hide a blushing smile.

"Then why do you look like you're about to piss in your pants?"

A muffled laugh burst from Henri's downturned face.

"Sir, I–"

"Call me 'Jake'," he said. "We use last names with our military riders, but we use first names for ourselves."

"Sir. Jake. Yes, I will call you 'Jake' from now on. All of us will. My men are ready for their first dive."

"I know it doesn't feel right," Jake said. "But you're always safer submerged than surfaced when you're hiding. We're running out of nighttime, and we need to get underwater."

"How can you be sure that the new hatch will hold?"

"For the same reason the Malaysians trusted the old hatch. It's designed for it."

Henri interjected.

"I have inspected the new hardware. Your countrymen were as skillful attaching the new hatch as they were in blowing through the old one. It will hold."

"And if it doesn't," Jake said, "we'll trust that this ship has the strength to reach the surface. What's our status, Henri?"

"The ship is rigged for submerging. Four Black Shark torpedoes are loaded in tubes one through four. Two Exocet anti-ship missiles are in tubes five and six. High-pressure air banks are at ninety-eight percent. The battery is at sixty-four percent."

Jake almost cracked a joke about the ship's former owners being sloppy with their battery energy management, but then he remembered that three Malaysians had succumbed to the attacking gas. Three dead on a mission where he had held child-like hopes of shaping regional boundaries without dealing out more death.

"Prepare to dive," he said. "Station two men with flashlights below the forward hatch to look for water leaks."

The men returned to the control station, and Jake awaited a glance from Henri. Although he had looked over every major system aboard the once-Malaysian submarine, he wanted his French ace's affirmation that he had inspected every safety detail and approved taking the *Wraith* below the waves for its maiden dive under its new command.

Henri gave him the look with a nod.

"Henri, submerge the ship," Jake said.

"Venting main ballast tanks," Henri said.

The enclosed steel world remained unchanged, save for the digital depth gauge ticking away meters.

"Depth is ten meters," Henri said.

"Take us to thirty meters," Jake said.

Showing his skill in distributing water throughout internal tanks, Henri balanced the submarine's weight and kept the deck level. His eyes glued through the control room's forward door to two men peering upward with flashlights, Jake ignored the ship's depth.

"Steady at thirty meters," Henri said. "Holding depth. Speed four knots."

"Maintain course, speed, and depth," Jake said as he stepped down from the conning platform.

He walked forward, sliding between bodies of Philippine sailors who apprenticed over the shoulders of French-trained mercenaries. When he reached Henri, a glance sufficed to raise him from his seat. Flores followed the Frenchman like a trained dog, and the tight space under the forward hatch became cramped with five bodies.

Pointing his finger at moisture that reflected flashlight beams under the hatch, Flores revealed his ignorance.

"Is that a slow leak, perhaps? Microscopic?"

"No," Jake said. "It's condensation. The temperature just fell a few degrees as we descended. Plus the hull has started shrinking ever so slightly under compression by water pressure. So there's less air volume to hold the moisture."

Flores had a sheepish grin.

"They didn't teach us this detail in our training, such as it was," he said. "I expect that I'll be learning a lot."

"Most nations that need to catch up in a hurry on their submarining abilities send their people to friendly nations to get trained," Henri said. "You unfortunately don't have that luxury."

"Not to worry, Flores," Jake said. "You and your team are getting the bonus immersion plan. Trial by fire–and water."

Jake looked upward and saw the hatch holding.

"How's it look to you, Henri?" he asked.

"Marvelous."

"Agreed. Head back to your station and take us to sixty meters."

After returning to the conn, Jake called Flores to his side.

"Yes, sir. I mean, Jake."

"Hang out with me. If you're going to be your nation's first submarine commander, you need to see the world through my eyes."

"Okay. Thank you."

"Ask questions when there's a break in the action. If I need to ignore you, I will."

"Yes, Jake."

"Henri," Jake said. "All ahead two-thirds."

"You don't mind me asking why you increased speed?"

"Before we go deep, I want speed in case we need to drive to the surface."

"Why didn't you speed up before coming to sixty meters, or even thirty meters?"

"There's a set of rules saying that you don't go fast near the surface or when you're really deep. The reason is in case you accidentally place the ship on an angle, such as if your stern planes get jammed in the wrong position. If you're going too fast when that happens shallow, you pop to the surface and risk hitting something before you could recover. If it happens deep, you know the rest."

"You would dive below crush depth?"

"Right."

"I've heard that submarines will travel at maximum flank speeds at any depth."

"Correct," Jake said. "Sometimes you just have to take your chances and hope nothing goes wrong."

"I see."

"Henri, make your depth one hundred meters," Jake said.

The deck dipped, and Jake grabbed the polished railing for support. Beside him, Flores stumbled for balance.

"The quickest way to change depth is with an angle on the ship and with speed," Jake said. "Henri took it easy on you thus far but seems to have lost his patience."

The shift in depth seemed fast.

"Showing off, Henri?" he asked.

"Just testing our new ship," Henri said.

Jake recalled that the *Wraith* lacked the air-independent-propulsion MESMA system of the *Specter*. The missing hardware limited the ship's underwater endurance but made it shorter in length and gave it a slight advantage in maneuverability.

The deck steadied.

"Henri," he said. "Rig the ship for deep submergence."

The Frenchman acknowledged his order and lifted a sound-powered phone to his cheek to pass the word to the engineering spaces.

"What is deep submergence?" Flores asked.

"I station sailors near the large-diameter seawater valves throughout the ship," Jake said. "Each one of them will be wearing a sound-powered phone headset so that they can announce a flooding casualty. When you go deep, you want those extra seconds of response time, in case it happens."

"But it won't happen, will it?"

"I'm going deep to test my new ship–not to kill myself. Follow me."

Jake led Flores forward through the control room, sliding around the central navigation table and between the bodies of mercenaries and apprentices. He stopped below the hatch and looked up at the glistening condensation.

"The hatch is fine. Let's go to the torpedo room."

He descended ladder rungs and faced a room stacked with rows of green cylinders, each with the mass of a sedan.

"Black Shark torpedoes," he said. "Except for over there, up front. You see four spare Exocet anti-ship missiles. They're launched from the tubes, just like torpedoes, except that you have restrictions on how fast and how deep you can be."

Feeding hydraulic fluid to the six tubes capped by breach doors, copper piping ran between liquid crystal displays and control buttons over the forward bulkhead. A French mercenary stood at the weapons control panel, a headset covering his ears. His uniformed Philippine shadow leaned against a weapons rack.

"You have communications with the control room?" Jake asked.

"Yes, Jake," the mercenary said.

"Good."

"The tubes?" Flores asked.

"Yup," Jake said. "Those count as holes that let water into the ship. Big ones. Twenty-one inches wide to be exact. Need someone watching them. Let's head aft now."

A minute later, Jake passed another mercenary-apprentice pair in the rear auxiliary machinery room. Atmosphere cleansing and refrigeration units whirred.

"You got communications with the control room?" he asked.

"Yes," the mercenary said.

"What's at risk for flooding in this compartment?" Flores asked as he craned his neck.

Jake pointed at two angled cylinders that resembled minitorpedo tubes as they jutted through the insulating hull lagging.

"The three-inch launchers," he said. "For shooting out bathythermographs to measure water temperature and the associated speed of sound. Also for communication buoys and, God forbid we need them, some of our anti-torpedo decoys."

Clenching his jaw and slamming his eyes shut, Jake waited for the haunting memories of his past reliance on decoys to clear. He then pointed to the other side of the room to a downward-aimed cylinder propped below a hydraulic compactor."

"Also there," he said. "The trash compactor and ejector."

"I see."

"One more stop," Jake said. "Let's go."

Reaching the hull section where his memory expected to see an air-independent ethanol and liquid oxygen MESMA plant, he found it unfortunate that the Malaysians had foregone this tactical gem in favor of a smaller, cheaper submarine.

He ducked through a watertight door and underneath the wide air ducts leading to the quad diesels. He saw the main motor further aft, hidden intermittently by a man pointing to gauges on a control panel. Four sailors–a mix of mercenaries and Philippine students–wore the dungarees of the engineering crew and surrounded their instructor, who shook his head.

"I don't like this, Jake. I don't like it at all," he said.

Jake respected Claude LaFontaine, a former engineer officer on the French nuclear-powered *Rubis* submarine who had become an expert on diesel power plants in Renard's fleet. He looked as thin and edgy as the French cigarette he cradled between his fingers.

"What's wrong, Claude? Don't like what I stole for you?"

"I don't like the temperature readings. Even with oversized heat exchangers, everything runs hotter than it should. We are operating in tepid seas."

"It's in spec, though, right?"

"Well, yes. It's just that I fear the lubrication oil will have less viscosity, making the diesels less efficient."

"So it's going to take a little longer than normal to charge the batteries, due to diesel inefficiency?"

"Possibly. I'll tell you more when I run them. But the salinity is horrible. Even with the extra salt filtering added to this ship, the cooling water chemistry is corrosive."

"So that's a long-term maintenance concern? You'll need to add fresh water to the cooling water more frequently?"

"Well, yes."

"The fresh-water still works?"

"Yes. So far."

"So no major problems?"

LaFontaine furrowed his brow.

"Well, no. But I still don't like it. And with no MESMA system, we'll place a greater strain on our battery. This ship makes me nervous."

"I think waking up and realizing you're still alive makes you nervous. That doesn't bother me. What would bother me is if nobody is on the phones when I take us for a deep test run. Get someone on the phones."

After returning to the control room, Jake stood at the polished rail. Despite his brave airs, going deep made him anxious, and doing so in a stolen submarine made it worse.

He called to a Philippine linguist who was seated, pouring

over logs and seeking updates in manuals.

"You see anything about limited operations?"

The linguist shook his head.

"You've looked at the captain's standing orders, the deck log, the latest updates to operations manuals?"

"Yes. All of them. There's nothing here limiting depth operations. This is a healthy submarine based upon the notes."

"Well, what did you learn? Anything?"

The linguist grabbed the Malaysian ship's former captain's standing orders and flipped pages.

"Here," he said. "You're not supposed to run the fresh-water still when ocean temperature is above twenty-seven degrees centigrade. It can't condense the fresh water adequately, despite being designed to work up to thirty degrees."

"All stills are temperamental. If that's all you see noted as a chronic problem, I'm ready to go deep."

He ordered the *Wraith* to two hundred meters, and Henri dipped the deck on a steep angle to get there. When the ship leveled, it felt strong around Jake, honoring its design. Respecting the dangers of depth, the mercenary crew remained quiet and alert to slow leaks that could rupture.

He gave it five minutes and then pushed deeper.

"Henri," he said. "Make your depth three hundred meters."

As the room bent downward, Jake felt a chill, which he credited to the coolness of the deeper water.

"Steady at three hundred meters," Henri said.

"Very well, Henri. Get a report from each station to verify that we have no leaks."

After a half minute of rapid conversations on the sound-powered phone, Henri confirmed the ship's integrity.

"Okay," Jake said. "Let's see what this ship can do. You ready, Henri?"

"Yes, Jake. So is the engine room."

"Henri," Jake said. "All ahead flank. Make your depth fifty meters, smartly."

Jake yanked the rail as the deck shot upward. The ship shuddered as it climbed, and a glance at the speed gauge showed the *Wraith* cracking twenty-five knots. As the deck leveled again, he appreciated and respected his new submarine.

"Henri," he said. "Get a secure message ready in our radio queue telling Philippine fleet command that the ship is shaken down sufficiently for its intended operations."

Beside Jake, Flores appeared enthused and offered his first smile.

"Feel like a veteran now?" he asked.

"It's good to have finally gone deep."

"Message is ready," Henri said.

"Antoine," Jake said. "Are there any close contacts on sonar?"

The Frenchman shook his toad-like head.

"Henri," Jake said. "Take us to periscope depth."

As the deck angled upward, Jake tapped a capacitive touch screen to command the periscope's ascent. A subroutine sent the optics into a rapid full-circle swivel, and a panoramic image of the sweep filled two adjacent monitors beside him.

The first pass had taken place with the periscope submerged, and the panorama contained hues of dark blue water. As the *Wraith* lurched in the surface swells, he commanded another full-circle optical scan, and the world above him appeared in his screens as a panorama of a starry sky.

"Raise the radio mast," Jake said. "I'm lowering the periscope."

"Radio mast is raised," Henri said.

"Very well," Jake said. "Transmit."

"Note is transmitted."

"Check for downloads."

"Already checking. Here comes some tactical information."

"Display it on the screen," Jake said.

He stepped down from the conn and bent over the room's central navigation plot. The Spratly Islands peppered an overhead view of the South China Sea.

Jake knew the Subtics tactical computer system could produce higher resolution graphics, but he preferred the classic two-dimensional symbolic representation of man-made assets. To the east, a crosshair represented the *Wraith*. One hundred and thirty miles to the northwest, a trio of red squares materialized.

"A Chinese task force," Henri said. "Three ships. A frigate and two smaller escorts."

"No shit," Jake said. "Just what we hoped for. They've been moving closer to us in their patrol pattern."

"Someone is blessing us with excellent intelligence."

Jake wondered how much debt Olivia McDonald believed he now owed her. Such real-time information carried a price.

"And here is a note from Pierre," Henri said. "It's a response to your report. He says the task force is expected to maintain its easterly track throughout the next six hours."

"That will put them in range," Jake said.

"That's what Pierre says. He's given his order to engage. I'm receiving a concurring message from Philippine fleet command now."

"Bingo," Jake said. "We have a target. Let's go hunting."

CHAPTER 5

Jake pointed a stylus at an overhead view of landmasses one hundred miles west of the Philippines. The crosshair of the *Wraith* inched away from a reef, attempting an intercept course with the trio of red square icons representing the Chinese task force.

"We're one hundred and sixteen nautical miles from the closest Chinese escort," he said. "And they're heading south, roughly, averaging eighteen knots on course one-six-eight."

"They're probably going faster than that but cutting back and forth in a submarine-evasion pattern," Flores said. "That's how I would transit when I commanded my ship."

"Makes sense," Jake said. "Hand me the printout, Henri."

The Frenchman stretched his arm across the table, and Jake grabbed the clipboard.

"And that's what the intelligence report supports. They're in a zigzag course, alternating their heading randomly for each ship. I guess when you get a satellite dedicated to watching a ship, you can see everything."

"There's no guarantee that this is satellite intelligence," Henri said. "But someone is giving us everything we need."

Jake looked back to the printout.

"It says here that the frigate is a *Jiangkai II* class," he said. "Respectable anti-air defense for a frigate. Thirty-two vertical launch cells with anti-air missiles, and a decent anti-air radar suite. No sense in shooting missiles at it unless we're in really close and don't give it time to react."

Flores looked at him and raised an eyebrow.

"You expected to encounter a *Jiangkai II*, didn't you? You certainly had advanced intelligence on the Chinese patrol patterns."

"Of course," Jake said. "But I'm not going to risk getting within sight of that ship. Without a MESMA system, we don't have the endurance anyway. I'm going after an escort."

He read further, scanning the section of the report showing

the capabilities of his target.

"Two *Jiangdao*-class corvettes. Minimal point defense against missiles. This one here is our target."

He tapped the stylus on the closest red square. A name appeared on the electronic chart.

"Impressive," he said. "Our intelligence is so good that we know which specific ship it is. It's the *Luzhou*. I intend to engage the *Luzhou* with two Exocet missiles."

"Just two missiles?" Flores asked.

Down deep, a part of Jake wanted his attack to fail. Although he accepted that he belonged on a submarine reshaping world boundaries, the killing had started to sicken him.

He credited–or blamed–the phenomenon on a god that his wife forced him to research. To his surprise, his fact checking had allowed the possibility of such a deity's existence, and a distracting inner Jake-God dialogue ran in his mental background.

He shut his eyes and looked back to the paper to clear his mind. He pushed away thoughts of a god, specifically his dubious Christian God, and silently requested of said deity that if He in fact existed, would He please guide his upcoming attack on the Chinese task force.

Either that, or could He at least stay out of the way.

"Yeah," he said. "Just two. If I launch all six, it's a sure kill. But if I'm trying to convince the Chinese that I'm a Malaysian sub trying to optimize my attack against a ship with weak air defenses, I hold back the other missiles to use against the other ships. There's a fifty-fifty chance that the ship is dark anyway."

"Dark?" Flores asked. "Do you mean EMCON?"

"Yes. Emissions control. Keeping its radars off so that nobody except people like us with access to satellite intelligence knows where it is."

"We don't know that it's satellite intelligence," Henri said. "It could be an American submarine trailing them for all we know. Or possibly a spying aircraft."

"I'm betting it's satellite intel, but we may never know. The point is, the target may be dark and won't even see it coming."

"Can't we use our own sensors to tell if the Chinese radar systems are transmitting?" Flores asked.

Jake considered the difference between a submarine's small-aperture radar mast perched a couple meters above wave tops versus a surface ship's elevated and larger radio frequency sensors. There was no comparison.

"I'll raise the radio mast before launching to see if I can sniff a radar system, but a submarine's electronic sensory measures suite is weak versus that of a surface ship. And we're disadvantaged since it's so low to the water and our horizon is only a few miles away."

"If they defend themselves?" Flores asked. "Then you will have wasted two missiles."

Jake found the Philippine future submarine commander annoying, but he blamed eager nervousness.

"If so, it won't matter. They'll realize what almost hit them, review the short list of people who could have fired at them, and *voila*, they'll be pissed at the Malaysians. This mission is accomplished just by making it look like a credible attack."

"I see. That's why you're not attacking the frigate. It wouldn't look credible. It would easily defend itself."

"Correct."

"Then why not go after the frigate with torpedoes?"

Jake reminded himself to remain patient. The entire Philippine submarine fleet's expertise rested on Flores' shoulders, and he gave him leeway in his questioning.

"You do realize from our mission brief that a torpedo attack isn't part of this phase?"

"Yes, I agree that there was no mention of a torpedo attack, but there was also no restriction against it. If you have a chance to sink a Chinese frigate and lay the blame on the Malaysians, I highly recommend it."

The concept struck Jake as viable, and he wondered if Renard had watered down his plan due to his request for humane slow-kill weapons and minimized casualties.

"I'll consider it," Jake said. "But let's see how the Chinese react. Torpedoes may end up being necessary in defense anyway."

"Thank you," Flores said. "I don't mean to second-guess you, but I see no other way to apprentice your skills."

Jake thought he noticed insincerity in the Philippine officer's gratitude, but he dismissed it as paranoia.

"It's fine. Better now than when I'm launching weapons. So get your questions out now."

"I have no more to add."

"Good."

Jake aimed the stylus at the plot again.

"We took over this submarine with the Malaysians in transit towards this Philippine reef," he said. "The deck log confirms they were making a straight shot for Commodore Reef, right?"

Cradling a handful of notebooks, binders, and manuals on his arms and the edge of the plotting table, the linguist nodded.

"That is correct," he said. "I also now have access to the former captain's safe."

"It's been cracked?"

"Sorry, Jake," Henri said as he leaned closer into the table. "I forgot to mention that. There was nothing surprising."

"What did you find?" Jake asked.

"Mission orders and captain's log," the linguist said. "The mission orders were to maneuver within visual range of landmasses to monitor for adversarial activity. They had inspected their own Malaysian-claimed holdings and had just passed within two miles of their Investigator Shoal before we intercepted them en route to the Commodore Reef."

"Did it say where they were going after Commodore Reef?"

"Yes. They were going to turn west and pass by a line of several Vietnamese-claimed holdings."

Jake studied the electronic chart.

"Interesting," he said. "That course is more or less the course we're going to take to intercept the Chinese task force. Are you sure there's nothing in there about engaging the Chinese?"

"Nothing," the linguist said.

John R. Monteith

"That doesn't rule out the possibility of a verbal order to the Malaysian captain," Henri said.

"I know," Jake said. "If there was an order to attack, it probably would come that way–given to their captain in person in a secure setting. But it also would require advanced knowledge of the Chinese task force's movements."

Jake let his imagination consider that Olivia McDonald's hand had extended to the Malaysians. He wondered if she had baited them into maneuvering their submarine within harassing range of the Chinese task force.

Had she promised them monitoring of Chinese naval movements in exchange for their patrolling of the seas around the Spratlys? Had she negotiated an oil-for-intelligence trade? If so, then she had orchestrated a scenario of manipulative elegance beyond his expectations by poising the Malaysians to fall into a pit of their own doubts about their innocence in the upcoming exchange.

"Whoever is pulling the strings on our intel," he said, "is working way over our heads. No need to speculate about it. Our orders remain clear."

"How soon until we are in range of Exocet missiles?" Flores asked.

"Good question," Jake said. "The irony is that you're as well prepared to answer it as anyone. Other than restrictions on our speed and depth when launching, the attack will be the same as if you were firing it from your patrol boat."

"I've studied long-range ship-to-ship missiles, but I've never used them in reality or in training. My vessels were all armed with short-range missiles."

"That's fine," Jake said. "The only difference is the time delay it takes for the Exocet to reach its target at long range. That creates a couple of challenges and opportunities. The challenges are that your target will cover more ground during missile flight, meaning that the missile seeker has a larger area to search when it gets near the target."

"And you could hit the wrong target?" Flores asked.

"Yes. And there's also more time for the targeted vessels to shoot down your incoming missiles, although that's offset in part by the fact that the missiles fly so low to the water, keeping them below the horizon of the targets as long as possible."

"What's the advantage, then?"

Jake tapped his stylus between two Vietnamese-held reefs.

"Waypoints," he said. "We'll send the missiles to the west and have them make a tight turn in front of Cornwallis Reef. That'll make the missiles seem to have come from a Vietnamese reef or from a vessel or aircraft in that area. It'll mess with their heads, and the last thing they'll expect is the truth."

"If we pull it off," Henri said. "Which we won't unless you charge the battery. We're at twenty-four percent. Remember there's no MESMA system. We have to reach our launch point and then slip away after shooting without air-independent propulsion."

Three hours later, Jake sat in the foldout captain's chair, feeling the diesel engines rumbling through the submarine's ribs and in his bones. The *Wraith* bobbed and rolled under the surface waves.

"Battery level?" he asked.

"Ninety-six percent," Henri said.

"Raise the radio mast and get me a communications download."

Above Jake's head, servomotors whirred to life, shifting high-pressure hydraulic valves.

"Radio mast is raised," Henri said.

Jake glanced at a display showing the strengths of radar signals that the *Wraith's* electronic sensory measures suite discerned from background electromagnetic energy.

"Nothing on ESM," he said. "Just a few civilian navigation radars from the shipping lanes to the southwest."

"Radio is synched," Henri said. "Download in progress. Scanning the message headers now. I see tactical data."

"Send it to the navigation chart," Jake said.

He stepped down and bellied up to the table. As Henri funneled the tactical intelligence into the Subtics system, the red Chinese squares time-warped to their updated positions on the chart.

"That's good enough," Jake said. "I'm shooting."

"Pierre agreed," Henri said. "I'm getting his narrative now. He recommends that you attack as soon as possible."

"Attention everyone!" Jake said. "I intend to launch missiles in five minutes. Henri, warm up the weapons in tubes five and six. Update them with the latest tactical data from Subtics. Make your depth thirty meters."

Henri acknowledged Jake's orders and set them in motion with a series of phone calls and taps on his control station screen.

"Do you want to man battle stations?" he asked.

"No," Jake said. "I don't expect any retaliation."

The deck angled downward and then leveled.

"Steady on depth thirty meters," Henri said.

"Very well, Henri. Come left, steer course two-seven-zero. Slow to three knots."

As the ship rolled through the turn, Jake heard inner demons condemning him for the pending slaughter of faceless men.

"Steady on course two-seven-zero," Henri said. "And we are at three knots."

"Very well, Henri. Weapon status?"

"Ready to launch the first weapon in ninety seconds. The second weapon needs another five seconds to warm up."

"That's good separation," Jake said. "I don't want them interfering with each other, but I want them arriving on target as close as possible. I will launch each weapon as it becomes ready."

Jake watched the targeted ship move closer to his trap.

"Ten seconds," Henri said.

"Silent countdown," Jake said.

His pulse racing, he watched Henri in breathless anticipation.

"Tube five is ready!"

"Shoot tube five!" Jake said.

The flushing whine of the launch system pushed the encapsulated missile from its tube for an airtight ascent to the wave tops and booster ignition.

"Tube five, normal launch," Henri said.

"Do you hear the booster, Antoine?" Jake asked.

His sonar expert nodded his confirmation that the missile had begun its self-powered flight.

"Tube six is ready!" Henri said.

"Shoot tube six!" Jake said.

"Tube six, normal launch," Henri said.

"Very well," Jake said. "Reload tubes five and six with Exocets. All ahead two-thirds, come left to course one-two-zero."

The ship rolled with hushed men absorbing the gravity of their actions. Next to Jake, Flores broke the quiet with a whisper.

"If we hit, will we hear it?" he asked.

"I'm honestly not sure," Jake said. "I've never attacked anything from so far away. Time will tell."

He glanced at the clock on the navigation table and did the math in his head, assuming ten miles per minute of missile travel.

"We'll know in about three and a half minutes," he said. "If we don't hear anything, I'll ask for an assessment report from fleet headquarters. I'm sure somebody is watching."

"Steady course one-two-zero," Henri said.

"Very well, Henri. Take us down to fifty meters."

The deck dipped and steadied.

"What if you miss, Jake?" Flores asked.

"The point is to convince the Chinese that the Malaysians attacked them. My attack was credible enough to demonstrate that."

"But you could turn around and–"

"Shut up."

Jake waited for his blood pressure to drop.

"Go hang out with Remy and put on a sonar head set," he said.

"You might become one of the few people to hear a live missile attack happening."

As Flores moved towards the sonar expert, Jake stepped up to the conn and sat on the foldout chair. He watched the toad-like head of Antoine Remy, headphones covering its ears, curl into its owner's chest as it absorbed the ocean's sounds.

Unlike his discovery of quiet submarines that rose into his mind, intermingled with memories and hallucinations before blossoming into audible reality, the *Luzhou's* fate struck Remy in an instant. He yanked his left earmuff to his neck and turned to Jake.

"Probable explosion from the bearing of the *Luzhou*," he said. "It's faint, but it has the characteristics of an explosion above the waterline. It was probably one of our Exocets."

Jake stood.

"Just one explosion? Listen for the other missile."

Half a minute passed, and Remy shook his head.

"That's fine. One missile is enough," Jake said.

"No sound of keel rupture or sinking," Remy said. "I might not be able to hear it from this distance, though."

Sensing he'd killed again, Jake swallowed.

"I'm sure it's a hit," he said. "Your best guess is as good as truth to me. This phase of the mission is accomplished."

CHAPTER 6

Qiang Wong stormed past the secretary and tensed his shoulder to bust open the door.

"It's open, commander," the secretary said. "The admiral has been expecting you."

The salutation calmed Commander Wong, and a quick sideways glance at the secretary, a young lieutenant who rose to his feet behind his desk, helped him regain his composure.

"I called him when I saw you down the passageway," the secretary said. "Go right in. He understands your situation."

"No one understands," Wong said.

As he passed through the doorway, hardwood yielded to carpet and the odor of stuffy, sterilized privilege. The admiral sat behind a mahogany desk with underlings seated around it. Token oil paintings framed in cherry wood lined the walls, ordered in an evolutionary chronology of the People's Liberation Army-Navy's surface combatants.

He tucked his cap underneath his arm as he stopped in the room's center and came to attention. Waiting for an invitation to relax, he grew perturbed.

"Remain at attention, commander," the admiral said. "Remember your military bearing. Remain silent until spoken to."

Wong clenched his jaw.

"I've authorized the creation of a task force to prosecute the submarine that attacked the *Luzhou*," the admiral said. "You and the *Chengdu* will be a part of it. You will have your opportunity to avenge your brother."

Wong's younger brother had died commanding the corvette that an Exocet missile had turned into a burning wreck. The missile had struck aft of the bridge, killing all in proximity.

"Thank you, sir."

"But remember that this is not your personal mission of retribution," the admiral said. "Your destroyer will be part of a warranted military retaliation. You will be part of a team, not a lone player nor the team leader. Captain Zhang will command the task force from the *Jinggang Shan.* He will give the orders, and you will follow them."

"I understand, sir."

"Do you? Your demeanor tells me otherwise."

"My brother is dead, sir."

"So are twenty-one other men."

"But none of their families have an obligation of vengeance. I command a vessel capable of retaliation. I have the right and responsibility to take action."

Wong considered the background politics. His father, a ranking member in the communist party, had exchanged favors to assure that he and his brother gained command of naval vessels. He considered his brother's death an opportunity to show strength in a decisive act of retaliation, adding momentum to his career aspirations. He saw no harm in turning his grief into gain.

Knowing that a call from his father would guarantee his involvement in the task force, Wong silenced himself and let the admiral muddle through the illusion of choice.

"I need to know that I can trust you to see through your anger," the admiral said.

"I can."

"You can, or you will?"

"I will, sir."

"You may not be able to deliver the death blow yourself. You may have to allow someone else to launch the fateful weapon of retaliation. Windows of opportunity for striking submarines open and close too fast to guarantee that the shot can be yours."

"As long as I am part of the task force, I will carry out my duties as the task force commander sees fit, sir."

"So be it. Make your ship ready to get underway. The mission briefing is in one hour."

Twelve hours later, Wong stood on the *Chengdu's* bridge, the setting sun casting an expansive black form onto the waves. The sleek shadow invoked childhood wonderment from pictures of

American *Arleigh Burke*-class destroyers, and he prided himself in commanding a vessel of lesser but comparable lethality.

Near the center of the transiting task force, Wong's ship sliced the ocean with restrained ease, withholding its propulsion prowess to let its posse keep pace. The amphibious transport dock, *Jinggang Shan,* bounced in the swells eight nautical miles away, squeezing every joule of energy from its combined diesel and gas turbine plant to propel its twenty thousand tons at twenty-four knots.

The massive *Jinggang Shan* served multiple purposes. It housed the group's commander, Captain Zhang, who ordered the ships on a southeasterly course away from fleet headquarters in Zhanjiang. The dock also allowed amphibious landings of troops with armored vehicles on any of the Spratly landmasses or on mainland Malaysian shores, if Beijing desired to threaten or exercise escalation.

For Wong, land attacks and escalation meant nothing. He valued the dock for one reason–its helicopters.

Submarines feared helicopters. Helicopters–five times faster than the speediest submarine, invincible against undersea attacks, unstoppable with their dipping sonar systems and air-dropped torpedoes. An anti-submarine helicopter needed to only overcome its victim's stealth, and like kryptonite, an aging airframe could subdue the most sophisticated naval asset.

The trick–discovery. Somewhere, within a thousand-mile radius, Wong expected the Malaysian *Scorpène*-class submarine *Razak* to be hiding from him. With a task force consisting of five surface combatant ships, a nuclear submarine, and a constant patrol of helicopters, he expected to find his target and have his vengeance.

A tactical display showed an overhead view of the group. The transport dock defined the center with his destroyer, the *Chengdu*, in proximity to provide protection. Two *Jiangkai II-class* frigates marked opposite corners of an outer square, and two anti-submarine warfare variants of *Jiangdao*-class corvettes set the other corners.

The nuclear-powered submarine, *Shang*, searched the forward waters. With speed rivaling that of a destroyer, the Chinese nuke operated ahead of the group. Wong trusted that its commander knew better than to stray within the task force's perimeter and risk becoming confused with their Malaysian target.

Tapping a screen to expand the chart, he brought the South China Sea into view. Six hundred nautical miles separated him from the northernmost Spratly landmass–the Philippine-controlled Northeast Cay–and another one hundred and fifty miles separated him from the site of the submarine's fatal attack near Cornwallis Reef.

Given the best sustained speed of a *Scorpène*-class submarine, he calculated that his Malaysian target could have passed the Northeast Cay if it sought aggression against its hunters, but the laws of physics kept it outside strike range of his task force. So he would delay his zigzag anti-submarine legs another three hundred miles.

Then he considered that his target could be running the other way, trying to achieve the safety of Sepanggar Bay. But his intelligence sources reported no sign of the *Razak* having returned to its home port.

Satellites caught no telltale signs of humps or wakes on the water's surface, and their orbiting sensors lacked any heat signatures of a skulking *Scorpène*. A Harbin SH-5 maritime patrol aircraft had unloaded its inventory of sonobuoys between the attack point and the submarine's home, but no audio peep of a submerged target materialized.

Although such technological search techniques included imperfections, human intelligence provided Wong's definitive answer. Chinese spies on the Malaysian island of Borneo, paid and threatened to watch the comings and goings of the *Razak*, reported no sign of it. While its older sister submarine, the *Rahman*, remained in dry dock undergoing maintenance, the *Razak* had been seen leaving port two days ago, but it hadn't returned.

And Wong knew the *Razak* had attacked his brother's corvette. Forensic evidence of the damaged ship and the radar signature of the incoming missile revealed an Exocet as the culprit. The debris of the second missile, which Wong's brother's ship had managed to knock down with its point-defense systems, also suggested an Exocet. Aerial and satellite searches of the area revealed no launch platform, and the process of elimination identified it as a submarine.

The only submarine on the planet that carried Exocet missiles which had deployed with enough time to reach the attack point was the *Razak*, and it remained at sea, telling Wong that it intended to continue fighting. If it wanted a fight, he reflected, a fight it would get. Either that, or it had been wounded. In either case, Chinese firepower was alerted and seeking vengeance, sealing his adversary's fate.

He felt edgy, but with half a day separating him from the earliest possible hostile encounter, he forced himself to block the hunt from his mind. An empty stomach reminded him of his pending dinner. He left the bridge, climbed tight flights of ladders until reaching his chambers, and ordered a simple meal of fish and rice.

With minimal tactical decisions to fill the night, he allowed himself an evening of rest.

After waking, he descended several decks to the exercise compartment and invested thirty minutes of treadmill time towards his health. He then returned to his quarters, showered, and donned a fresh uniform. Downing an apple as his breakfast on the run, he reached the bridge to greet the sun rising on the *Chengdu's* port side, behind the task force's epicenter, the *Jinggang Shan*.

The sun's azimuth seemed too northerly for his tastes until he recalled that the task force followed a circuitous, shallow-water route towards the Spratly Islands. Confining the adversarial submarine to a two-hundred-meter seafloor robbed it of deep acoustic layers that could hide its sound and exposed it to the surface combatants' active sonar systems. He judged the extra half day of travel worth avoiding the oceanic trenches that favored his enemy.

His executive officer, a tall and lean man with a gaunt face, caught his attention.

"Sir," he said, "we are ten nautical miles from the edge of the *Razak's* extreme possible range of an Exocet missile attack."

"Send a recommendation to Captain Zhang to verify that our air defenses are optimized and to begin anti-submarine legs within the next thirty minutes."

"Aye, aye, sir."

When the maneuvering order arrived, Wong fantasized about kicking his destroyer into high gear, leaving the task force, and hunting the submarine himself. He then reminded himself he needed every resource at his disposal–helicopters, a friendly submarine, and the other combatants.

"Commence anti-submarine legs," he said.

The ship rolled through a turn, and the floating dock drifted past his aft bridge window. After a dozen minutes, a flanking corvette appeared as a blur on the horizon. Then, following a prescribed turning cadence designed to appear random to any submarine that might shoot intercepting torpedoes, he felt the ship roll through a turn in the opposite direction.

Hours of monotonous zigzagging passed, testing his patience. Although he expected a multi-day hunt, he wanted his vengeance. He wanted his glory. But as the horizon swallowed the setting fiery orb, he conceded the first full day of hunting to his hidden adversary.

As darkness filled his windows, he sank into his captain's chair in the bridge's corner. He noticed movement, and his executive officer's boney visage appeared, ghastly in the red lighting.

"Sir," the executive officer said. "There's flash message traffic, your eyes only. Would you like a hard copy?"

Wong slid his buttocks aside and reached into his trouser pockets for his phone. He pulled it out and noticed he had left it silenced.

"No, I'll read it here," he said.

His subordinate nodded and marched away, and he read the note from fleet headquarters.

Beijing had authorized strikes against Malaysian military targets as retaliation for the unprovoked attack on the corvette *Luzhou*. Kuala Lumpur denied the attack and countered by offering support in a search for the true, unidentified assailant. Wong muttered to himself.

"Meaningless political misdirection."

He slid his phone into his pocket, placed his shoes on the deck plates, and brushed by his executive officer.

"You have the bridge," he said.

"Aye, sir. I have the bridge. Good night."

Twenty hours later, Wong reached the bridge after dinner and received a report from his executive officer.

"Sir, the lead ships have visual contact on the Prince Consort Bank."

A landmass near the Spratly's southeastern extreme, the Vietnamese-held property was a watchtower perched on a submerged mound. Though remote and helpless, the tower let the Vietnamese see the task force as a warning to stay out of the way.

"Very well," Wong said. "Ready the main cannon. Head below to the combat control center and prepare for gunnery operations."

After ten minutes, he looked down to the forecastle as the *Chengdu's* main gun turret rotated clockwise. The barrel rose up and then descended, holding its true elevation in perfect counterbalance to the destroyer's roll. Quick strides brought him to the starboard bridge wing, where he tasted moist salt air.

Earmuffs protected the hearing of the young, husky petty officer standing on the wing. The sailor held binoculars to his face and aimed them between the horizon and the setting sun. Wong raised his voice to get the youngster's attention.

"Do you see it?"

The sailor turned, nodded, and pointed.

"There, sir. And also the watchtower on Prince Consort Bank."

Wong lifted binoculars from his chest to his face, and he saw an orange cubic target drawing a wake through the waves. He then shifted his view a mile forward of the orange target and saw the frigate that towed it. Continuing further ahead, he noticed the Vietnamese watchtower cresting the horizon, giving him his first view of a Spratly landmass since joining the task force.

"Very well," Wong said.

Closing a door behind him as he reentered the air-conditioned coolness, he looked to his officer of the deck, a lieutenant.

"Is the operations officer ready to fire?"

"Yes, sir."

Wong stopped at a console and cast his gaze to a monitor. He extended his finger and flipped through camera views, shifting between the cannon, the target, and the Vietnamese watchtower. Settling on the target, he lifted a sound-powered phone to his check.

"Operations officer," he said, "This is the captain."

"Captain, this is the operations officer."

"This is for demonstration and target practice. Don't use guidance on the shells. Let's test our true marksmanship."

"Yes, sir!"

"Commence gunnery operations, release one round for spotting."

A deep thud shook the windows, and a flash of lightning filled Wong's peripheral vision. He counted silent seconds until water splashed behind the bright cube.

"You're off target," he said. "Report your adjustments."

"Adjusting one and a half degrees left azimuth, half a degree downward elevation, sir."

"Very well. Release one round for spotting."

The polycarbonate windows shook, and the next round tore a hole in the cube's fabric.

"Excellent," Wong said. "Release ten rounds. Fire at will."

Wong offered his crew a ceremonial nod of approval for hitting the target eight out of ten times.

"Secure gunnery operations," he said.

Through the forward window, the pillars of the Vietnamese tower jutted above the horizon. Other ships in the task force had already turned east, and he needed to join them.

"Officer of the deck," he said. "Set new fleet course of zero-nine-zero. Come left to course zero-nine-zero. Recommence anti-submarine legs in five minutes."

An hour later, a navigational aid atop the Vietnamese-held Grainger Bank appeared as a white flash in the dusk, warning ships to avoid its underlying shallows. Like all major navigational aids in the Spratly Islands, human beings lived inside it, peering back at him. Even as he drove the *Chengdu* forward in unlit blackness, Wong recognized his vulnerability to infrared optics.

As the light drew to the destroyer's starboard and then disappeared into the encroaching darkness, he moved to an electronic charting table and studied the Spratly Island's southern landmasses. Passing by Prince Consort Bank and Grainger Bank had given Vietnam the warning to stay out of the way, but a continued easterly course would only broadcast the task force's trajectory to people outside the Chinese sphere of influence.

Assuming the Malaysian submarine to be hiding near its home waters, he decided that his hunt needed to veer southeast, away from the landmasses and towards the open shallow waters west of the Malaysian mainland. He picked up a radio handset and hailed the *Jinggang Shan*.

"This is the captain of the *Chengdu*," he said. "Get me Captain Zhang."

After token protests from an underling about bothering the task force leader, Wong's persistence won out.

"This is Captain Zhang."

"Sir, this is Commander Wong. I recommend setting fleet course at one-three-five."

"What's the meaning of this? Why would you challenge my orders?"

"The present course runs us by manned Vietnamese land-masses. They may see us, and they may warn the Malaysians."

"I am fully aware of that, Wong. Do you think me an idiot?"

Yes, he thought. *You earned your rank as a glorified taxi driver for real men who carry rifles.*

"I am doing my duty of sharing my anti-submarine fighting expertise."

"And how many submarines have you successfully hunted?"

Arrogant ass, he thought.

"You know the answer, sir. Only a few lucky men have had the opportunity. But their lessons are part of my training, and I know how to–"

"Fleet course is zero-nine-zero, commander."

Silence filled the line, and Wong cursed.

He slept fitfully, instincts waking him in the middle of the night as his ship passed the next occupied Vietnamese land-mass. To calm himself, he crept to the bridge and glared through binoculars at the white flashing luminescence pulsating from the lighthouse atop Vietnam's Rifleman Bank.

Trusting his anti-submarine legs and good fortune, he returned to his stateroom and napped for three hours, waking with gratitude that a Malaysian torpedo hadn't cracked his keel. After showering and choking down breakfast, he reached the bridge in time to see the lighthouse of Amboyna Cay.

With the sun risen, he also saw the first dry land of his Spratly Islands hunt–all four acres of it. As the cay drifted aft and the *Chengdu* rolled through another anti-submarine leg, the lighthouse of Barque Canada Reef came into view. The fifteen-mile reef held a small Vietnamese military detachment.

I understood a demonstration of firepower to warn the Vietnamese, he thought, *but this has decayed into folly. They could almost feed targeting data to the Malaysians.*

He grabbed his phone and hailed the floating dock, which

passed closer than his ship to the militarized reef.

"Captain Zhang."

"Sir, this is Commander Wong. We are in a compromised tactical position for hunting a submarine. I recommend setting fleet course at two-two-zero to reposition ourselves to unmonitored waters. If the Vietnamese so much as give a hint of our presence–"

"That's exactly what I want them to do, commander."

"I don't understand, sir."

"Prepare for naval gunfire support. You and the frigates will give my landing teams naval bombardment support."

Wong scanned his memory banks for a target and connected Zhang's intent with the nearest Malaysian landmass–Mariveles Reef, which contained a naval garrison.

"You mean Mariveles Reef?"

"Yes, commander."

"And you want my gunfire support? You would have me and the other combatants be pinned down under possible return fire from shore cannons, while a Malaysian submarine has free reign to attack us at will?"

"You have a nuclear-powered submarine defending you and at least two anti-submarine helicopters airborne at all times."

"This is madness. This isn't how you hunt a submarine! How can we accomplish our primary goal–"

"Who said that hunting a submarine was our primary goal? I don't know what the admiral told you, but I have my orders, and you have yours. We're taking Mariveles Reef from the Malaysians. Submerged targets are secondary. I'm landing my troops, and your ship will support. Do you understand, commander?"

Wong grit his teeth.

"Yes, sir."

"Good. One other thing, commander. I will give the order when you can fire. You will hold your fire until I say. Do I make myself clear?"

"Yes, sir. May I ask one thing, sir?"

"Make it quick."

"Why did you broadcast our movements to the Vietnamese?"

Wong heard an arrogant chuckle.

"Because, commander, I want that forward base on Mariveles Reef as my own, and I can't use it if I have to destroy it. I expect the Malaysians to know we're coming, and I expect them to realize that there's nothing they can do about it."

"You don't expect their submarine to challenge us?"

"I have sufficient assets to oppose any submarine, at least long enough for the assault team to land. And don't you consider this a perfect opportunity to lure out this submarine you seek?"

"If by luring out, you mean offering it easy targets for its torpedoes, then yes."

"Sarcasm doesn't become you, commander."

Nothing Zhang said registered as sanity for Wong, but he needed to try to understand.

"What of the garrison then? Don't you expect them to sabotage the garrison with explosives?"

"These are reasonable men with no motivation to lose their lives defending a rock. I let the Vietnamese see our approach so that they would warn the Malaysians, as I'm sure they have."

"Why? Why did you want the garrison warned?"

"To give adequate time for escalation to the highest echelons of Malaysian command. To give Kuala Lumpur a chance to show its real intent in defying me."

"Defying us, you mean. Defying our nation."

A moment of silence proved that Wong's accusing barb had struck Zhang, but he expected the man's conceit to compel him to ignore the comment.

"Look at your tactical picture, commander."

"I did just before I called you, sir," Wong said.

"How many Malaysian surface combatants and aircraft did you see rising to the garrison's defense?"

Wong felt foolish for missing the subtlety.

"Zero, sir."

"You see. We have Kuala Lumpur's answer. No matter what missteps in logic or assumptions led them to attacking your brother's ship, we now know they are willing to concede land-masses."

"It doesn't make sense, sir."

"Precisely. It's an inconsistency I exposed by my challenge. Prepare for naval gunfire support, commander, and remember to keep your weapons tight until I say otherwise."

CHAPTER 7

Standing atop the surfaced *Wraith*, Jake Slate squinted in the darkness. Restricted from civilians, the black shoreline offered no orientation. He trusted his GPS data and the dim green and red lights atop channel buoys to guide him. A wide, forgiving channel simplified his navigation, and a turn past a jutting rock revealed a concrete waterfront.

The Philippine Navy's newest construction project was an infrastructure to house its future submarine fleet. Cliffs backstopped the property, separating it from unwanted visitors. Jake expected to be the fledgling base's first tenant, ensconced with the *Wraith* under a covered wharf.

Seen through binoculars, the first pier supported little beyond shack-like buildings. It lacked the life support systems for naval vessels, such as cranes, fuel oil tanks, electric cables, and mooring cleats. Undernourished by the rocky land, the installation appeared to be growing behind whatever schedule governed it.

As the covered wharf's four-story opening came into view, he confirmed his hopes of seeing pier-side facilities under the roof. But he glared at a dark mass in the water that shocked him–a submarine tied to the first berthing area.

Honoring radio silence, he resisted the urge to hail Renard on his cell phone, but as he passed the surprise vessel, he saw the Frenchman standing on the concrete pier, a cigarette hanging from his mouth. A smallish Philippine man with a shiny scalp stood beside him, and a uniformed Caucasian man with an athletic build flanked the Filipino.

Men wearing white Philippine sailor uniforms trotted along the pier towards cleats and motorized capstans. A quick glance across the basin showed nothing but barnacle-covered wooden pillars holding up a sheet metal wall, reminding Jake that he wanted for tugboat support.

He lifted a sound-powered phone to his cheek.

"Henri, send line handlers topside."

"Well ahead of you, Jake."

The blended crew of Philippine sailors and mercenary Frenchmen appeared atop the *Wraith's* back. They fielded rubber balls tossed from the pier and then pulled the thin lines wrapped around them. Nylon mooring lines followed, and Jake's crew wrapped them around the submarine's cleats.

Capstans bolted to concrete twirled slow coils of rope, spitting water from two tight lines and drawing the *Wraith* towards its berth. An overhead crane crossed the roof's network of inverted tracks and dangled a steel walkway above the vessel. Seeing his exit, Jake raced down the ladder rungs of the musty, confined conning tower, and then he ducked, stooped, and twisted his way to the back of the ship.

Supervised by Henri, two of his sailors guided the walkway to the deck and then knelt to bolt it into place.

"The brow is ready, Jake," Henri said.

Jake trotted across its girders, his steps echoing off water and steel. On solid concrete, he felt the odd disorientation of stability. As he moved towards his reception party, he took slow steps to familiarize himself with terra firma.

Learned habit compelled him to grasp Renard's shoulders and kiss the air beside his cheeks. The Frenchman stank of body odor, nicotine, and expensive cologne.

"Leave it to you to steal yet another submarine, attack a Chinese combatant, and comport yourself as if it were a mundane week at the office."

"The adrenaline rushes came and went. You know how it goes. I assume there's a bar around here?"

"Of course, my friend. All in good time. I'd first like to introduce you to my new associates. I believe you know of President Andrada's chief of staff, Mister Virgilio Navarro."

Jake shook hands and noticed a glint of shrewdness in Navarro's eyes.

"And this is Commander Terrance Cahill," Renard said, "commanding officer of Her Majesty's Australian Ship *Rankin*."

"Call me Terry," Cahill said. "Ready to help with the cause."

Though much less muscular than Jake, Cahill offered a firm grip and an air of boldness. He sensed that Terry Cahill would do things Terry Cahill's way, and he wondered if he had encountered his Australian clone as he shot a sideways glance at Renard.

"I've briefed him of your background," the Frenchman said. "He knows your real name."

"Seems like everyone knows what's going on except the guy who just brought home your new toy," Jake said.

"Slight change of plans," Renard said. "Nothing to be alarmed about. Mister Navarro is investing in joint operations with the Australians, and Commander Cahill is here to oblige."

"So I'm a diplomat for rent now?" Jake asked. "I didn't sign up for this."

"Well, mate. How do you think I feel, having to interact with mercenaries?" Cahill asked.

"Nobody's forcing you," Jake said.

"I'm under orders. Unlike you, I report to a democratic nation in me chain of command."

Jake reflected upon his mental encyclopedia of the world's submarines and their capability.

"I don't want to turn this into a 'my penis is bigger than yours' conversation, but I just stole a submarine that's better than anything that Australia has, and..."

He looked to Renard.

"Does he know about our hardware situation?"

"He knows of the *Specter*."

"And this is my backup submarine. My primary sub could bring down your entire fleet if I felt like it."

Cahill glared back at Jake.

"You really think you're that good?"

"I've proven it. Because I'm a mercenary, I get all the action. More than all Australian submarine commanders combined."

"You have no loyalty to a cause other than money."

"Gentlemen!" Renard said. "You've just met. The least you can do is enjoy some drinks together before you commit yourselves to lives of mutual hatred."

Jake folded his arms.

"I got nothing against the Australian Navy," Jake said. "I just don't like having changes rammed down my throat."

"Me crew and I were heading home for leave when we got our orders to show up here," Cahill said. "So we weren't exactly thrilled when we got turned around. But we're here, and I'm ready for a coldie."

"I can always go for drink," Jake said.

"It's settled, then," Renard said. "The club is only halfway completed, but there's enough seating for both crews. It's a modest walk from here."

During the moonlit trek on a bleak stretch of asphalt leading to squared buildings in varied states of construction, Jake sensed Renard lagging. He slowed his gait.

"You having trouble keeping up?" he asked.

"No," Renard said. "I was actually hoping that we could speak in private."

"No shit, Pierre. What the hell's going on here?"

"That's not what I mean. There's plenty of time to discuss the factors governing this situation. You don't need to deploy to sea for another two days."

"Great. Then you're flying the wives in, right?"

"You know I can't do that," Renard said. "If the crew's wives knew where we operate, they'd become targets for those whom we've wronged. We can't risk it."

"I was just kidding. What's on your mind?"

"I want you to try a new medication."

Jake reflected upon the antiretroviral drugs that had kept him alive since an accident on the USS *Colorado* had nearly killed him and left him HIV-positive.

"I feel fine. I get the best medications money can buy. It's a nonissue."

"That's not what I meant. I meant a medication for addressing cravings for alcohol."

Jake stopped walking, causing his Philippine and Australian companions to look over their shoulders.

"We'll be along soon," Renard said. "Please, continue and warn the owner that two thirsty submarine crews are approaching."

The duo continued up the road's slight incline. Jake glanced to the waterfront at a gaggle of Australian sailors who began their journey to the bar. Beyond the Australians, Henri led a mixed group of Filipinos and Frenchmen from the *Wraith*.

Jake's words issued as a raspy retort.

"Your wording was clever. You didn't call me an alcoholic. You didn't say I have a drinking problem. You phrased it cerebrally to pique my interest in it scientifically. Nice try, but I'm offended."

"I only took interest because you yourself have lamented on many occasions that you wish you drank less than you do."

"I only say that when I've got a hangover."

"Regardless, I grew concerned and conducted exhaustive research. I found a medication that reverses the brain's learned patterns for desiring alcohol."

"Proven on lab rats?"

"Well, yes. Followed by tens of thousands of humans since the nineteen nineties."

"Well, Pierre, I'm not an alcoholic, and don't give me a diagnosis-by-denial. So I'm not ready to deal with liver damage, brain damage, or any other side effects."

Renard pulled a Marlboro from his blazer's breast pocket.

"No need to mock me for the irony," he said. "It doesn't work for cigarettes. Nicotine addiction works differently."

"I'm not taking another pill," Jake said.

"You mentioned side effects. There are none."

"Bullshit. Every drug has a side effect."

"If you must know, the drug blocks your opiate receptors, which require three days to decay and be replaced. So if you have any pleasurable experience like a runner's high or sexual intercourse, your brain will fail to link any instance of such an experience with pleasure."

"Meaning I become a zombie for life?"

"No," Renard said. "You take the pill an hour before you drink, meaning you only take it if you're going to drink anyway. So, yes, if you're drinking every day, the medication will prevent your brain from wiring itself towards certain positive activities. But then again, you'd be drunk every day."

"I don't drink every day."

Renard flipped open his gold-plated Zippo lighter and sparked flint into flame below the cigarette's butt.

"Precisely. Take the pill at least an hour before you drink, and its chemicals will prevent the alcohol from stimulating your opiate receptors. After several months of repeating this, you unlearn the craving for alcohol by unwiring your brain, so to speak."

"No nausea? No liver damage?"

"None at all. And you still feel drunk. It's gentle and slow, which is why it takes months to minimize cravings."

It sounded too good to be true. Jake wondered how such a medication could remain a secret, but then he remembered the absurdity of the world's medical system. Multi-billion-dollar treatment systems would implode without addicts.

"What happens after a few months if I take it?"

"You just take one before you would drink, if you drink. There are other protocols where the drug is taken multiple times a week or even daily, but for you, I believe that would be overkill."

"Did you consult a physician about this?"

"Three of them. The best. And given your drinking patterns, they suggested the approach I now offer you. Forgive me for approaching medical counsel on your behalf, but I've known you long enough and assumed you'd permit me."

"But you're still talking about using the drug forever. Sounds like a pharmaceutical company is creating its own revenue stream."

"Not that you care about money, but it's an inexpensive drug. Patents have run out."

"Costs aside, forever is still a long time."

"You already take drugs every day to stay alive. For you, this is easy. People with much less personal discipline are doing it, and if you stop drinking, you stop taking the drug."

"Fine. I'll order some when I get home."

"I happen to have some of the medication with me."

"I should have guessed."

The Frenchman reached into his blazer again, pulled out a pill bottle, and extended it.

Jake grabbed it and read its label.

"Naltrexone," he said. "I'll have to research it for myself before taking it. Do we get cell phone reception around here?"

"Yes, of course. You'll find many ways to use the drug, and not all of them effective. For you, I recommend The Sinclair Method, which I essentially have already described to you."

"Sinclair. Got it," Jake said.

"But will you trust me for now?"

"Sure," Jake said. "As long as you take one first, just to show how trivial the side effects are."

"Agreed."

Bare drywall and a construction tarp serving as a wall revealed the sailors' premature use of the building, but Jake's Franco-Philippine crew and that of the *Rankin* seemed comfortable. After half an hour of segregation between the disparate populations, beer's influence brought the men together and loosened their tongues. He overheard exaggerated stories of deep dives, equipment breakages followed by heroic marathon maintenance, and–from his French veterans–torpedo evasions.

Cahill drew his attention to the table where they sat with Renard and Navarro.

"I think you're going to win it, mate."

Jake slurped his third diet cola dry.

"Win what?" he asked.

"That wager you had with Pierre. That you couldn't make it an hour off your submarine before starting your first coldie.

You're going to make it, but you've got some catching up to do."

Glancing at his phone, Jake noticed that he had given the naltrexone fifty-five minutes to work its way into his brain cells. He nodded at the club's owner, who balanced a half dozen brimming glasses of amber fluid between his chest and fingers in a cloud of cigarette smoke over a table of thirsty sailors.

"By the time that overworked guy can bring me a beer, I will have won," he said.

He didn't feel comfortable yet with the Australian, but the commander's demeanor had softened with alcohol.

"Congratulations, Jake," Renard said. "Your first round is on me."

"All the rounds are on you."

"Precisely. Consider it a gentleman's wager."

When his beer arrived, Jake gulped half of it. As the fluid mixed with the cola in his stomach, he belched and watched Navarro adjust his jacket lapels as he stood.

"Gentlemen," the chief said, "If I attempt to keep pace with drinking sailors, I will regret it tomorrow. I must excuse myself."

As Jake stood with the others to shake hands at Navarro's departure, he flagged down the waiter for his next drink. He returned to his seat and finished his first beer as his second arrived. Just as he thought that Cahill may turn out to be an okay guy, he opened his mouth to confirm it.

"Half of me wishes I could blow a few Chinese ships out of the water. Those mongrels are going to take over the entire Pacific Ocean if we don't stop them."

"You'll have your chance," Jake said. "I'm sure there'll be plenty to share. Tactical brief is tomorrow, right?"

Cahill looked to Renard.

"Jake," Renard said. "We should discuss the rules of engagement."

"No shit, Pierre. No offense to our new friend here, but you still haven't told me how an Australian submarine helps us."

Cahill's cold glance shifted to Jake, but he remained silent.

"Commander Cahill is under strict orders from the Australian admiralty to avoid engagement with Chinese military assets. You can imagine the implications if he were to enter in a hostile exchange with them."

"Yeah, I can," Jake said. "But so what? You can't change the world without blowing people up."

"I couldn't agree with you more, mate, but I have me orders. I'm here to provide you intel. Nothing more."

Jake gulped half his beer. An extra submarine worth of sensors and ears could aid his quest, but a single mistake by the Australian could ruin the mission and get him killed.

"What's your take on this, Pierre?" he asked.

Renard flicked ashes into a tray.

"I'll keep your submarines separated to prevent the accidental discovery of one from compromising the other. And with Jake having the only authority to launch, there will be no interference of weapons."

"Good," Jake said.

"I've already heard most of it," Cahill said. "And I don't like it either. Paring up isn't right for submarine warfare, but Renard's done a fine job planning for us, given that we have to."

"I'm sure," Jake said. "He always does. What about using the slow-kill torpedoes?"

"Renard already asked me about it. It's still potentially lethal, and that means me orders prevent me from using it. And what would you do if I asked you to put another mercenary's homemade weapons in one of your tubes?"

Jake reflected on the worst potential disasters of an unproven torpedo—accidental detonation in the tube and mistakes of guidance sending the weapon back at him.

"Fair enough," he said. "I wouldn't take them. But what about an acoustic limpet torpedo?"

"The design you based your slow-kill on?"

"Yeah. I've already proven the design in the field, so to speak."

"So to speak," Cahill said. "Argentina."

"I gave him a summary of our operations history," Renard

said. "He needed to know that our status as a mercenary fleet is more a benefit than a detraction. Though our team is small, most of our sailors have seen real combat."

"I can't argue with your success," Cahill said. "But it's still a lot to deal with, partnering with mercenaries. None of me boys are sure about this, but I must admit they're all excited about tracking real Chinese targets. And so am I."

"That's the first thing you've said about wanting to be here," Jake said.

Cahill tipped back his beer.

"Let's say I am. Let's say I really believe in this mission."

Jake slammed his beer and waved down the waiter for more.

"Okay," he said. "Let's say you want to be here. What does that mean?"

"Right," Cahill said. "Let's say I want to see the Philippines stand up to China. Let's say I want the experience of tracking Chinese targets. Let's say I'm honored to command the submarine that was chosen for the first joint exercise with a Philippine submarine crew, even if it's only a partial crew training on a mercenary vessel freshly stolen from Malaysia. What of it?"

"I would say that you're pissed off that you're not allowed to fire weapons."

The stone of the Australian's face melted with a smile that yielded to an alcohol-fueled staccato laugh.

"What's so funny?" Jake asked.

"All the shit I've been through just to get here undetected, snorkeling God knows how many times and crawling at slow speed so nobody would hear me. All the shit I'm going to put up with following orders from a mercenary. And all the Chinese shit that's going to be within launch range of me submarine, and all you can think that's pissing me off is that I don't get to shoot!"

"Well, when you put it that way, I guess it's funny. But not that funny."

The waiter plopped full glasses in front of the submarine commanders, and the Australian took a deep gulp.

"Didn't mean to offend you," Jake said.

"No offense taken, mate. There's just a little problem with your observation."

"Oh yeah? What's that?"

Cahill focused his eyes on the infinite distance.

"The problem is," he said, "you're bloody well right."

CHAPTER 8

"You're making the right decision," Jake said.

From the pier, he watched the overhead crane dangle the green cylinder over Cahill's submarine as Australian sailors reached and steadied its descent into the *Rankin*.

"I shot a couple exercise weapons when I was deployed," Cahill said. "Plus I had a spare weapons rack. So I've got room in me torpedo room for three limpets. May as well take them."

"Limpets don't kill," Jake said. "But they sure as hell scare the piss out of whoever you shoot at, and it keeps them away once you tag them."

"You're sure I can use them like any other torpedo?"

"As far as the weapon is concerned, it still thinks it's a Black Shark," Jake said. "I've shot two in combat with no problems."

Cahill crossed his arms and looked down.

"Well," he said, "I probably won't get a chance to use them. I think you'll have all the fun, mate."

"If all goes well, I won't need to shoot, either. I'll just be an insurance policy."

Jake gulped from his water bottle, nursing the dehydration of the prior evening's alcohol excess. His first use of naltrexone felt like a placebo, and he remembered behaving like a drunken sailor.

"You know," he said. "In all our story swapping last night, we never talked about how you trailed the *Razak*. I mean, I assume it was you."

Cahill smiled and winked.

"How's the saying go? I can neither confirm nor deny."

"Thanks," Jake said. "I guess I wouldn't even have the *Wraith* now if you didn't help me find it."

"No hard feelings, mate."

With Cahill taking three limpet torpedoes and Jake needing to remove Malaysian weapons from the *Wraith* to make room for his mix of limpet and slow-kill weapons, crane operations would consume the entire day's activities under the covered wharf.

"Pierre offered to show us the railgun module. They're running the final test today."

"I'd like to see that."

"I'll call him," Jake said. "We need a helicopter ride."

Two hours later, the helicopter's shakiness stopped as its wheels touched down on an anchored freighter. Jake jumped to the deck and ducked as he trotted from the rotor wash, which died as the pilot cut the engine.

Expecting Renard, he frowned when a junior Philippine naval officer greeted him.

"Mister Slate, Commander Cahill, I am Lieutenant Sanchez. Mister Renard sent me to escort you to the railgun module. Please, follow me."

Trailed by the Australian, Jake followed the Filipino down girder stairways. The muggy heat became stifling as he descended into the ship's superstructure until an air-conditioned boundary brought relief.

Upon reaching the bridge, he walked by its expanse of windows and took in the vessel's enormity, its deck extending the length of two football fields below him. He and Cahill reached the vessel's captain, a Philippine naval commander.

"Is the bridge secure?" Jake asked. "Can we talk?"

The commander glanced at the door to confirm it was shut.

"Yes. Everyone here is part of the sailing crew."

"You're heading to the Second Thomas Shoal, right?"

"Yes," the commander said. "I'm delivering the payload to the shoal. Holes for the support columns have already been dug, and I sincerely hope to be anchored there for less than twelve hours."

Jake looked again through the forward windows. Eight decks below, a gray circus tent concealed the payload, but he knew what rested under the canvas.

"It's heavy," he said. "Can your cranes handle it?"

"They already loaded it from the pier."

"Do you have divers to help guide it into place onto the reef?"

"Divers are stationed aboard the *Sierra Madre* to assist."

Jake recalled the shoal's status–uninhabited except for the Philippine landing craft, grounded in its shallows for two decades. With the installation of the railgun module, the landmass would embark on a transformative era of military occupation, providing a defense for a vast region of drilling fields.

"If something goes wrong on the way over, is that module operational? I mean could it defend your freighter?"

"The module will remain hidden. But if needed, I can use it. It's self-contained and fully functional. The only time the module will be useless is when it's suspended from my cranes."

"Gentlemen," Lieutenant Sanchez said, "we should go. I don't want you to miss the test."

Jake followed the young lieutenant deeper into the superstructure. A final flight of stairs brought them to a door that issued to the sultriness.

An obstacle course around capstans, supports, winches, and cables brought them to the entrance of a tent that gave concealing shade to the railgun module, in addition to shielding it from distant prying eyes.

Underneath the fluttering curtain, the module dominated the freighter's deck, spanning the area of a doublewide mobile trailer and standing four times as high. At first glance, it was a concrete obelisk atop thick pillars that would root the structure in a seaborne landmass. Chained to the deck for stability during transport, the self-contained weapon system appeared impregnable.

"There's an eye-opener," Cahill said.

"No shit," Jake said. "It could probably take a few punches from five-inch shells."

"Wouldn't have to," Cahill said. "Nothing would get within gun range against it. Not before it gets cut into Swiss cheese."

Jake silently acknowledged the railgun's range which, per Renard's explanation, reached beyond one hundred miles. He realized that the hand of the CIA's fastest rising executive, Olivia McDonald, extended across the globe. He could fathom no other explanation for the American-controlled BAE Systems hardware's existence in the Philippines.

"Entry is from above," Sanchez said. "There are stairs in the front."

The steel steps rang with Jake's footfall as he ascended the rectangular module. Half way up, he followed a horizontal plank outward to overcome the outer wall's seaward slant, which minimized the impact angle of incoming weapons. At the top, he found a view in stark contrast to that from below.

From his study of the module, he recognized that hydraulic lifts had raised the upper weapons subsection. Atop the covering layer of pre-stressed concrete, he saw a fraction of a canted phased array radar. Below the concrete, a layer of plastic housed compartments of fluid designed to slow incoming weapons and to dissipate their heat, in case a projectile penetrated that far.

Under the fluid layer, a final defense protected the twin railguns and the crew and equipment below it. Used on Abram tanks, British Chobham armor erected a barrier of metal plates, ceramic blocks, and open space. The ceramic material would absorb blast heat and impact energy. Empty air pockets would relieve and redirect hot gases or the metal shards of an explosion.

Jake knew the advanced armor surrounded not just the hydraulically raised roof, but the entire module. The defensive covering would stop a five-inch round from a naval vessel, but how many rounds it could take in a successive pounding remained untested.

The twin guns were unimposing, deceptive in their lethality. With their barrels poking through the gap created by their hydraulic elevation, the guns appeared smaller than he expected. The greatest mass rose behind the breaches to absorb recoil, and as he walked deeper inside the module, he thought he could touch the top of the weapons standing on his tiptoes.

But a Phalanx close-in weapon system, complemented by an

eleven-cell Rolling Airframe Missile launcher, blocked his path to either railgun. The point defenses of the Gatling gun bolstered by the RAM launcher added protection against airborne assailants.

"Impressive," Cahill said.

"No shit," Jake said.

"You think those railguns can hit incoming attack aircraft?"

"Yeah. In theory. The munitions are GPS guided."

"Then why the RAMs?"

"My guess is that nobody's tested the guns against anything more complex than a drone. A real pilot with his life on the line is going to juke and jive to get away. Not to mention incoming anti-ship missiles. Better to be safe than sorry and have the RAMs."

"What about those?" Cahill asked.

Jake followed the Australian's arm towards one and then the other of devices that resembled oversized surveillance cameras. Dumbfounded, he stared at them, pondering their purpose, until the truth sank in. Awareness of global weapons technology came with his job, and he recognized the United States Marine Corps' ground-based version of advanced naval weaponry.

"Huh. Pierre didn't tell me about those."

"Does he always tell you everything?"

"Good point. He's a sneaky bastard, and I think he snuck a couple laser weapons onto this thing without telling me."

"Makes sense," Cahill said, "especially if you consider that this module's purpose is to turn electricity into cheap weaponry."

Jake glanced at the Philippine lieutenant to see if he could confirm his assumptions, but Sanchez shrugged and added what he could.

"I don't know the full testing history of all the systems on this module, but I can confirm that those are Ground-Based Air-Defense laser weapons designed to attack air threats as fast as supersonic missiles. They use targeting information from the Phalanx close-in weapons systems, and they use energy from the railgun capacitors."

"Awesome," Jake said. "Keep going."

The lieutenant appeared chuffed with Jake's appreciation of his knowledge, and his voice climbed half and octave.

"The lasers and the Phalanx close-in weapon systems can extend beyond the module's armor when deployed," he said. "They can rotate and extend to either side of the module, depending on the axis of the incoming threats. Unlike the guns, they can remain extended outside the armor when the weapon subsection is lowered so they provide defense while the armor protects the module."

Jake noticed the flexed robotic arms holding the lasers and the coiled power lines feeding them. A quick visual confirmed that each weapon could reach outside the pre-stressed concrete armor during combat.

"What about chaff?" he asked. "I thought I saw a couple canisters around the base of the RAMs."

"You did, sir. And since the module obviously cannot maneuver to hide under it, the chaff can be launched into incoming winds, to allow the metal shards to float over the module and create a confusing cloud for terminal-homing radar systems."

"Clever," Jake said. "It's a pretty solid air defense."

"Solid, but not impregnable. No defense system is. For example, a squadron of bombing aircraft could saturate the defenses, but that's where deterrence applies. It would be a suicide mission for many of the aviators."

"And you also have no way to oppose submarines. Granted, the shoals would make it a tough torpedo shot, but submarines could get close and launch missiles, right? Submarines are the one thing the guns can't attack."

"Yes, sir," Sanchez said. "A future phase of defense may include hydrophone fields in the shallow waters around the shoal. Then the anti-submarine rockets may be installed to deter submarines. But this is speculative at this point."

After he led Jake down a ladder, the lieutenant rotated a handle, unlatched a lock, and pulled open the hatch. As air-conditioned coolness wafted over him, he looked down and saw a scene that reminded him of a submarine control room. Artificial lighting, stale air, and the whir of fans seemed familiar.

So too, did the silvery hair of the Frenchman who looked up at his arrival.

"Welcome, gentlemen," Renard said. "Enter and close the hatch above you."

Within the command center, Jake discovered more elbow room than anticipated, although the compartment carved a small square within the outer armor's larger rectangle.

Two enlisted Philippine sailors sat before consoles on one end, and their counterparts sat in front of similar electronics at the other end. A lone operations officer patrolled the space between the operators, looking over their shoulders and stopping to toggle views and glance at screens dedicated to his supervisory view.

Jake felt the ancient but poignant discomfort of being a newbie on a submarine–of being useless but consuming valuable square footage with his body mass.

"Gentlemen," Renard said. "Over here."

The Frenchman backed into a wall of consoles and gestured for his fellow observers to join him. As Sanchez, Cahill, and Jake crammed against the screens, Jake appreciated the room's spaciousness. Then the hatch opened, and three senior uniformed Philippine officers descended into the compartment.

A naval captain nodded at the visitors with a grim, weathered face and then uttered a command to the module's operations officer. The three evaluators then moved in front of Jake, limiting his view.

"Final inspection team?" Jake asked.

"Correct," Renard said.

A cruel look from an inspector compelled Jake to lower his voice to a whisper.

"If this fails?" he asked. "Then everything has been in vain?"

"True," Renard said. "But there's no need for concern. I've witnessed the pretests. This final inspection is a mere formality."

The test commenced without ceremony as the quiet click of

a servo-valve resonated through Jakes shoes. He recognized the pneumatic-hydraulic system handling its load.

"They're lowering the weapons subsection," Renard said. "The test starts from the module's non-alert state."

"Hunkered down like an armadillo," Jake said.

"Correct," Renard said. "Except that contrary to common belief, most armadillos don't retract their heads."

A clunk announced the sealing of the armored boundary.

"The weaponry's impressive," Cahill said. "But where's all the power coming from, and what's the manning?"

Jake realized the Australian lacked access to the system diagrams that Renard had shown him. Given that electric power served as the heart of everything, he rendered a thorough answer.

"The whole module runs on direct current electricity."

"Right. You need that for the railguns."

"You need it for everything. This is a tightly knit weapons system. On the deck below us are the ammunition stores, then below that is the living quarters. One more deck below are two Rolls Royce gas turbines. They only run when they're either charging the railgun capacitors during combat or recharging the batteries."

As he finished speaking, he noticed most of the module's crew curving around a bank of monitors, and then he heard their clanking footsteps as they descended stairs. He realized that the test he was observing evaluated both the equipment and the readiness of the people supporting it. The off-duty men had to simulate being rousted from their living area.

He surveyed the room and saw the senior enlisted sailor standing in the center and a sole junior enlisted man seated at a console, establishing what he concluded was the standard two-person watch section.

"Yeah, I noticed there weren't any capacitors above—just a bunch of electric cables. They're below as well?"

"Yes," Jake said. "The capacitors are on the same level as the turbines. Then there's what I'd call a half-deck, about six feet high, that houses the battery cells. It's about what you'd see on a submarine."

"I get it," Cahill said. "Not nearly as much load as a submarine, but you need it all to run on battery power most of the time. Air conditioning, electronics, cooling water, radar systems."

"It's supposed to get early warning radar support from high-flying aircraft," Jake said. "That's the only way it can use its long-range gunning advantage. But when needed, it's got its own radar, running on the battery."

"What about fuel?"

"Everything below the battery cells is one big jet fuel tank."

A red pulsating light spurred the two-man watch section into action. The senior enlisted man stepped forward to a supervisory console and tapped a button. Jake heard the servo-valve click that signaled the rise of the weapons subsection.

Screens came to life showing views of the outside world. Though limited to the artificial lighting under the tent, cameras showed multiple angles. Three cameras covered each railgun, giving the operators clean views of the weapons.

Designed to function outside the armor, the Phalanx-RAM units deserved only one camera each. Watching one, Jake saw the opening in the concrete expand and then steady, followed by the air-defense unit sliding outward through the gap.

Another view, through downward looking cameras, covered a full circle around the base of the structure, allowing manual control of the Phalanx guns to shred any frogman, marine, or small boat that attempted to approach. He also considered that the electric fence that would surround the module offered additional anti-personnel defenses.

He heard the high-pitched whine of the first gas turbine coming on line twenty-five feet below, and he noticed the operational staff climbing back into the room.

Men took their combat stations and tapped control buttons. The officer relieved the senior enlisted sailor, who took a place at a console. For minutes that flowed with impressive choreographing, verbal reports flew back and forth in a rehearsed routine as status lights flashed, camera views changed, and weapons moved.

Servomotors whined overhead and camera views showed the guns rotating, demonstrating coverage around the module's full azimuth and spanning sixty degrees in elevation.

As unceremoniously as it had started, the test ended. The captain uttered a few words that Jake couldn't hear, but the nod and stiffened back of the operations officer conveyed the meaning. The team was deemed ready.

"What?" Cahill asked. "No live firing?"

"No need to announce to the Chinese that we're here. This module needs to be a surprise."

"Correct," Renard said. "This final test demonstrated every system except actual live fires. The three-man engineering team brought the gas turbines online, capacitors were charged, weapons were maneuvered, and guidance systems were energized. The team performed satisfactorily."

"So that's it?" Cahill asked.

"I'm quite afraid so," Renard said. "The show is over."

Jake smelled the tobacco from Renard's Marlboro as the Frenchman accompanied him on the return walk to the helicopter. The heat had become sweltering, limiting conversation. Once in the air-conditioned boundary, Cahill spoke.

"Is it just me perception, or are the guns rather small for taking on full-size naval vessels?"

"No, you are correct," Renard said. "These aren't the anti-ship or land-attack weapons you would see on a *Zumwalt* destroyer. These are smaller guns using smaller, simpler, cheaper rounds. They are designed to hit aircraft as well as surface targets. Though they lack explosives, they are guided rounds moving at Mach 7."

"What's that?" Jake asked. "Just over five thousand miles per hour?"

"Indeed," Renard said. "A man can carry the munition in the palm of his hand, and the unit stores almost a thousand of them.

It's a matter of quantity, kinetic energy, and precision more so than explosives. There are, in fact, no warheads."

"Satellite-guided, right?" Cahill asked.

"Yes," Renard said. "There's inertial guidance, too, improving the marksmanship. Even though the damage to large vessels is only the punching of holes, enough holes can sink the largest ship, not to mention what the guns could do to the annoying Chinese installation on Mischief Reef."

"So this is what it's all about," Jake said. "This is what we're fighting for."

"It's a land grab," Cahill said. "Held with the most advanced weaponry on the planet."

Renard blew smoke.

"It's much more than that," he said. "The location is strategic in that it covers promising drilling sites for the Philippines. The first drilling platform is already afloat and waiting to be towed to its first site."

"Waiting for what?" Cahill asked.

"Waiting for this railgun module to be installed and operational for protecting the drilling platform's first deployment."

"What about after the platform is deployed?" Cahill asked. "Railguns can't stop a Chinese submarine from attacking it."

"The platform will have its own anti-submarine helicopters for that very purpose. And should that defense fail, the structure's base is reinforced to withstand a torpedo attack."

"Really? Has it been tested?" Cahill asked.

"In simulations," Renard said. "But no need to test this feature in reality. All you have to do is protect the railgun during its installation. Beyond that, you may trust that the Philippines will deploy the drilling platform and at least triple its oil output."

"Triple?" Cahill asked.

"At least, based upon the geological research. As you may note, Commander Cahill, I rarely take on a client unless I can benefit him well beyond my fees."

Cahill smirked.

"I assume your fees are hefty."

"Quite. And I shall soon earn a good portion of them once we touch down at the submarine base."

"And how's that, mate?"

"By enthralling your crew and that of Mister Slate with the genius and insight of my operational plan for your submarines. The brief begins after lunch."

CHAPTER 9

After the tactical brief, Jake accepted the Australian submarine's presence. If Cahill's crew found anything worth sharing, the *Rankin* would provide intelligence. Beyond that, the surprise accomplice would stay out of his way.

And that's how he liked it.

Following the brief, he descended the dark asphalt road to the wharf. He bypassed the gaping hole of the open weapons loading hatch and entered his submarine.

A status report with Henri and a brief tour of the torpedo room satisfied him that the *Wraith* would be armed per his desires. Two weapons remained to be loaded, and he knew his crew would finish before stopping work for the day.

Retreating to the privacy of his stateroom, he sat at his fold-out desk and grabbed his laptop, which employed a temporary Internet connection wired to a pier-side router. He typed his password to his encrypted communications site and waited for his wife to respond.

Linda Slate appeared, her smile spread across wide, ruddy cheeks that he wanted to reach out and pinch. He considered his wife an anomaly among the Chaldean people with her rosiness glowing through her perpetually tanned skin.

"Hi honey!" she said.

"You look tired," he said. "Did I wake you up?"

Since unpredictability surrounded his days, he wired ringers in his home to wake his wife when he called. With her natural smooth swarthy skin and dark eyelashes, she required no makeup. Only the vessels in her eyes revealed that he had rousted her from her slumber.

"It's okay. I'm glad you called me. I miss you."

"I miss you, too, cutie."

"How's work?"

He knew how to tell her what she needed to hear without exposing her to tactical secrets.

"It's fine," he said. "You know Pierre. He wouldn't sign me up for anything unless he knew it was safe."

"The last time you left me, you said it would be your last. You said you were done."

"We've been through this a thousand times. You know I can't stop. This is who I am."

"I don't like it. You make me worry."

"Don't. I'm fine."

Sadness cast shadows over her face.

"Pierre says hi," he said.

"Hi to Pierre."

The sadness remained. He switched tactics to his French crewmen. If she felt comfortable about their wellbeing, she would accept his safety.

"Henri is doing well. I think he's getting younger every time I see him."

"Good for Henri."

"Antoine is doing well, too."

"Okay. Is Claude talking to you? You said he's been standoffish the last year or so."

"Claude is standoffish to everyone except his tapeworm."

She giggled.

"How are you feeling? Are you still angry?"

He had accepted anger management counseling from his wife's former priest, now a bishop. His Excellency, Francis Kalabat, Eparch Emeritus of Saint Thomas the Apostle of Detroit, had helped by guiding Jake in his fledgling spiritual journey. But first he had to navigate through a decade of deep anger.

"I didn't think of it until now," he said. "But I guess I've been kind of calm during this whole assignment."

"Really? That's good. Are you sure you haven't lost your temper even once?"

"Sometimes it happens so fast that I don't notice. But nothing major, at least for me."

"That's unusual."

He reflected upon a checklist of life's aggravations, and he started with the frustration of needless death.

To ease his conscience, he had invented the slow-kill weapon, based upon the non-lethal limpets that had proven invaluable in his Falkland Islands campaign. Although he had attacked the Chinese corvette, those souls had been destined for death before he arrived in the region. Accepting their loss as a necessary expense for regional stability, he was at peace with the level of violence in his Spratly campaign.

Next, he wondered if his role as a slave still infuriated him. He had made half-hearted attempts to leave Renard's mercenary team, but each time a power greater than himself had driven him back. Guilt, camaraderie, and the CIA kept him inside the Frenchman's submarines. But a candid session with a mirror revealed that his free will would place him under his mentor's employ. Captive or not, he belonged where he was.

But being in the right place fell short of knowing his purpose, and the philosophies he studied left him empty. The godless beliefs seemed inconsistent and lacked satisfaction. Zen Buddhism rejected intrinsic human desires, which struck him as nihilistic. Though he could afford all luxuries, materialism lacked fulfillment. Taoism left him in an infinite loop with man and nature seeking purpose from each other. And Ayn Rand's objectivism promoted personal responsibility but marginalized the morality imprinted upon his human soul.

The monotheistic views required a willing suspension of disbelief to accept a god. But he had seen enough of the world to give credence to the supernatural, leaving the door open for a deity. He had started studying the major offerings of Judaism, Christianity, and even Islam, but he hesitated before pursuing an off-the-shelf belief system. The first step was examining the evidence for a single, ruling god.

But anger delayed this journey as every fact he digested in favor of a god crashed against the walls of his past emotional pain.

A lackluster childhood had included a deceased father he hardly knew and a mother who had driven herself to an alcoholic's death before he graduated high school.

When success at the U.S. Naval Academy and the submarine fleet had promised him a distraction from his suffering, a malicious move and cover-up after an accident had left him with HIV and no chance of a naval career. Anger had tormented him until the then-mysterious Renard had recruited him to steal his Trident missile submarine and sell its warheads to Taiwan.

Ten years ago, he had stolen the USS *Colorado*, but to protect a friend and an American submarine crew, he had stopped short of warhead delivery. His anger had lingered in the background until six months ago, when his rage exploded in a bar fight, driving him to kill a man with his bare hands. Then–like a cancer in remission–it had receded. It simmered in his heart, and he knew it could erupt without warning. But, for the moment, he felt himself free to maneuver without fury.

With that freedom, he pondered his purpose.

His wife's priest had earned her trust during the darkest moments of her divorce, and Jake grew to respect him. He also offered Jake counsel while respecting his boundaries–by omitting the peddling of Jesus and the recitation of Catholic rules.

Jake's mother had raised him Catholic, but he escaped prior to confirmation, the anger of his youth leaving him too disillusioned to fathom a caring god. His dialogue with Kalabat lingered at Question One–the existence of God–and that question kept him off balance enough to diffuse his anger.

"I'm fine, actually," he said. "The anger is there, but it's like it's on the back burner."

"Really? That's great, honey! That's a lot of progress."

"Yeah. I guess all this stuff I've been reading and talking to Bishop Francis about is making me think."

"Why don't you call him? He'd love to hear from you."

"A bishop wants to hear from me?"

"He loves you. I think you're his favorite student."

"I wasn't sure that asking him for advice every six months earned me the status as his student."

"It doesn't matter. He likes your questions. Plus, you've donated enough money to him that I think he'd take your call any time of the day."

"That money went to help oppressed people in Iraq. None of it went into his diocese."

"But he appreciates it. That's where he wants it to go."

"I don't want to talk to a priest, I mean a bishop. At least not now."

"Will you do it for me?"

He knew where she was going, and resistance was futile. She wanted him to receive a blessing to keep him safe.

"Okay, honey. I'll get hold of him."

"Yay! Thanks."

"You sound tired."

"I'm exhausted. I worked until almost ten last night."

She didn't work for money, but, as an immigrant born in Baghdad to parents from Al Gosh and Mosul, she volunteered to help her countrymen who suffered prolonged persecution.

With a nine-figure net worth, Jake silently matched all funds she acquired in her charity work. But he would never pay for it all and rob her of the satisfaction of making a difference.

"What did you do last night?"

"Oh my God, Jake. I think I found an attorney that will work for free to bring orphans into the country for adoption."

"That's wonderful."

"He can't have kids with his wife, and they want to adopt kids for themselves."

"Not a bad tactic to find pro bono support."

"Nope. You didn't marry no dummy."

She yawned.

"Should I let you go back to sleep?"

"No, I miss you!"

She knew better than to ask how long he'd be gone, but she seemed to sense when he would leave for days or even weeks.

"I'll be fine," he said.

The tears started.

"I said I'll be fine, honey."

"Promise me you'll ask for Bishop Francis' blessing."

"Honey, you know how I feel about that."

"You have to promise!"

Resistance–futile.

"Yes, dear. You'll have to log him in to our secure site, though."

"Let me know what time."

"In four hours."

A knock on his door startled him.

"Come in."

Cahill appeared in the doorway.

"Mind if I join you?"

"I think you already have," Jake said. "But no, I don't mind."

"Good-looking ship you got here."

"I have to credit our Filipino hosts for the handiwork. I lost track of the number of faceplates they've swapped out from Malaysian to English."

"Look, mate," the Australian said, "I don't mean to be paranoid, but I'd like to take a look inside those limpets I loaded, just to convince meself there's no explosives inside them. I didn't want to open them up without one of your guys watching."

"That's not paranoid," Jake said. "I imagine I'd do the same thing. Let's go."

"Don't you need to bring one of your technicians?"

"No," Jake said. "I helped design them. If you let me borrow your power tools, I'll have you inside them in twenty minutes."

On the pier, Cahill pulled a *Rankin* officer's ball cap out of his pocket and extended it.

"A gift."

"Thanks," Jake said.

The sensation of a ship's ball cap felt alien after not having donned one since wearing an American naval officer's uniform.

Following the Australian over the *Rankin's* brow, he heard a sentry announce over the vessel's public address system Cahill's return. The tradition addressed him by the name of the ship he commanded.

"*Rankin*, arriving."

Jake wondered if the sentry would salute him and stopped breathing as the young sailor announced his arrival.

"*Wraith*, arriving."

Instinctively, he returned the salute that accompanied the announcement. In that moment, he sensed his twelve-year sentence of shame dissolve. He no longer commanded a mercenary ship, but he was a legitimate submarine commander.

His treason with the United States Navy prevented his homeland from acknowledging this, and the clandestine acts he had committed during a decade of redemption pushed him outside the bounds of any national navy's public recognition. But here, by a concealed wharf and united by shared secrecy, an Australian vessel recognized him for the first, and probably last, time.

He knew that Cahill had arranged the gesture, having spoon-fed him the ball cap to allow him to return the salute.

"Thanks for that," Jake said.

"What? Announcing your arrival? It was nothing, mate."

"You do remember that I stole that thing, right? You just had one of Her Majesty's Australian Ships approve that theft."

"And I can't confirm nor deny that I helped you steal it, right? Let's just say that I give you more credit for what you've done with that submarine alone, never mind what you've done with your other submarines, than I give meself and all me colleagues back home. While we've been busy training, you've been busy doing."

"Thanks. I don't know what else to say."

"Buy me a beer when we're done with this and celebrating the oil flow into the Philippines."

Jake hardly remembered navigating the *Rankin's* corridors to its torpedo room, opening up the limpets, and waving a flashlight over the harmless noisemakers.

He bid a satisfied Cahill farewell and floated across the brow, anger and anxiety leaving his body as the *Rankin's* sentry saluted and proclaimed his authenticity again with a final salutation.

"*Wraith*, departing."

Three hours later, he finished a stir-fry dinner loaded with the fresh vegetables he would miss at sea, and then he walked to the torpedo room with Henri. He remained silent, already knowing that his ace French mechanic had loaded the new weapons per his orders.

To the untrained eye, the compartment appeared unchanged since the *Wraith* had slid under the wharf's covering canopy. But Jake noticed the subtleties.

A clear white ring encircling the torpedo's circumference atop its warhead section identified it as a limpet. Beside it, he recognized a slow-kill weapon's telltale gray ring. Then behind the two custom torpedoes lay their twins.

On the other side of the room, four more custom weapons rested in their racks, ready for the automated hydraulic system to reload them into tubes. Behind the custom armaments, a yellow ring identified a drone of the type that DCNS, the European naval construction company that had launched Renard's private career, had been producing for Jake's use for a decade.

"No need to show me what's in the tubes," Jake said. "After eight years, I'm willing to trust you."

"Thank you," Henri said.

"The crew is all aboard?"

"I need to take a final muster, but all hands were aboard prior to the evening meal."

"We cast off in two hours. Take muster and remind everyone to be ready."

In his stateroom, he read a book on his computer to distract himself while awaiting his wife's call. A future earth had polluted itself to the verge of extinction, and cartels of the wealthy elite battled the government's military for control of humanity's new future on a terraformed Mars.

A popup window showed his wife's attempt to contact him.

He accepted the call and typed his passcode to connect with her, but a man's gentle and wise face appeared. Jake recognized the man seated in front of his refrigerator.

"I didn't know that bishops did house calls."

"Whenever needed, brother," Bishop Francis Kalabat said.

Linda slid her face in front of the camera, smiling as if Kalabat's presence assured her husband's safety.

"Hi, honey!" she said. "Look who's here. He came right over when I called him this morning."

"Thank you, Bishop Francis," Jake said.

"My pleasure. Linda says you need a blessing before you head off on another endeavor."

"That is indeed what she says, and I'm not about to argue."

"Well said. Shall we?"

"Sure," Jake said.

He bowed his head out of respect to the bishop and his wife's beliefs.

"Dear God, I ask you to guide Jake with wisdom, compassion, and decisiveness and to bless him on his upcoming endeavor. Amen."

"That's it?" Jake asked.

"Do you want more? You're normally looking for the tersest answers I can give. I figured you'd be happy if I kept it short and sweet. God knows what I'm wishing for you in my heart."

Jake had seen the bishop render passionate homilies and knew he could speak as long as needed to inspire anyone who listened. He considered him the ordained Energizer Bunny with eyeglasses, a gray beard, and a miter.

"No," he said. "That was perfect. Thank you, father. I mean bishop. I mean… Your Excellency?"

"All of it works for me. I answer to a lot of things. How are your studies going?"

"I got sidetracked by work, so to speak. But it's starting to sink in, the evidence for a god, I mean."

"Great!"

"Doesn't mean I'm picking a side of the argument. Just digesting the facts."

"Fair enough. Do you have anyone to talk to on your crew?"

As best he could tell, his main French accomplices were Christians. Antoine Remy had revealed his belief, but Jake also suspected Henri Lanier and Claude LaFontaine.

"Yeah. There are a few guys. I might have some down time with them to chat. Thanks for the idea, actually."

"My pleasure."

Jake glanced at the clock on his wall and let thoughts of his mission creep into his head.

"You look like you need to leave us, Jake," Kalabat said.

"I'm afraid so. I need to say good bye. Will you assure Linda that everything will be okay?"

She shifted the camera to her face and tried to hold on to the moment. The vision pained him, but the bishop mitigated the suffering.

"I will help her find the strength and courage to trust in the outcome," Kalabat said, "so that you can go and do God's work."

Four hours later, Jake slid the *Wraith* under the waves, thirty minutes ahead of the *Rankin*. He then drove his submarine at an economic speed of six knots towards the Second Thomas Shoal in preparation for another showdown with the Chinese Navy.

CHAPTER 10

Pierre Renard suppressed a frown as he saw the observatory's fluorescent lighting reflecting off the chief of staff's scalp.

"I'm still a bit underwhelmed by your command center," he said. "I trust that your leadership is trained well enough to manage their naval assets within these limitations."

Navarro kept his gaze fixed through the glass on the room below.

"I assume that you grew accustomed to superior equipment working in Taiwan," he said. "But you have nothing to worry about here. Admiral Torres is competent, and our command center is sufficient for our needs."

Renard looked down on the small center. Torres, the solitary flag officer, overlooked a handful of mid-grade and senior officers seated at consoles, one of which remained vacant for the Frenchman's use managing the submarines. The central hub of the Philippine Navy would fill half the tactical operations room of an American destroyer, but he conceded its adequacy.

"From what I can see, it appears that everything is running smoothly," he said. "The submarines are in transit to their stations, the conventional arms and construction equipment are en route to your islands, and the railgun module is en route to the Second Thomas Shoal."

"Correct," Navarro said.

"I don't see signs of air support, in the event that it is needed."

"That's controlled by our air forces. We have communications with their command center, but there's no direct control from here."

"You have a man in charge of your air forces that you trust, I assume?"

"Yes," Navarro said. "The Secretary of National Defense. He served the president's father in various assignments for decades. His loyalty is impeccable."

"Excellent. I understand why you would have him monitoring your air forces. They're your greatest military asset."

"He's verified that our general has fighters airborne for radar support and that he's ready to scramble every aircraft, if needed."

"I pray that such a reaction remains unnecessary."

Turning his attention to the laptop on a table, Renard leaned forward and tapped keys to bring up an overhead view of the Spratly Islands. The Chinese task force that had overrun a garrison on a Malaysian landmass had turned southwest to search for the *Wraith*, under the false assumption that it searched for the *Razak*, hiding in waters close to its homeport.

"The task force is almost a full day's transit away from being able to respond to our moves," he said. "The plan is working perfectly thus far."

"Thus far," Navarro said. "But the Chinese will notice our activity soon enough, and they will respond. I will need you in communication with the submarines during the crucial hours."

"Of course. I promise you that I won't stray far and that I shall return long before you need me."

"I don't assume that your absence is negotiable?"

"I consider every conflict to be negotiable," Renard said, "unless I'm dealing with powers I don't understand. I fear that I've lost sight of Officer McDonald's influence and motivations."

"Then appeasement is best."

"Agreed. Excuse me. I shan't keep her majesty waiting. She is arriving soon, and she has beckoned."

Two hours later, Renard stirred in the back of a limousine parked on a private airstrip. Olivia had texted him about her pending arrival, but her true landing came ninety minutes later than her declaration. Having worked with Asians, the Frenchman had developed a calloused patience against petty power plays, but the CIA officer's game irked him. He expected better from her.

His driver appeared comfortable reading an electronic book, and Renard mimicked the man's decision. He withdrew his phone and indulged in a novel, opting to rest the overworked scheming and analytical section of his mind.

A futuristic detective story took him to an orbiting annulus where a hero sought to unravel a web of politics, crime, and nanotechnology. When the lights of the landing jet shone through the windshield half an hour later, he stepped from the vehicle, stuffed his phone in his pocket, and watched the airplane taxi to a stop.

The aircraft halted but then remained dormant long enough to test his nerves. As a fuel truck approached and hooked up its lines, he withdrew his phone and began reading again, attempting to hold down bile as her gamesmanship forced him to wait.

As he sensed his endurance buckling, a door flipped open followed by stairs reaching to the tarmac. Ghoulish red light flowing from the cabin backlit a man of average stature who called out.

"Mister Renard?"

"Who else might be standing here with infinite patience awaiting a summons from her majesty's lackey?"

Olivia's assistant adjusted the lapels of his tailored suit.

"Come," he said. "She is waiting."

As the Frenchman ascended into the cabin, he thought he ventured into a night club.

Two suited men he considered too handsome and young to be useful beyond toys for Olivia sat on a couch opposite their leader. The one who had beckoned him into the airborne den appeared to be the designated adult, the only occupant free of chemical influence.

An emptied bottle of Kettel One vodka on the glass tabletop revealed a shameless admission of her traveling style. The unfocused eyes of the handsome duo and of their priestess sprawled on the opposing leather couch were saucers dilated wider than the soft red light warranted. Renard suspected her Ecstasy habit and hoped she experimented with nothing harsher.

At his arrival, she curled into a ball and then rose to her feet. She slinked towards him, her stiletto heels tracing sultry arcs as each exposed knee slid towards him in a practiced, seductive rhythm. A smile spread across her face as she lifted graceful arms to his neck.

"Pierre," she said. "It's been too long."

Her cherry red lips appeared black in the redness, and they caught him off guard as she pressed them against his. He tasted the moisture of her opening mouth as he grabbed her bare shoulders and pushed her back.

"Young lady," he said. "I'm old enough to be your father, and I am happily married."

She seemed dazed.

"Olivia?" he asked. "Are you not engaged? And why are you wearing an evening dress? Should you not be showing more restraint?"

Her throaty laugh sounded ghoulish as she stepped back. Then her face turned venomous in the dark light as she angled her chin at her handsome underlings, dismissing them with a nod through a curtain to the aircraft's rear. The sober babysitting assistant remained, lowering himself to his queen's couch as she sat and gestured for Renard to join her.

"Engaged?" she asked. "That's what the press would have you believe. Maybe I will marry him and become Misses Argentina. But for now, President Ramirez and I are just enjoying the benefits of being a power couple."

"I fear that I no longer know who you are."

"Come on, Pierre. Can't a girl have a little fun? I deserve it, after all I've been through."

Despite his present sentiments, he agreed.

Undercover a decade ago, she had survived being raped and contracting HIV while busting a human trafficking ring. Reward for her survival and success earned her an assignment in entrapping Jake Slate, the escaped traitor, as his lover and in catching her greater prey–the Frenchman who protected him. With her seductive skills, she had toyed with Jake, but she also had erred and had started to love him.

When the realization struck her that the CIA had exposed

her to unnecessary danger leading to her rape, her loyalties had turned murky. Instead of taking Jake and Renard into custody, she had chosen to side with them in their mission of taking an *Agosta* submarine in pursuit of a renegade Pakistani vessel. She had then used her analytical skill as a psychologist to predict the Pakistani traitor's motivation to help her new friends stop him from nuking Hawaii.

Years later, as her career trajectory in the CIA targeted the moon, she had led a team in assessing the dossiers of a rogue Israeli submarine's crew. Frustrated, she had found no sign of treason, leading her to discover a broader and deeper terrorist group working within and against the United States. She had enabled Jake and Renard, who had access to a *Scorpène* submarine through the Frenchman's shipbuilding connections, to join forces with the United States Navy and save countless lives.

Finally, less than a year ago, she had lent her growing sphere of influence to Renard's plan of arming Argentina to retake the Falkland Islands. When treachery revealed that she had joined him in choosing the wrong side, their coolness working together under pressure, combined with Jake's heroism commanding the Frenchman's *Specter* submarine, had allowed Renard to declare victory in his mission.

In his wake, she had extended her influence across South America, including a publicized romance with Argentina's new playboy president.

She had suffered, and she also had met Renard's high standards of intelligence and efficacy. He had thought she had recovered from her victimhood, but success appeared to destabilize her and subject her to something more debilitating than chemical abuse—power and a hunger for more. He wondered if only a psychologist as brilliant as herself could rescue her.

"Much as I would prefer to prove you wrong," he said, "I cannot dispute it. You have been through a lot, my dear. And I cannot argue with your results."

"Good. I didn't come here to argue."

She floated her arm into the air and offered a slow flick of her thin fingers as a command for him to sit opposite her. He walked around the short table, adjusted his blazer, and sank into the couch.

Brightness flowed into the cabin as her underling adjusted a remote to energize overhead bulbs. He noticed that her pitch-black gown swallowed light and made her red hair appear like flame in contrast.

"Why did you come here?" he asked. "You could have simply called me."

"Where's the fun in that, Pierre?"

"I'm not one for excesses in leisure. Not for decades, at least. I've been through that phase in my life."

"I have a generous travel budget. Why not use it?"

"You do seem to enjoy traveling in style."

"Don't be judgmental. Would you like to compare dossiers, or can we agree that amassing your personal fortune included arming the wrong side more than once?"

"I have my regrets, but at least I regret them. As a friend, I counsel you to beware of your rapid rise within the CIA. Rapidly begotten power is stressful in its own right. I can't imagine what it does to someone so young."

She shifted in her seat and curled her legs underneath her, signaling that his warning had failed to take root.

"You make it sound like I might fall as fast as I've risen. I'm two levels below the director of the CIA, I'm literally in bed with the president of a South American nation, and my mentor is going to be elected President of the United States in four years."

"I meant no offense. Perhaps I overreached the bounds of good discretion."

"No offense taken. The reason I came here was simple. I wanted to see you in person at least once before you take on this little assignment for me."

"Fair enough. This is a large undertaking, even for me."

She spread her arms across the cabin, her raised nose implying that the gesture extended to the entire South China Sea.

"I made all this possible," she said. "I made state of the art military hardware accessible to Navarro, I made Australian and American intelligence available to you, and I helped Navarro finance this entire operation. But you've never asked me why?"

"I saw no wisdom in challenging my good fortune."

"Bullshit. You analyze everything."

"Yes. Of course, I thought of it. But I saw no wisdom in expressing my thoughts to you when you were obviously enthusiastic to support my mission."

"Indulge me."

"Very well," Renard said. "You saw excellent returns on investment. Navarro will enjoy the oil revenues and improved defenses. You, I assume, will enjoy a negotiated share of his oil for American import. And I, of course, will enjoy my fees and my new submarine."

"Typical Pierre," she said. "Always thinking about military advantages and making money."

"You make it sound like a crime."

"You're missing the big picture."

He feared he would lose his cool if she lectured him on global affairs and politics.

"Forgive me if I don't indulge you by guessing at your meaning."

"I mean control," she said. "Controlling the Philippines. Controlling China's expansion in the South China Sea. Controlling the oil."

"Ah. I see. You may as well complete your thought and include controlling me."

She shifted her knees and leaned forward. He craved a cigarette as his blood pressure rose, but he decided it would show weakness.

"Do you really want to have that conversation?" she asked.

"Perhaps we should. The last person in your organization to threaten me outright was your old boss and mentor, the expected future president, and that was years ago. I had considered our relationship one of ongoing mutual benefit, if not candid friendship, at least for my part."

She leaned back, her discomfort in holding any position betraying her edginess, or perhaps her aloofness. He couldn't tell which.

"I never said anything about controlling you," she said. "You brought it up. You accused me of it."

"I'm usually quite effective at identifying motivations. You are more of an enigma than most, but I believe I finally see you for who you are."

"Do tell."

"You're obsessed with control."

"So? Isn't everybody? I'm just honest enough to admit it. You should be grateful that I don't bullshit you."

"Then you do wish to control me."

"No shit, Pierre. What woman trying to make her mark in the male-dominated intelligence community wouldn't want to have her own private mini-navy?"

"Need I remind you that I am a mercenary for hire? You may always purchase my services provided you meet my price and provided I can live with the consequences of my endeavors."

Again she fidgeted, this time causing her lackey to slide to the edge of the couch.

"Don't pretend that you operate in a free market. That's exactly the point I came here to make. You don't have that freedom anymore."

"You need not even ask about having the right of first refusal with me," he said. "If I ever have a conflict in my schedule, I shall always prioritize your needs at the top. This I will do freely out of loyalty."

"Not good enough."

He forced himself silent to buy time to think. Reaching into his blazer, he awaited a command to restrict him from smoking, but it never materialized. So he withdrew a Marlboro, lit it with a gold–plated Zippo, and then rested it on a tray. Challenged, he considered the cigarette a show of defiance.

As the aircraft's ventilation inhaled the smoke, he broke the silence.

"What more do you demand?"

"I demand veto power."

"Meaning that you want me on a leash? You want the right to tell me to reject business?"

"Exactly," she said. "If you're going to be useful to me, then I can't have you getting your submarines destroyed or have you making more enemies than you already have. I've been using disinformation to try to hide your existence from the world, but that has its limits. You're becoming a known entity."

"I need to keep my crew fresh. I need to keep them active to keep them proficient. You can't stash me behind protective glass and wait until you need me."

"That depends how you define protective glass," she said. "I'm no idiot when it comes to submarines. You'll have your missions, even if I have to spoon feed you easy ones."

He exhaled smoke and calmed himself. Tactical retreat seemed his best option.

"We've been through a lot together. I see no reason to dive into more detail at the moment. It would only lead us to destructive paths of speculation and hypotheticals. Shall we delay clarifying the definition of your intent until a later date? I need my focus on the present mission."

Her smile came too easily for his tastes. In her mind, he deduced, her veto carried absolute power, and he would gain no ground attempting to argue it in her aircraft.

"Of course, Pierre. I believe we understand each other as far as we need to for this chat. However, I do want to be obvious about one detail."

"Go ahead."

"No matter what happens in the Spratlys, I want Jake to come back alive. If you need to make a choice, the *Rankin* is expendable. The Australians can always buy another submarine."

"Do you mean Jake specifically, or do you mean the *Wraith*, as the asset at your disposal?"

"Don't be dramatic. Can you separate the two? I can't."

"Fair point."

She stood, and he mimicked the gesture, recognizing the signal that his audience with the queen was concluding. Slinking around the table, she raised her arms to embrace him.

"Don't worry, Pierre. I won't do anything to upset Marie. I'm not in the habit of making wives jealous."

He accepted her hug and air kisses aside his cheeks. Resisting the allure of her perfume, he disengaged and walked to the door where he descended the stairs and then sensed the tarmac beneath his shoes.

As the jet taxied away, he stood by his limousine door and watched his old friend-turned-tyrant depart. Between puffs of a fresh Marlboro, he wrestled for a perspective on his new relationship with Olivia McDonald.

As her airplane alighted in the distance, he surprised himself by uttering a simple summary of his assessment.

"Bitch."

CHAPTER 11

Commander Wong checked his chart.

"It's time to change course," he said.

His gaunt executive officer presented a plasticized face.

"Sir, I agree that the lead ships should soon turn. However, I mark our own ship's turn around the Louisa Reef in thirty minutes."

"No," Wong said. "That's not what I meant. I mean this back and forth across the Malaysian land masses is wrong."

"These waters are the most likely place where the *Razak* is hiding. You declared this yourself, and I agree. The Malaysian submarine lacks the endurance to transit far from its home."

"Precisely," Wong said. "And there's been no sign of it despite our task force, maritime aircraft, and satellites hunting it for three days. We have a hundred conscripted men on fishing vessels, and they've seen nothing. We have passive sonar systems on merchant ships, and not a sound–including no sign of it imploding or sinking. We haven't even sniffed a radio broadcast or navigation radar transmission that could be mistaken for the *Razak*."

"This takes patience, sir, as you've taught me. The *Razak* will make a mistake. It's only a matter of time."

Wong tapped the chart and expanded its view.

"I know what I've taught you, and the lesson still stands. But that logic only applies if you're hunting in the right place. I believe that we have been duped and hunt nothing."

"The evidence is damning that the *Razak* attacked your brother on the *Luzhou*. The evidence is also convincing that the *Razak* has not returned to any Malaysian port. Our coastal spies are numerous and attentive, but they've seen nothing. Our target remains at large, sir."

"Agreed. And since it has no air-independent propulsion system, it must snorkel soon. It must. In fact, it should have snorkeled already."

"Per our estimates of its battery potential, it could have remained submerged since we entered the landmasses, but only if it has drifted without propulsion to conserve energy. It must snorkel soon."

Wong thought of the stifling life inside a submerged diesel-powered ship. Even deep, the tepid waters guaranteed discomfort to a crew condemned to sip energy from its battery. Electrical systems and the minimal atmosphere-purifying machinery would consume every precious watt.

Deprived of air conditioning, fans, and showers, men would stink. They'd eat uncooked meals from cans. Garbage bags would accumulate in corners, reminding the sailors that danger prevented them from compressing and ejecting their trash. Shared toilets would fill with rancid excretions, with relief coming only after a sonar search suggested safe solitude. The stench of fear–a warranted fear–would pervade the vessel.

Wong accepted that time worked against the *Razak* and that a change of the hunting parameters would lead to its discovery.

"I would agree with you," he said, "except that I challenge one of your assumptions. I believe the *Razak* hasn't tried to reach its homeport. Its commanding officer foresaw our response and attempted an alternate tactic. He knew that our maritime aircraft would block his route home, he knew that our task force would come, and he knew that we would hunt him in the waters closest to his home."

"It's possible that he considered these factors. But if so, then where is the *Razak*?"

"Either a neighboring state is harboring it, or it remains north of us, hiding between the Spratly Island landmasses, praying that we lose patience searching for it and decide to take out our vengeance elsewhere, as we have begun to do with our assault upon the garrison on Mariveles Reef."

"But why? Either case would only prolong the inevitable. The *Razak* doesn't have the endurance to outlast its hunters, and our nation has the resources to continue pursuing it. And a collaborating state could only hide it for so long before it would be discovered."

"I can't answer that," Wong said. "Nor can I fathom the insanity of that accursed submarine attacking my brother without cause. None of this absurdity makes sense, but I swear to you that sinking that vessel is the only answer that will bring me peace."

"Then let's find it, sir. You mean to search elsewhere?"

"Right. We are wasting our time looking between the Malaysian-owned Spratly landmasses and the Malaysian mainland. The *Razak* is not here."

"What do you suggest, sir?"

Wong saw a newfound use for the floating dock that he once had blamed for slowing his task force. It provided the amphibious firepower to support a plan he would recommend to fleet headquarters in Zhanjiang.

"We send the *Jinggang Shan* and the frigates to threaten the local nations. They approach their populated coasts, regardless of their diplomatic standing with Malaysia, and we have our national leadership threaten shore bombardment and landings. Let our politicians glean information from the military pressure. Fear drives men to talk."

"If the *Razak* is harbored by another nation, then I agree that threating amphibious military action is beneficial. But why did you mention just the frigates to accompany the floating dock?"

"I wouldn't deprive the dock of frigate support. But I'm taking our nuclear submarine and the corvettes and breaking off to search for the *Razak*."

The executive officer's eyes glowed with suspicion.

"I see, sir. That will give us better search speed. But how do we make it happen? The task force commander receives suggestions unfavorably."

"I will go over his head. I will make use of my connections."

An announcement of flash message traffic drew the executive officer's attention.

"I understand, sir. Will you excuse me while I investigate our new message?"

"Yes. Brief me after you've read it."

Wong sipped tepid tea and gazed through the window at the moon's reflection shimmering atop the waves. Moments passed in an instant, and his executive officer marched back into his view.

"Sir!"

"Something interesting?"

"Yes. There is heavy shipping movement around a Philippine-claimed Spratly landmass."

"The Philippines?" Wong asked.

Wong reached into his trouser pockets for his phone. He pulled it out and digested the report.

Several amphibious docks had made landfall–rather, their landing craft had made landfall while the docks loitered beyond the coral reef–on the Philippine's largest claim, Thitu Island. Satellite photographs showed pictures of truck-mounted mobile anti-air systems, identified as American Avengers and also pictures of bundles of shoulder-mounted American Stinger missiles.

Parked excavators and slipform pavers appeared in a makeshift construction zone, poised to extend and concretize the island's runway and its causeway. The small military presence seemed to be taking over the island.

Wong's mind worked in bursts, drawing a rapid conclusion.

"Do you see a coincidence that a Malaysian submarine draws our attention to the southern fringe of the Spratly Islands while the Philippines multiply their military presence on their largest island to the far north?"

"I would, sir, if I believed in military coincidences."

"Well said. I do not believe in military coincidences either. Forget my plan of splitting the task force. We have a new ground zero. This entire task force must head to Thitu to challenge this Philippine uprising."

"What of the *Razak*, sir? Retribution for your brother?"

"The *Razak* will be near Thitu, defending it."

A watch officer announced the arrival of a new message. Orders from the task force commander aligned with Wong's wishes. The Chinese ships would leave the Malaysian waters and head north.

Ten minutes later, he turned the *Chengdu* north and joined his task force's journey to Thitu and its new potential adversary.

As the sun set on the following day, shimmering shadows stretched over the sea. Wong paced across his bridge, fearing that the *Razak* had somehow passed through the layered defense of his task force and lurked below him, awaiting its perfect timing to deliver a death blow.

Recognizing his paranoia, he stepped into the moist air, leaned, and pressed his palms atop a bulwark. A deep sigh escaped his lungs, and he lowered his head between his shoulders.

As the door opened, he craned his neck and saw his executive officer.

"We have our new orders, sir. We're officially attacking Thitu within three hours."

"Is Captain Zhang ordering us to provide cannon support for his landing teams?"

"Yes, sir. Just as we did against the garrison at Mariveles Reef."

"There are civilians on Thitu. One errant round of ammunition will destroy any diplomatic leverage we have. For the moment, the international community sympathizes with us for the unwarranted attack on my brother. But if we kill Philippine civilians, we would force the United States to become involved, working against us with international support."

"Given Captain Zhang's personality, I don't think he considers those factors."

"He's an imbecile," Wong said. "He's going risk political destruction of our mission while he sets up the naval combatant vessels as targets against the *Razak*. I won't die and fail in my revenge due to his stupidity."

"What can you do, sir? You know he is stubborn."

"Have you shared these orders with anyone else?"

"No, sir."

"Good. Get our helicopter ready for personnel transport and

watch what I do."

As the sun dipped below the horizon, Wong stood on the bridge wing and watched his helicopter angle towards the *Chengdu's* fantail. He ducked through the door and darted out the back of the bridge. Moving with determined agility, he traversed the length of the destroyer and stepped out the rear of its superstructure.

Rotor wash whipped his face as he approached the crew that assisted the helicopter's landing. Once his men lashed the aircraft to the deck, he ducked and trotted to its door.

Within its cramped cabin, he recognized the four commanding officers of the task force's frigates and corvettes seated behind his two-man flight crew. The occupants stirred at his arrival.

"Stay seated gentlemen!" he said.

The commanding officers, all junior to him, obeyed. He turned to his flight crew.

"Except you two. I need privacy with your passengers. But don't go far. I need you to return them to their ships in ten minutes."

As the aviators stepped out, Wong crouched in a tight huddle with his surface combatant colleagues.

"You've all received orders from Captain Zhang to provide gunfire support against Thitu, have you not?"

A chorus of confirmations of the order and its absurdity filled the cabin.

"We agree then," Wong said, "that it would be foolish to bombard Thitu and that limiting our maneuverability to launch that attack would make us easy targets for the *Razak*. We got lucky when the *Razak* failed to appear at Mariveles Reef, and I don't expect we shall see such fortune again at Thitu. Instead, I expect that our submerged target will expose itself in defense of this Philippine-claimed island."

"So you believe the Malaysians and Philippines are united against us," a lieutenant commander asked.

"It's the only solution that makes sense, other than random coincidence, which I refuse to accept."

"I agree," a second lieutenant commander said. "But we face the challenge of our task force commander's myopia on the amphibious assault."

"I have a solution for that," Wong said. "That's why I flew you here in person. We are going to disobey his orders, and I will take personal responsibility for the deviation."

Silent heads nodded, their faces blank with disbelief but flush with hope and relief.

"As commander of the surface combatant contingent of this task force, I will deal with this. By protocol, Zhang will be trapped. Once he issues the order for us to provide him gunfire support, you will all then technically report to me and must follow my instructions on how to carry out his order."

"I don't see how that solves the problem," a commander younger and subordinate to Wong said.

"When you are all under my instruction, I will issue an order to conduct anti-submarine warfare operations prior to beginning bombardment. I will cite the reason as protecting the task force."

"That's logical, but risky," the commander said. "What if the forces at Thitu resist Captain Zhang's landing teams? We will have failed to weaken them, causing casualties to our own comrades."

"I thought of this already," he said. "You make a good point, but there is a flaw in your rebuttal. Did you look at the intelligence photographs of Thitu closely?"

"Of course."

"I know what you saw," Wong said. "But what did you not see?"

Shoulders shrugged, and eyes met across the cabin, seeking insight but instead confirming a shared ignorance.

"What?" the junior commander asked.

"You didn't see any offensive weapons added to the island. Not one cannon. Not one anti-ship missile. Not one rifle. Everything we saw was either construction equipment or air defenses."

"Deploying those weapons is still an act of aggression," the junior commander said.

"Of course, it is" Wong said. "But to what end? Did Manila expect us to ignore their build up? I think not. They knew we would respond. And what does a lack of offensive firepower tell you?"

"Either they underestimated our resolve to respond," the commander said, "or they have a dangerous surprise for us."

"Correct," Wong said. "Even if I didn't suspect the presence of the *Razak* working in conjunction with the Philippines, I would draw the latter conclusion that we are walking into a trap."

"But we are walking into it, like it or not," the commander said. "I agree that we must implement anti-submarine warfare tactics, but whether or not there are new offensive weapons on Thitu, there is a military force present on the island to resist our landing teams. We must acknowledge our obligation to provide the gunfire support."

"I do," Wong said. "I acknowledge it just as I acknowledge the situation we saw at Mariveles Reef. There was a military force present there, but they simply surrendered."

"And you expect the same at Thitu?"

"Not necessarily a surrendering, but a trap," Wong said. "There is no other explanation for the increased activity at Thitu. I suspect the *Razak* as the concealed danger awaiting us, but its presence may not comprise the entirety of the ruse. There may be more to it. However, since the Philippine forces were smart enough to expect us to use naval gunfire support, I expect that such bombardment will fail to counter whatever surprise awaits us."

Heads nodded their agreement.

"Therefore," Wong said, "we must search for the *Razak* at Thitu, and we must remain on high alert for other surprises. Gunfire support is all but irrelevant."

"Logical," the commander said.

"Do I have your support?" Wong asked.

"I support you," the commander said.

"As do I," a lieutenant commander said.

"As do I," another lieutenant commander said.

"I support you as well," the last officer said.

"Good," Wong said. "When you return to your ships, look to your tactical systems for further instructions, which I will transmit personally. I will avoid the main circuits for establishing our anti-submarine warfare search plan around Thitu. I don't want Zhang to overhear that we are united in overcoming his stupidity."

John R. Monteith

CHAPTER 12

Jake glared at Lieutenant Commander Flores.

"Approach the conn," he said.

The Philippine officer stepped below him, and Jake leaned over the polished rail to hold a private conversation.

"Yes, Jake?"

"You look seasick. Being shallow on a submarine is difficult when the swells rock us. Don't worry, though. We'll go deep soon."

"No, I'm fine."

"You don't look fine."

"It's not seasickness."

Jake studied him.

"I see," he said. "You're afraid. You've never been in real combat."

Jake realized the banality of his observation. Flores' nation barely had a navy.

"It's okay to be afraid your first time."

"I was hoping it wasn't obvious."

"Nobody here wants to die," Jake said. "We'll be okay, and everyone expects to come home alive."

"I do, too."

"Then you need to start looking like it. Your men will feed off your confidence or your fear, depending which dominates you."

"I understand."

"Remember that we have the tactical advantages of surprise and superior positioning. Heck, if all goes well, we'll be just an insurance policy. This could all be one big training exercise."

"I know, Jake. Forgive me for doubting. I know of your history and experience. If anyone can lead a submarine into a successful battle, you can."

"I appreciate the vote of confidence. Everyone I've ever taken to sea on a submarine has come back alive. Well, unless you count people killed by firearms inside one of them. Or, I guess you have to count the collision I had with an ice wall that killed one guy from impact and another from the fire that broke out after it. But other than that, I have a clean record for ten years."

A shadow crept over the Philippine officer's face.

"I wasn't aware that people under your care had died."

"Technically, only two were mine. The rest turned against me and had it coming."

"Only two men? Then every submarine you've taken to sea has returned safely?"

"Yes. Sort of. There was the one I abandoned because, well, because I had to. I tried to scuttle it, but then it got hit by a torpedo. Then there was the one I used to absorb a torpedo to save an American destroyer. So I guess I've actually lost two submarines to torpedoes."

Flores stared at him.

"But there was nobody aboard when they got hit," Jake said. "I managed to get everyone off them."

"So other than two casualties from a collision, everyone else has been safe under your command? You've lost two ships, but everyone survived those loses?"

"Right. Oh, wait. I had to abandon ship one other time, but I ended up evading that torpedo and keeping that ship. It's called the *Specter* now, and I know you've heard guys telling stories about it. I got really lucky, though. I should have died, along with half the French guys on this ship."

Flores appeared more spooked.

"May I return to my station?" he asked.

"Sure. I hope our little chat has helped."

"I think I have a better sense about my odds of survival."

Flores fled for a seat in front of a Subtics monitor. Moments later, Henri came to Jake.

"I don't know what you said to him, but he looks worse than he did before your conversation."

"I was trying to boost his confidence," Jake said.

"How so?"

"I just told him a bit about our history and how we've managed to survive."

"That explains much of his dismay."

"I didn't want him playing twenty questions with me like he did before I attacked that corvette."

"I see," Henri said. "You may have succeeded in deterring him from asking you questions, but I fear that you've incapacitated him with worry."

"He'll be fine when the action starts."

"I'm unsure if I agree with you, but I concede that there's nothing to be done about it."

"I have faith in him because I have no choice at the moment. Sometimes he's annoying, and he looks scared now. I always encourage you to call me out when you think I'm missing something. Do you see a red flag here?"

"Perhaps. It's difficult to tell in these situations, and I don't quite see any cause for alarm," Henri said. "I am merely asking you to watch him closely."

"If he does lose his cool, there are enough of us with combat experience to keep him in line."

Jake moved around the railing and stepped down from the conning platform. He bellied up to the navigation table in the center of the *Wraith's* control room. Beside him, Henri tapped the horizontal screen, pulling tactical information from the Subtics system onto the chart before them.

"You must thank Miss McDonald for the information she has made available to us," Henri said.

"I'd rather keep my distance," Jake said. "From what Pierre tells me, she's become a she-devil."

"Nevertheless, we are in her debt."

"That's the problem."

"Shall I raise the communications buoy for updated data?"

Jake looked at the digital clock on his chart. The latest download had aged ten minutes. With his buoyant communications suite tethered below the waves, it remained hidden from airborne and orbiting spies, but its temporary stealth made it useless.

Slithering across the sea's surface, a wire trailed behind the

Wraith, invisible to hunters. It handled low-frequency and low-bandwidth data, designed as an alarm system to get Jake's attention. He likened it to a paging system.

"No," he said. "Let's see what the world looks like ten minutes ago and then determine if we need an update. If something big happens, Pierre will page me."

The eastern section of the irregularly shaped Spratly Islands appeared with the crosshairs of the *Wraith* at the center. Thirty miles southeast of the submarine, a blue square indicated a freighter at anchor beside the Second Thomas Shoal.

Within his horizon, the Chinese-held Mischief Reef appeared as a blob of a landmass. Despite watchful enemy eyes, he considered the adversarial stronghold to be innocuous as long as he kept his masts and antennas below the water's surface.

One hundred and twenty nautical miles to the northwest, red lines sprang from squares of the Chinese task force, indicating the motions of its ships towards Thitu Island. Land masses dotted the water between the *Wraith* and the task force, as did a half dozen red squares representing Chinese fishing vessels suspected of carrying spying equipment.

Also dotting the water, blue squares represented Philippine fishing vessels that carried friendly spy equipment. The closest one ten miles away served as Jake's communications conduit to the command center. When he raised his buoy, he could keep its transmission power minimized and directional to avoid detection while reaching the nearby craft.

A corner of the chart showed the latest photograph of the railgun module from the perspective of the *Sierra Madre*, the vessel that Philippine maritime forces had grounded in the shallows.

The unmoving winch from the freighter had just freed itself from bearing the railgun module's weight. Pontoons held the structure buoyant as tugboats positioned its pillars above its final location at the northeast tip of the landmass. The latest update reported that divers were checking the final placement and that it would be operational in thirty minutes. From the look of the Chinese task force, the timing would be ideal.

Additional blue icons of interest represented the nearby friendly gunboats, but he expected them to provide negligible crippling force due to the limitations of their weapon systems. To his west, an inverted semicircle represented the *Rankin*, which served no purpose in his mind other than staying out of his way and then usurping whatever political credit the Australians needed to claim.

To his southeast, a blue square showed the frigate *Gregorio del Pilar* standing guard behind the *Wraith*. Ten miles from the *Pilar*, its sister ship, the *Ramon Alcatraz*, offered to serve as part of the final barrier to any would-be assault on the module at the Second Thomas Shoal.

Despite his fond memories of the *Pilar's* role in his acquisition of the *Wraith*, he doubted its use beyond serving as an accidental missile sponge. The aging frigate and its sister ship, the *Alcatraz*, positioned southeast of the module, lacked defenses against cruise missiles beyond rudimentary retrofitting of Vulcan Phalanx close-in weapon systems.

The ancient former United States Coast Guard cutters faced an uphill climb trying to survive modern combat. But Jake respected their commanding officers' desires to participate in protecting the railgun. In the event of surface combat, he hoped that the frigates' cannons and the gunboats' small-caliber armaments might provide enough harassment against the Chinese to create a protective fog of war.

"I can't predict what's going to happen," he said. "But I think something interesting's about to take place. We need to get ready."

"Shall I prepare a drone?" Henri asked.

"Prepare them both. We're digging in to play defense."

Jake had used drones to his advantage in past encounters, but they incurred a significant cost. Since they transmitted information back to their host vessel by a wire connected within the torpedo tubes, each one's use precluded reloading a tube. Using two drones limited him to four available weapons.

But he had loaded two drones during his Philippine port call, knowing that he would want them out in front of his submarine, protecting it and extending his acoustic detection radius.

"Where do you want them?" Henri asked.

"Ten miles out, forty-five degrees off our bow in either direction. Straight runs at eight knots."

"I shall take care of it."

Henri slid behind Jake and leaned over the shoulder of the newest young man recruited from the French Navy. Henri had assured Jake of the new crewman's training and ability with operating drones. The sailor appeared confident while he exchanged words with the mechanic.

Henri returned to Jake.

"He entered the data," he said. "The drones are initiating and will be ready in ninety seconds."

"His name is Durand, right?" Jake asked. "The new kid running the drones?"

"Correct," Henri said. "His commanding officer in the French Navy said he was the best weapons control operator he had seen. At the end of his enlistment commitment, Renard plucked him away by offering the usual tripled salary versus the military pay scales."

"Thanks, Henri" Jake said. "Take your station."

He returned to the conning platform, stood before a monitor, and called up a miniature overhead view of the tactical chart. He raised his head and watched Durand turn his chin towards his shoulder. A tiny line jutting from the man's freckled skin revealed that he approached his thirties.

"Drone one is ready," Durand said.

"Very well," Jake said. "Launch drone one."

"Launch drone one, aye."

Jake appreciated the subtlety of a drone launch. Unlike many torpedoes, which high-pressure air thrust from the tubes, drones operated free of the safety interlocks that required rapid accelerations to disarm. The *Wraith* maintained its whisper-like silence as its first mechanized spy swam into the sea.

"Drone one is launched," Durand said. "Normal launch, all systems normal, normal control."

Jake watched the inverted blue semicircle separate from the crosshair of its host submarine. It veered off forty-five degrees to the left of the *Wraith*, which floated silently with the ocean current.

"Drone two is ready," Durand said.

"Very well," Jake said. "Launch drone two."

"Launch drone two, aye."

"Drone two is launched," Durand said. "Normal launch, all systems normal, normal control."

Fed by a combination of onboard battery power and electricity delivered up its control wire from the *Wraith*, the second drone accelerated to eight knots. Its blue icon veered forty-five degrees to the right.

The air in the control room thickened, and Jake realized that the simple act of drone deployment had given half his crew their first major taste of undersea surveillance.

He waited until the drones reached two miles from his ship to make his next move.

"Henri," he said. "Raise the buoy and get a download."

A servomotor whispered above his head, extending the length of the buoy's tether.

"The buoy is surfaced and linked," Henri said.

"Send incoming data to Subtics."

The red squares of the Chinese task force inched closer to Thitu. A notable exception from Jake's view was the *Shang*-class nuclear submarine suspected to be part of that task force but hiding beyond the reach of friendly detection systems.

"I see the new data on the task force," he said. "Can you get me video of the railgun?"

"Yes. I'm streaming it now."

Live video from the beached landing craft showed the concrete obelisk taking root in the shoal, its compact solidness standing in defiance of any threat.

As the freighter raised its anchors and departed, the module's lid rose, exposing its air defenses and its railguns. The opened gap exposed opaqueness through the camera's night vision, but Jake knew the firepower the shadows hid. Cutting edge technology pointed northwest towards Thitu and the task force that threatened it.

The image became clearer as the camera adjusted for ambient moonlight, and the muzzles appeared as black lines pointing outward. They then rose upward in elevation, preparing to send shells within miles of their maximum distance.

A voice from the control room speaker startled him. As he recovered his bearings and reached above for a handset, he recognized it as Renard's.

"*Wraith*, this is Fox Den, can you hear me?" Renard asked.

"Fox Den, this is *Wraith*. Go ahead," Jake said.

"Nothing urgent," Renard said. "In fact, all thus far is going per plan. However, I needed to inform you that the festivities are about to begin."

"The task force is taking the bait?" Jake asked.

"It appears so. I don't have the authority to make that determination, but I expect that landing craft will be deployed soon against Thitu and that you'll hear friendly retaliation within an hour."

"Good to know."

"I recommend that you remain ready to lower your buoy and seek maximum stealth if you hear the guns fire. Chinese satellites and any available surveillance aircraft will soon be looking in your general direction, if they aren't already."

"Got it," Jake said.

"Good luck, my friend," Renard said. "As always, I trust you will optimize my planning and improvise where needed."

Jake bid his friend and mentor farewell and faced his crew. A dozen pairs of eyes looked back at him for confidence. He felt a twinge of doubt, due to the pending uncertainty of combat, but he forced his features to take on a rugged look of fearlessness as he sat back on the foldout captain's chair.

"Get ready, gents," he said. "The fun is about to start."

CHAPTER 13

Wong tapped coordinates into the *Chengdu's* tactical data system, ordering the task force's other four surface combatants into their submarine search geometry. Through the destroyer's mast-mounted night vision camera, Thitu appeared as a warm glow on the horizon, and his system showed his task force surrounding it.

"Flash traffic, sir," his executive officer said.

A glance at his phone told him that Captain Zhang wanted confirmation of his gunnery orders. He ignored the task force commander and slid the device back into his pocket.

"Noted," he said.

The executive officer released a wry smile, marking the first time Wong had seen the corner of the man's mouth rise.

Watching the tactical display, he saw the frigates and corvettes fan out and encircle Thitu, supported by three helicopters that completed an octagon around the island.

A voice boomed over the bridge's loudspeaker.

"*Chengdu*, this is *Jinggang Shan*. Over."

"Anyone who answers Captain Zhang will spend eternity in the brig," Wong said.

The voice rang out louder.

"*Chengdu*, this is *Jinggang Shan*. Answer me!"

Admitting his cruel joy to himself, he suppressed a smile.

"Damn you, Wong! What do you think you're doing?"

He reached up for the radio and turned it off. Returning his attention to the tactical view, he tapped his finger against a liquid crystal display, ordering all available assets to shift their active sonar frequencies and duty cycles to avoid interfering with each other.

"Set active sonar at half power," he said. "Set the ping interval to allow a maximum search range of twenty nautical miles."

The deep chirp of three-kilohertz sound resonated through the ship's hull.

"All ahead two-thirds," he said. "Begin submarine search legs."

As the deep chirp resonated again, the deck tilted under him, and he held a railing for support. With the *Chengdu* maneuvering itself on a preset zigzag course within its defined search area, a sailor carried out Wong's order with the press of a button.

For a moment, fear gripped him, and minutes elapsed like hours. Ten minutes into the search, he called each commanding officer, including those of the helicopter air crews, for status.

Nothing.

Sensing his executive officer next to him, he verbalized his frustration.

"I'm starting to suspect that I was wrong," he said. "The *Razak* may have simply vanished."

"Don't give up hope yet, sir."

Wong repeated his fruitless plea to the unit commanders ten minutes later. Then, as a half an hour of futility seemed like an exhaustive eternity, he capitulated.

"Secure from submarine search legs," he said. "Position us for gunfire support."

When his ship reached fifteen miles from Thitu, he ordered an ovular course, alternating broadsides to the island. As he noticed the other vessels in position, he sent a tactical message to the *Jinggang Shan* declaring the task force's readiness for gunfire support.

On his display, he noticed landing craft exiting the floating dock and sprinting towards the island. He noticed an absence of air assault craft, a sign of respect for the Philippine forces' bolstered air defenses. Orders from the floating dock flooded his display, telling him where to lay down gunfire.

"So it begins," he said. "Prepare for gunfire support!"

Bowing his head and bracing himself for a beating, he turned on the radio. Worse than knowing what awaited him was the sick twisting in his stomach questioning if he deserved it.

"*Jinggang Shan*," he said, "this is *Chengdu*. Over."

The replying voice sounded deeper than Zhang's. Wong felt momentary relief but knew it was the captain's way of extending the anticipation of the agony.

"*Chengdu*, this is *Jinggang Shan*. Standby for the task force commander."

"*Jinggang Shan*, this is *Chengdu*. Standing by. Over."

The new voice that replied carried an eerie calmness of vengeance in mid-satiation. Excess formality compounded Wong's inner agony.

"*Chengdu*, this is task force commander. With whom am I speaking? Over."

He knew that Zhang recognized his voice but relished the buildup to the final blow that would likely cost him command of his ship. Even if his connections back home could save him, he doubted he deserved being saved. He had gambled by disobeying an order from a superior officer, and the *Razak* had not appeared.

"Task force commander, this is Commander Wong of the *Chengdu*. I await orders to commence fire. Over."

"Commander Wong," Zhang said. "Did you think your submarine hunting stunt would go unnoticed?"

"No, sir. I thought it wise if–"

"Silence!"

Wong clenched his jaw.

"Why should I think you are smart enough to recognize a rhetorical question when you're not smart enough to carry out a very simple order?"

He found himself in a scholarly trap. If he answered, he reinforced his accuser's point, but silence would seem like insubordination, doubling Zhang's fury. He chose to inflict more rage rather than admit stupidity.

"So, Wong. You have nothing to say for yourself?"

"I must apologize, sir. I made a decision that I deemed prudent for the defense of our forces, but the search proved unnecessary."

"Don't you apologize to me, Wong! Do you think that showing meekness now, after you've defied and embarrassed me, will give you a shred of hope of retaining command of your vessel? Do I need to remind you that I indeed have the authority to strip you of your command, replace you, and have you tossed into the brig?"

As Wong pondered another scholarly trap, a sonic boom cut the night, and a small explosion illuminated a landing craft off his port quarter.

"What was that? Task force commander–out!" Zhang said.

Wong exhaled as he realized that divine providence rained down destruction upon his countrymen, killing his comrades but preserving his command–at least until his next conversation with Zhang.

As long as the *Chengdu* remained his, he would command it, and he switched the radio circuit to an internal network.

"Operations center," he said, "tell me what's going on."

His operations officer replied with a tense voice.

"I'm not sure, sir. It's unlike anything we've seen."

Another boom ripped through the air, and another explosion shot from the same landing craft.

His subconscious mind taking over, he realized something odd about the attack. The explosions seemed too small for warheads, and whatever struck the landing craft hadn't destroyed the tiny vessel with two hits. But the weapon struck with accuracy, as if guided.

A fuzzy image of a potential weapon formed in his mind, but nothing real registered.

"Is it coming from Thitu?" he asked.

"No, sir," the operations officer said. "It's coming from the southeast."

"What's out there to the southeast?" Wong asked.

He looked on his display, seeing but disbelieving the answer.

"Nothing, sir. Absolutely nothing!"

Another boom and explosion, followed by reports of a fire breaking out on the landing craft, which continued onward but at reduced speed.

"Something is launching weapons at our landing vessels. Give me information. Speed of the weapon. Trajectory. Radar cross section. Give me something!"

Another boom and explosion hit a second landing craft, as if guided by divine eyes. Wong began a silent countdown in expectation of the next hit.

"There must be an error, sir."

"Tell me what you have."

"The projectiles are moving at Mach 7."

Another boom and explosion. Five seconds separated the rounds.

"Say again."

"Mach 7, sir. Their radar cross sections are smaller than three-inch cannon rounds, and we can barely detect them. The other ships with inferior systems can't even track them. Only we can."

Boom.

"Do you have the trajectories? Can you trace them to their source?"

"Yes, sir. Due to the speed and small radar cross sections, this is rough, but the source is over a hundred nautical miles away."

"Are these self-propelled projectiles?"

Boom, but the second craft under assault continued towards Thitu undaunted. He overheard reports of the craft's hull being punctured by tiny holes and its armored vehicles being punctured as well, but the boat maintained its propulsion and structural integrity.

"No, sir. We would see contrails or exhaust plumes or something on infrared. We don't see anything but hot air heated by friction, and the incoming weapons are following ballistic trajectories."

Boom.

"Nothing without self-propulsion can follow a ballistic trajectory that far except..."

"Yes, sir?"

While he struggled to utter his thoughts, another explosion cut its target, and an engine on the second craft caught fire. Half the landing force had been slowed before reaching a fourth of the way to its destination.

"A railgun," he said.

Another boom and explosion, this time on a new victim. A third craft suffered a puncture wound in a fuel tank, setting off a deafening explosion that echoed across the waves.

"There are no railguns deployed, sir, except for the American *Zumwalt*-class destroyer, and every *Zumwalt*-class ship is accounted for. It can't be a *Zumwalt*."

Boom, and a small explosion rose from the final landing craft.

"There's a Philippine frigate in the general area of the launch platform, sir. It may have been fitted with a railgun."

Boom.

The thought of a fifty-three-year-old converted coast guard cutter ruining his already tragic day sickened him. Groping for a solution, he realized that the shells were hitting rapid targets with alarming accuracy, even as he overheard his comrades' failed attempts at evasive maneuvers.

Boom.

Something guided them, and that meant that their guidance could be thwarted. He sought a countermeasure.

"Can you detect any guidance communications?" he asked.

"Hold on, sir," the operations officer said. "I need to scan for that. Give me thirty seconds."

Boom.

While his staff sought jamming frequencies, he considered a simpler solution–the electromagnetic befuddlement of chaff.

He switched frequencies to the hail the task force commander.

"*Jinggang Shan*, this is *Chengdu*. Over."

"*Chengdu*, this is task force commander. What's going on? You have the best sensory systems in the group. Tell me who and what is attacking us!"

"Sir, I believe it's a railgun, most likely mounted aboard the Philippine frigate, *Gregorio del Pilar*."

"My landing force is being assaulted by hypervelocity munitions, and you tell me a relic over a hundred miles away is responsible?"

"They must have stolen or purchased American technology,

sir. But I have an idea. Send the entire task force northwest to open range from the attack. Even railguns have limits on their reach."

"I know that! I'm already heading northwest, you moron!"

Wong's stomach tightened as he realized that he dealt with a frightened idiot.

"I mean the entire landing force, including what's left of the landing craft. Have them slow down, pop chaff, and hide under their chaff. Have them huddle together under a combined chaff cloud and then work their way northwest as fast as the chaff will allow."

"Wait," Zhang said.

Another craft became hobbled but able to limp forward.

"I have given the order," Zhang said.

"You must also order the nearest frigate to sprint towards the landing craft and escort them northwest. The frigate may have enough chaff to carry them out of harm's way."

Four more rounds struck targets, and Wong feared that Zhang would relieve him of command as he watched his landing force die a death of a thousand cuts.

Then, as shards of floating metal hid the huddled and slowed landing craft from electronic targeting, a shell splashed into the water. The convoy slipped northwest at absurdly slow speeds for maritime assault vessels, but then the next round missed. Then another, and yet another.

He glanced at a tactical display and confirmed his suspicion. His ship's electronic sensory measures suite detected electromagnetic energy from a Philippine C-295 airborne early warning and control aircraft that circled beyond the range of his surface-to-air missiles.

Until the rounds landed, the distant airborne radar energy had meant nothing. But as the picture cleared, he realized that the aircraft provided targeting data for the railgun, and as the projectiles started to miss their targets, he realized that chaff disrupted the radar energy, degrading the targeting data.

"Chaff works, sir!" he said. "They can't guide the projectiles if they can't get radar return on our ships!"

"Now what, Wong?" Zhang asked.

"Have the landing craft continue to make best speed to the frigate," he said. "Order all other vessels to escape northwest under their own chaff."

"Your idea had better work!" Zhang said.

"It's our only hope, sir. We know the railgun projectiles are arriving from greater than forty degrees of elevation. We're near the edge of the weapon's maximum range."

"Very well," Zhang said. "I will give the order to evade."

As the diverted and battered landing force escaped northwest, a frigate sprinted to intercept them and offer its greater supply of metallic cloud coverage.

The vessels took turns popping aluminum shards, prolonging their collected protective coverage, but as ships designed for minimal combat at sea, they carried few canisters and ran out. Their final chaff cloud draped the water with metallic slivers, exposing them to the incoming projectiles.

As Wong's contentment of having protected the landing force ebbed with the exhaustion of chaff canisters, a railgun shell sliced through a fuel tank, setting another vessel ablaze. The fire, combined with the collection of harsh puncture wounds, sent all survivors overboard.

Rounds continued to pelt their targets. As he began to give up hope that the landing craft would reach the frigate's chaff coverage, his operations officer hailed him.

"Sir! We may have a useful jamming frequency. We're attempting jamming now."

"Excellent! What frequency?"

"Military Global Positioning Satellite, sir. There's frequency hopping, but I believe we can jam enough frequencies to disrupt the targeting."

"Do it!"

"Already in progress, sir!"

Despite no chaff cover, the next shell missed. Then the next. Given the ninety-second flight time of each projectile and the five-second spacing between them, only three of the next eighteen rounds impaled landing craft. Wong considered the hits to be random luck as his ship jammed the incoming guidance data.

Then the barrage ceased, as the assailants adjusted to Wong's active electronic countermeasure.

"Apparently, our attackers have realized that we have found a defense," Wong said. "Excellent work down there."

As his operations officer responded, he heard cautious and subdued cheers from the operations center deep within his destroyer.

"Thank you, sir. But we're not out of trouble yet. Whoever is attacking us is already thinking of a way around our chaff and jamming. And our chaff won't last forever."

"That's an astute observation," Wong said. "Railguns can hold huge magazines of shells, since they are cheap and small. Our chaff won't last forever, but the incoming rounds will."

"I'm afraid I agree, sir."

"Then we must take aggressive action. In fact, I have an idea."

He hailed his task force commander.

"Sir, I believe we can destroy that railgun."

"Really?" Zhang said. "How can you be so sure of yourself?"

"Sir, I believe that the Philippines have performed a strategic blunder. Our *Shang*-class submarine is impervious to the railgun and can defeat the *Pilar*."

"Have you forgotten that there's a hostile submarine out there? Or is that perhaps your intent—to have a nuclear submarine handle your personal vendetta against the *Razak* while attacking the frigate?"

"No, sir. I'm focused on the railgun now. Thitu is unreachable while the railgun is operational. We must all continue evading northwest while our submarine sinks the *Pilar*."

"It will disappoint you then," Zhang said, "to learn that I have just received satellite photographs of the gun that just attacked us. It is not, as you brilliantly surmised, the *Pilar*. It is instead a newly installed concrete-armored stronghold placed atop the Second Thomas Shoal."

The report hit him like a punch in the stomach. Without needing to see the picture, he realized that a torpedo would be useless against his assailant. If the Philippine military had gone to the trouble to mount a railgun on a shoal, they would have been sure to strengthen it with reinforced concrete.

Like airdropped bombs that bounced off German submarine bunkers in World War II, a torpedo exploding next to–but not underneath–a concrete edifice would deliver at best a glancing blow, and that was if the weapon could pass above the shoals and through wiring or netting that was sure to surround the structure.

"Does the stronghold appear vulnerable to submarine-launched missiles?" he asked.

"You tell me. I'm transmitting the picture to you now."

The night vision satellite image showed a huge block of blackness. Annotations by intelligence analysts called out what little his countrymen knew of the new threat, but they suggested concrete surrounding all sides.

"No, sir. Submarine-launched missiles may have an effect, but I wouldn't expect to inflict meaningful damage on that structure without landing a large salvo of missiles or naval bombardment."

"What about air power?"

"It's close to Philippine airspace, and they have two new squadrons of respectable Korean-designed TA-50 fighter aircraft. I also expect that the railguns themselves can attack air targets."

"That's not a recommendation, Wong."

He clenched his jaw and then continued.

"If air power is available, sir, we would need bunker busters to make a difference. But I'm sure they were smart enough to include anti-air defenses as part of the structure to mitigate any air attack we could launch. So it would need to be a large-scale air assault, but I expect it would succeed."

"Other than running away and hoping that a submarine or squadron of bombers solves the problem, what do you plan to do about it?"

He wanted to keep command of the *Chengdu*, he wanted to find the *Razak*, and he wanted to destroy the railgun. He believed that he could accomplish all three goals with one new mission.

"Sir, the Philippine forces on that shoal surprised us with new technology, but I've already found two countermeasures with chaff and jamming. Let me take the surface combatants and the *Shang* and launch an attack on the structure on the Second Thomas Shoal."

"Just a subset of this task force? Against a railgun?"

"The time to take this on is now. When else will our nation have the guns of a destroyer and two frigates this close to the railgun? When else will the *Razak* likely be working with the Philippine forces and ripe for hunting by a *Shang*-class submarine and five surface ships capable of anti-submarine warfare?"

"So you consider yourself a hero?"

"I'm no fool, sir. I will want a coordinated air strike as part of the assault, so as to saturate the stronghold's defenses."

"You don't even have an idea about its defenses. I will not seek air support based upon your speculation."

Wong knew that he could use his connections to work around Zhang's noncompliance.

"I'll use the resources at my disposal then."

"If you want to commit suicide and take hundreds of men with you, it's on your conscience."

"I understand, sir. I will take my chances. The lives of all men involved will be on my conscience."

Boom, and a round hit the floating dock.

"Damn you, Wong! They're attacking the *Jinggang Shan* now. I thought you were jamming their projectiles!"

"I am, sir."

Another shell hit.

"Then why are they hitting my ship?"

Another round punctured the floating dock, creating the tiniest burst of light in the night outside Wong's bridge window. He realized the obvious problem.

"Sir, you're driving in a straight line. You haven't changed course since you started popping chaff. They're sending the projectiles ahead of your path and waiting for you to drive under them. They don't need guidance to hit you, and chaff and jamming won't help until you commence zigzag legs."

Five more shells punctured the floating dock before it could alter its trajectory, and then every fifth round hit the hull as the railgun operators played a guessing game predicting the position of Zhang's ship.

Wong enjoyed the fear in the task force commander's voice.

"Very well, then, Wong. Keep command of your accursed vessel, and you can have the surface combatants and the *Shang*, provided their commanding officers volunteer to join you."

"And as many helicopters as my ships can carry."

"Yes, damn you, Wong! I don't want your death lingering over my head for having deprived you of helicopters. My task force is hereby dismantled. You have command of a new task force, staffed by anyone who is foolish enough to join you."

"Thank you, sir."

Wong's sarcastic salutation lingered unanswered as he tapped keys on his display inviting the surface combatants to rally to him under a new task force for attacking the Second Thomas Shoal.

All four commanding officers responded with courage and zeal, and Wong planned to wait until the *Shang's* next communications check to invite the submarine to join.

His ships cutting random lines in the water to evade railgun rounds, he began his nautical march to the southeast.

CHAPTER 14

Renard pushed back his chair from the console and reflected upon the unfolding military activity. A long drag from his Marlboro calmed him as he sorted his thoughts.

When he understood all the moving parts and the chain of responses he would recommend, he stood and turned to the elevated row of monitors behind him. From above, Admiral Torres glared and then motioned the Frenchman to join him.

He stepped to the stairs of the room's side passageway, climbed, and paced to the flag officer. Before he could speak, he saw Navarro enter the control room and begin descending stairs on the center's opposite side.

"Let's wait for him," Torres said.

The Philippine admiral, a tall chain-smoking man with a curving upper back, had shown his coolness while ordering the railgun module's attack. Before Renard could verbalize the suggestion, Torres had capitalized on the opportunity to damage the floating dock as it fled on a constant course and speed.

"Agreed," Renard said. "We have time to react, but we must be of one mind."

Navarro moved beside the admiral, who stood a full head taller.

"You and your staff have done well thus far, Admiral Torres," he said. "The management of communications, the timing of your attack with the railgun module, the adjustment to the chaff and jamming countermeasures–all excellent."

"Thank you, sir."

"But I am concerned," Navarro said. "Five combatant vessels appear willing to attack the Second Thomas Shoal, and American intelligence reveals signs of bomber and fighter escort activity mobilizing on air bases in the Guangzhou Military Region. I suspect a coordinated attack."

"The five Chinese combatants have forty anti-ship missiles and over one hundred anti-air missiles that can be used in a surface-attack mode," Torres said. "A full assault would overwhelm the railgun module's air defenses and test its armor beyond its design. I know what I must do to deter this, but deterring bombers is outside my reach. I will need fighter support if the Chinese bring bombers."

"Leave the bombers to me," Navarro said. "If the entire Chinese air force wishes to attack the module, we cannot turn them all back. However, our pilots are ready to meet whatever force comes, and there are surprises awaiting our adversaries if they approach the area. Maintain your focus on naval matters, and trust your aviator colleagues."

The admiral's voice sounded hoarse from decades of cigarette use.

"I will, sir," Torres said.

"The general is scrambling an entire squadron to intercept the incoming bombers before they can reach the Spratly Islands," Navarro said.

With the *Rankin* and the *Wraith* in holding patterns, Renard had observed the action, enjoying a silent celebration when the railgun module proved its efficacy in deterring the landing force at Thitu. But his hyperactive mind and inflated ego compelled him to contribute, and he recognized the task force's aggressive turn towards the module as his opportunity.

"Remember the *Shang*-class submarine that is suspected to be part of the task force," he said. "It remains outside our means of detection, but I must assume that it's leading the attack."

"How does that impact our tactics?" Navarro asked.

"If the railguns can find their targets, it will mean nothing other than the handful of its onboard anti-ship missiles to contend with," Renard said. "My greatest concern is if the surface combatants continue to evade the railgun rounds. In that case, the *Wraith* will then need to attack the surface ships, doing so while the *Shang* hunts it. It's nothing impossible, but it's tricky business to hunt surface ships while being hunted by another submarine, even for Jake."

"What of the *Rankin*?" Torres asked. "It is illogical to leave its weapons unused. Now that our need for defense is real, can it not be permitted to engage the Chinese?"

"I would lose credibility if I were to ask the Australian Minister for Defence," Navarro said. "But I agree and will ask an intermediary who might intervene with the minister on our behalf."

Renard realized that the chief intended for him to call Olivia McDonald. The Frenchman silently agreed, and he would call her at his next chance, but he knew that the conversation would lead nowhere. Jake and the *Wraith* were alone against the *Shang* and the surface combatants.

"Agreed," he said. "But first, we must adjust the railgun module's tactics. Since there's no shortage of rounds, you should recommence firing. At the very least, you'll force the task force into erratic maneuvering, which will slow its progress."

Torres nodded, gained the attention of an underling, and ordered the railgun module commander to attempt to predict the Chinese destroyer's course and hit it, assuming unguided shells.

With seventy seconds now separating the first shot from its result, Renard wiggled his phone in front of the Filipinos.

"Please excuse me, gentlemen," he said. "Let me see if I can use my connections with the Americans to improve our situation."

Each man nodded in apparent trust of his intent.

A quick series of leaps brought the Frenchman to the top of the stairs where he passed through a door. The observatory brought privacy and reduced background noise. He dialed Olivia's number and heard the background whine of jet engines.

"Miss me already, Pierre?" she asked.

"Woefully. Separation from you is agony."

"You're too cute."

"I am when it suits me."

"You didn't call me just to flirt, did you?"

"No, young lady. I am carrying out the wishes of my client. I don't imagine you feel comfortable reopening the dialogue with the Australian Minister for Defence?"

"Reopening a dialogue? You mean asking him to change his position about allowing the *Rankin* to shoot weapons at the Chinese?"

"Precisely."

"You're not letting another one of your missions get out of hand, are you?"

"The Chinese response is extreme but still within my foreseen parameters."

"But you sound anxious."

Decades of conditioning allowed him to mask his emotions under pressure, but he believed she possessed abnormal perception.

"The combination of factors is challenging," he said. "The entirety of the Chinese task force's surface combatants has committed to attacking the railgun module. They have an advanced nuclear submarine with them, they have optimized their jamming defenses, and a full squadron of bombers with fighter escort appears ready to join the attack."

"Make that two squadrons," she said. "I just got an update. You really know how to piss people off."

"Damn."

"No, Pierre. I'm not reneging on my agreements with the Australians just because the shit is hitting the fan. You assured me that you had planned for all contingencies. Now that you're facing them, face them."

"Fair enough, young lady. However, I could use one favor from you, something well within your reach."

"Name it."

"If you have in the region a satellite capable of detecting surface wakes made by submarines, please use it. I suspect the *Shang* submarine will be making twenty knots or greater in Jake's general direction. It may be detectable from above."

"I'll see what I can do. No promises."

"There are no promises in submarine warfare. I appreciate the help. Enjoy your flight home."

Sliding his phone into his pocket, he faced the control room. Through the glass, he looked at the main monitor.

Consuming the entire front wall, the screen showed an overhead view of landmasses, military machines, and merchant craft spanning across Thitu, the Second Thomas Shoal, and the nearest Philippine mainland. Three-dimensional artwork showed unambiguous representations of the moving parts.

Signifying the lead railgun round of the latest volley, a projectile-shaped icon embedded within a shifting ballistic arc drifted to the northwest. Renard's hope rose as it approached the icon of the Chinese destroyer, but the projectile disappeared from the screen.

Five seconds later, another shell disappeared, followed by the next. Eleven shells splashed into the water around the destroyer before a red pulsating orb rose from the screen.

He darted back into the control room and heard the admiral announce the success.

"Very well," Torres said. "I have acoustic confirmation from a merchant observer with a sonar system. One round, and one round only, has impacted the Chinese destroyer."

"No sign of secondary fires or loss of speed?" Renard asked.

"No," Torres said. "Radar tracking data shows the destroyer is maintaining its speed."

Renard felt grateful that the defense of chaff no longer concealed his adversaries since they needed speed that precluded staying under the clouds of slivers. Plus, the chaff magazines were finite, and a prudent task force commander would reserve them for closer proximity to the stronghold.

"Still," Renard said, "one well-placed round can make a difference. Your team is doing well to get the hit and should be able to land more, even at this extreme distance."

"The railgun module reports that its ammunition is down to seventy-five percent," Torres said. "I am ordering its rate of fire reduced by a factor of four until the targets are within forty miles and yield higher chances of hits."

"I understand," Renard said. "I was perhaps hasty in recommending that you fire at will. I admit I had considered your magazine to be large enough to ignore its capacity."

A mid-grade officer seated beside Renard's empty console waved him over. The Frenchmen descended steps and sat.

"Yes?" he asked.

"The *Rankin* is hailing you."

He slid an earpiece over his head.

"This is Renard," he said.

"How's your evening, mate?" Cahill asked.

A clock revealed that time had slipped past midnight.

"Another day in paradise has just begun," Renard said.

"It looks like you've angered every mongrel in the Chinese military. The scene looks really busy in me tactical data system."

"Busy, yes. But within foreseen parameters."

"You know, mate. I think I could be of better use if I repositioned meself a bit to the northwest."

"What's on your mind, commander?"

"I thought I could get a bit closer to those buggers."

"Dear God, man. Why? You aren't permitted to release weapons."

"I can still help the cause."

"How?"

"Let's say I get meself discovered. I can give the Chinese a submerged target to deal with. A little confusion. A little distraction."

"No. You'd have helicopters hunting you down to seal your doom. You might also get the *Shang* trailing you as well, for good measure. It's suicide. I won't allow it."

"Do you have any better ideas on how I can help?"

Renard sighed and reached in his blazer pocket for a fresh cigarette.

"Don't be a hero," he said. "I won't let you kill yourself and your crew."

"There's too much firepower coming down on Jake and the others. You have to admit that you expected the Chinese to run away when railguns struck them. You may have contingency plans, but you really didn't expect them to turn straight towards us and fight."

"What's your point, man?"

"I'm not sitting by idly and doing nothing."

"You're observing the scene and sharing intelligence."

"I'm gathering nothing where I am. I need to get closer."

"You could make a mistake, upset the balance, compromise the effort."

"How could I do that?"

"Damn it, I have no idea beyond generalities and conjecture. I just don't want you taking foolish risks."

"Make me a promise, Renard. Just one."

He exhaled smoke from his fresh cigarette.

"What?" he asked.

"If you notice a Chinese helicopter that looks like it's getting ready to drop a torpedo on a submarine, assume that I'm the poor bastard underneath it, and send a round or two into it for me."

"What about the surface combatants? What about the *Shang*? I can't do anything about it to protect you."

"Leave it to me. I know how to hide from their kind."

"You won't listen to reason, will you?"

"No, mate. Me mind's made up."

"Very well. I have a good idea of their helicopter anti-submarine search patterns. If I recognize an aggressive attack maneuver by one of their helicopters, I'll see that you're protected."

"Thanks, mate."

Renard switched frequencies and hailed Jake.

"*Wraith*, Fox Den. Over."

"Fox Den, *Wraith*. Over," Jake said.

After establishing communications, Renard felt comfortable dropping the formalities.

"I'm curious, Jake," he said. "Did you by chance hear a railgun round impact the *Chengdu*?"

"No. It must be too far away. That's good news, though. I was afraid I'd have to take down the entire task force single-handedly."

"Perhaps not. God willing, you shall remain an observer."

"I'm standing by. Is there anything you need me to do now?"

"No. I just wanted to inform you that Commander Cahill was overcome by a fit of optimism and has decided to drive northwest to intercept the task force."

"He's been authorized to launch weapons?"

"Sadly, no."

"Then what's he thinking?"

"He was rather cryptic and wouldn't let me talk him out of it, but I believe he's going to attempt to distract the incoming force."

"Shit. That's ballsy."

"Or foolish," Renard said. "The worst of it is that he'll lose his covert communications with friendly civilian vessels. If we need to speak with him, he'll have to transmit with enough power to be detected."

"He seems like a sharp guy, Pierre. Give him a chance. Let's see what he does."

"Unfortunately, I don't enjoy the liberty to share your outlook. I feel somehow responsible for him."

Renard sensed motion around him.

"There's activity here," he said. "Excuse me. I will contact you again soon."

He swiveled his chair and looked up. Torres pressed an earpiece to his head and raised a finger to hush any question the Frenchman might ask. Then, with a glint in his eye, he pointed to the screen.

"Another hit," he said. "This one showed a secondary explosion forward of the destroyer's bridge."

"You may have hit the vertical launch cell or perhaps the main gun's magazine," Renard said.

"I will seek a damage assessment from American satellite imagery," Torres said. "The task force is not yet within visual range of our merchant spies."

A mid-grade officer two consoles away startled Renard with a shrill announcement.

"Missile launch detected!" the officer said.

"Details!" Torres said. "Which ship launched it? Missile

Speed? Intended target?"

"Launched from the destroyer, sir. YJ-8 anti-ship missile. It's heading southeast, but it's too soon to know its target. With waypoints, it could be any of our ships or the railgun module. Our C-295 early warning and control aircraft is tracking it on radar."

"How many missiles are in flight?" Torres asked.

"Just the one, sir."

"The leader of the task force knows that long-distance launches provide more time for your defenses to engage his incoming missiles," Renard said. "He would prefer to get closer, but your last hit with the railgun has shown him that you can destroy his missiles before he wishes to launch them. A solitary missile launch is a test of your defenses."

"Then we shall pass the test and reveal as little of our defensive structure as possible," Torres said.

In addition to managing the submarines, Renard served as an advisor on the railgun module's abilities. He felt the liberty to question the flag officer's intent.

"Do you wish to seal the module?" he asked. "Lower the weapons subsection for protection?"

"No," Torres said. "I wish to maintain the firing cadence of twenty-second intervals. I don't want the task force commander to think that he can restrict my firing rate by launching a single missile. The railgun module will remain at full capacity."

"The destroyer is eighty-five nautical miles away," Renard said. "The missile travels one mile in roughly five seconds. I recommend using just the laser defenses and to engage with the close-in weapon system only if the lasers fail."

"Agreed," Torres said.

"You'll have almost seven minutes of missile flight time before it's in range of your defenses," Renard said. "It's a frustratingly slow missile when used at distance. You'll need to be patient."

"I've waited an entire career for my chance to stop China from spreading its dominance around my home waters," Torres said. "I can wait another seven minutes."

Seven minutes later, a mid-grade officer announced the uneventful success of the laser defense.

"The inbound missile is destroyed," he said. "The first laser hit it. No firing of the second laser defense system was required."

"Excellent," Torres said.

"Missile launch detected!" the officer said.

"Again? Details!" Torres said.

"From the destroyer again, sir. It's heading southeast. Our jets are tracking it on radar. This one is supersonic, though. Approximately Mach 4."

"How many missiles are in flight?" Torres asked.

"Just the one, sir. Only one again."

"He's testing you again," Renard said. "He's using an anti-air missile in anti-surface mode. He knows the warhead will have negligible damage, but the weapon's kinetic energy may be a risk."

"A fragile airframe against reinforced concrete?" Torres asked. "His anti-air missiles have no penetration capability."

"I agree in theory," Renard said. "But even with only half its fuel remaining, the missile will weigh roughly a ton. None of us wishes to see how many three-thousand-mile-per-hour, one-ton blows the module can take."

"The incoming weapon is too fast for anything except lasers as trustworthy defenses," Torres said. "I don't trust close-in weapon system bullets."

"The close-in weapon systems may surprise you with their accuracy, and they have twice the range of your lasers," Renard said. "I recommend using them at the cost of only several dozen tungsten bullets. If the Chinese task force commander wishes to test your defenses, then let us see how they stand up."

"So be it, Renard," Torres said. "But this time, I will lower the weapons subsection. Preserving the railguns is worth the concession of letting the task force commander know that he can temporarily silence them with his first anti-air missile."

The overhead icon-based view of the landmasses receded to the corner of the front wall's screen, as a night vision image of the railgun module from the beached landing craft took focus. With impressive speed, the twin railguns and the upper meters of concrete armor descended into the sealed obelisk. Exposed, the close-in weapon systems and laser weapons remained outside the armor.

Ninety seconds passed, and the supersonic missile reached the module's defensive perimeter. As Renard watched the concrete bunker assume its full armored posture, the Gatling guns of the close-in weapon system belched rapid flashes of gunpowder. Seconds later, he assumed that the lasers joined in the defense with their invisible bursts of weaponized light.

"The inbound missile is destroyed," the mid-grade officer said.

"Which weapon system destroyed it?" Torres asked.

"They're not sure, sir. It happened so fast."

"You may want to have weapons and sensor logs analyzed," Renard said. "You'll want to know which systems are effective against the anti-ship missiles. Given the complexity of this engagement, you'll need all the tactical knowledge you can acquire."

CHAPTER 15

Commander Wong leaned into a console and glared at the tactical display. The first railgun strike had punched linear holes from the deck of the *Chengdu's* forecastle, through berthing areas, and into the sea. His crew, which stood by at battle stations to combat fires and flooding, shored the small hole in the bilge and reduced the first shell's cut to a meaningless scratch.

The second strike changed everything.

Impacting on a ballistic arc, the projectile had cut through three cells in his vertical launcher, igniting a rocket propellant fire and stripping him of three Eagle Strike anti-ship missiles. Leaving nothing to chance, he decided to employ his weapons before giving the Philippine forces a chance to reduce his inventory further.

Seeking a saturation strike, he ordered all five ships to launch missiles in an orchestrated aerial dance that would climax with simultaneous arrivals at the stronghold, overwhelming its defenses. To exacerbate his enemy's predicament, he organized the Eagle Strikes to form four groups in flight, turn at preset waypoints, and slam into the obelisk on the Second Thomas Shoal with ninety degrees of separation.

He wanted the timed arrival of multiple weapons spread across four threat axes to overpower the stronghold's defenses and seal its fate.

Making the three major ships preserve two missiles for use against Philippine ships, and the corvettes to hold back one each, he ordered the group to unload the rest of its Eagle Strike arsenal. With eight of the forty weapons held back, he looked at a display showing the future paths of the four groups of eight missiles that would silence the railguns.

Content with the flight plans and with the automated launch sequence that his destroyer would control for all the missiles, he straightened and reached for a handset.

"All ships," he said, "report readiness for anti-ship missile launch."

As verbal confirmations arrived in parallel with updates in his tactical system, he tapped a key that gave him control of a five-ship arsenal. He toggled a switch and sent his voice through a circuit to speak to his crew.

"Standby for ripple launch of fourteen anti-ship missiles, cells ten through twenty-four."

Without further fanfare, he tapped a key and waited for rocket exhaust plumes to decorate the sky.

The fireworks began as a frigate created multicolored orbs over the horizon. The missiles that would angle behind the module and attack from its rear flank sprang from their canisters first so that they could complete their longer journey while achieving simultaneous impacts with the others in the salvo.

Then, as the ship cut to the right to evade the next railgun shell, he watched plumes illuminate a corvette ten miles off his starboard beam. Caught spectating, he cringed when his executive officer cried out.

"Eye hazard! Look away!"

He ducked his chin to his chest and bent forward, the rim of his helmet shielding his vision from the controlled inferno of the *Chengdu's* ripple launch. When the bursts of brilliance subsided, he looked up and watched smoke billow into the night under the last rocket booster.

The deck lurched, and he grabbed a console for balance. He looked at his executive officer, who appeared abnormally thin underneath his battle stations helmet. Steel groaned, and the now-familiar sonic boom of an incoming shell thumped against the windows.

"I had to order a hard left rudder and reverse the port engine," the executive officer said. "The latest projectile just missed off our starboard quarter."

"Very well," Wong said. "Continue the submarine evasion legs with adjustments to avoid incoming railgun projectiles."

He knew the railguns would become harder to avoid as he approached them. If he stopped at the destroyer's maximum cannon range of twenty miles to attack the concrete garrison, fourteen seconds of flight would separate him from each railgun projectile, giving him questionable time to dodge them. The frigates would fare worse, needing to get closer to make use of their three-inch guns.

Part of him wanted to test his courage with a brazen exchange of blows against the concretized Philippine stronghold, matching his destroyer's maneuverability, his ship handling, and his crew's gunnery accuracy against the upstarts on the Second Thomas Shoal.

To support shore bombardment responsibilities, his ship and the two frigates carried armor-piercing rounds. Those would crack and penetrate the concrete, exposing his enemy's guts to the high-yield rounds with less penetrative power but more explosives.

But his rational mind wanted the anti-ship missiles to silence the railguns and let him return to his hunt for the submarine that had killed his brother. A glance at his display encouraged him as it revealed all thirty-two missiles grouping into the prescribed four salvos.

Five minutes to impact.

"Left twenty-degrees rudder," the executive officer said.

The deck dipped as the destroyer dodged another projectile. Red icons straddled ballistic arcs on the tactical display, showing the barrage of incoming shells, the closest of which disappeared milliseconds before its sonic shock wave shook the *Chengdu's* bridge windows.

"Rudder amidships," the executive officer said.

Wong recognized the ship handling expertise of his second-in-command, and he trusted him to avoid the incoming shells. He excused him for the two projectiles that had driven puncture wounds through the hull since the radar system had lost momentary track of the high-speed objects.

The executive officer's river of rudder and engine commands drifted back into Wong's subconscious mind as the tactical display drew his attention. Four anti-ship missile groups raced southeast in a box formation towards his target.

Four minutes to impact.

Fifty nautical miles separated him from the Philippine stronghold–thirty miles from his maximum gun range. No matter the fate of the flying missiles, he vowed to dedicate armor-piercing rounds from his cannon's magazine towards silencing the railguns.

Three minutes to impact.

His heart leapt into his throat as one of the helicopters sweeping ahead of his five-ship line reported a possible active return from an unidentified submerged contact. But as suddenly as the evidence of a hostile submarine appeared, it vanished.

Two minutes to impact.

He reached for his handset and connected with the pilot of the helicopter. Rotor blade chop and turbofan whine hissed through the circuit.

"This is Helicopter Three, sir."

"Helicopter Three, this is the task force commander," he said. "Continue searching for the submerged contact for ten minutes. If you find nothing, then return to your patrol pattern ahead of the convoy. If you confirm a submerged target, sink it."

"What if it's the *Shang*, sir? What if it had propulsion or navigation problems and drifted into my path?"

"Then I pity our countrymen. My order stands."

One minute to impact.

A voice from the loudspeaker startled him.

"The railgun module has ceased fire," his operations officer said. "It fired its last shell thirty seconds ago."

He shifted the handset circuit.

"Very well," he said. "They must be bracing for impact. This is a good sign."

His eyes burned as he watched the two lead groups of Eagle Strikes veer wide of the Second Thomas Shoal, flanking his victim. As the box of thirty-two flying warheads encircled and pointed towards the railgun module, his operations officer's voice rang over the loudspeaker.

"Jamming frequencies, sir," he said. "Coming from the railgun module. They're trying to disrupt our missiles."

Wong considered that a stationary target had no chance of masking its position, but enough electromagnetic energy at the right frequencies could block the satellite data missiles used to judge their positions in flight. Left to its inertial guidance, the accuracy of a missile's self-assessment of its position would degrade.

"Can you overpower their jamming and guide the missiles from here?" he asked.

"Negative, sir. We're too far away."

He realized that the Philippine defenses included a phased array radar strong enough to mitigate his attack. As he watched his missiles begin to turn towards unwanted targets, he cursed under his breath.

"Missiles are tracking false targets," he said. "Report wayward missiles!"

"Wayward missiles are just now separating, sir," the operations officer said. "I count only three thus far, all from the same group. They're targeting the *Sierra Madre*."

Wong hoped that the remaining twenty-nine missiles would find their intended target while he conceded that the errant three would rid the planet of the landing craft the Philippines had beached on the shoal seventeen years earlier.

"Very well," he said. "Twenty-nine missiles are sufficient for the task."

"Sir, four more have gone wayward from a different group. They're tracking the *Alcatraz*."

A tingling reverence gave Wong goose bumps as he realized that the frigate had driven towards the shoal to defend the stronghold at the risk of absorbing missiles. He glanced at the display and noticed similar behavior from the *Pilar*, but it escaped the seekers of wayward weapons.

"Very well," he said. "Twenty-five missiles will suffice."

"Chaff clouds detected!"

"Very well. Chaff poses minimal concern."

"Point-defense missiles!"

"Damn! How many?"

"Ten already. More are being fired. Probably American Rolling Airframe Missiles."

"Damn!"

"Vulcan Phalanx close-in weapon system radar detected!"

He had expected the Phalanx radar, since the Philippine forces had used it against his solitary anti-air missile test shot, but the Rolling Airframe Missiles surprised him.

Bent over the display, he watched his salvo reach its terminus as defense missiles, Phalanx bullets, and laser defenses knocked his weapons out of the sky.

Questioning his judgment, he rebuked himself for keeping anti-ship missiles in reserve. As he scanned numbers tagged to each icon, he noticed that twenty-two Rolling Airframe Missiles sought his inbound weapons. Quick math, subtracting the wayward seven Eagle Strikes and assuming perfection from the Philippine point-defense missiles, suggested that his attack would yield nothing.

But Rolling Airframe Missiles could miss their targets, and saturation attacks could allow missiles to slip between Phalanx bullets and laser beams.

Two missiles punctured the *Alcatraz*, and two more transformed the rusting landing craft into a burning wreck. Then, icons representing his missiles–signs of hope that his strike would bear fruit–merged with the back corner of the stronghold.

"Three missiles have hit the primary target!" his operations officer said.

"Damage assessment?"

"No smoke on infrared. No sign of secondary fires."

He collected himself.

"Send a helicopter to high altitude for a long-range visual inspection."

A minute later, a railgun shell appeared on his screen, and he doubted that he had accomplished anything. The next round followed within ten seconds, and then a third ten seconds later.

"They have increased their firing rate from twenty to ten seconds, sir," the operations officer said.

Wong wrestled to understand the significance of the ten-second separation between shells. He wondered if the Philippine forces had halved the interval in defiance of his attack. But he hoped that he had instead silenced one of the guns and had scared his enemy into firing every round as fast as possible from the remaining muzzle.

The radar return of an approaching merchant ship captured his attention.

"Officer of the Deck," he said, "bring the translator to the bridge. I want that ship hailed in every possible language and warned to stay twenty miles away."

The translator arrived and rattled off orders in a multitude of languages over the radio, calling for the vessel at the targeted coordinates. With no response, Wong grabbed his handset.

"Operations officer, ready the ship's cannon."

When the encroaching ship reached the limit of his gun, he gave the order.

"Fire! Eye hazard! Look away!"

He looked at the deck as the muzzle flash illuminated the night and bridge windows thumped against their frames.

"This is a warning shot," Wong said. "Land the round fifty meters in front of the vessel."

Equipped with guidance fins, each cannon round could adjust its flight path with targeting data from the destroyer. He waited for the round to splash.

"Hail them again!" he said.

The translator obeyed. No response. Wong shot another round.

"Fire! Eye hazard! Look away!"

After the muzzle flash, his stomach twisted with another critical decision.

He wanted to set the approaching vessel ablaze and send it to an aquatic tomb, but his admiralty had issued the order to avoid innocent civilian casualties. Commanding officers needed freedom to apply judgment within gray areas, and the definition of innocence swirled in his head.

"This is another warning shot," he said. "Land the round twenty meters in front of the vessel."

The round splashed, and the translator attempted another hailing. Nothing.

As the deck lurched to avoid the new volley of incoming shells, he braced for another sonic boom shaking the bridge windows.

"Fire control radar!" the operations officer said. "Coming from the approaching merchant ship!"

There was no time to jam the next shell, and Wong cringed as fire shot up from the screaming steel of his punctured vertical launch system.

"Fire! Fire at will until that merchant vessel is destroyed!"

"Firing, sir! Attempting jamming of incoming shells!"

Eleven shells turned his vertical launch system into twisted metal before his cannon ignited flickering flames on the horizon. Multicolored hues pulsated into the night, and then the sea swallowed the merchant vessel and its unwelcome fire control system.

"Seal all compartments around the vertical launch cells," Wong said. "Keep damage control parties away from them. Let them flood. They are lost."

The *Chengdu* rode lower in the water, and Wong noticed a slight sluggishness as the executive officer recommended the railgun evasion legs.

As he caught his breath, he found solace realizing that his enemy had targeted his vertical launch cells. With the merchant vessel within visual range, the Philippine forces had free reign to choose any section of his destroyer, but they had taken out his arsenal of anti-air missiles.

They had spared his propulsion, and they had spared his cannon, allowing him to continue driving within range of his armor-piercing rounds. His enemy knew that, and still they had targeted his anti-air missiles.

Their fear of his anti-air missiles, weapons with tiny warheads and negligible hardening for penetration, suggested an exposure.

He had cracked the armor.

And though the latest shells had broken his magazine, he wasn't alone. Two frigates in his group carried thirty-two anti-air missiles each.

Regardless how wide a wound he had punched into his prey, he trusted that at least one of the anti-air missiles could find its way inside. A ton of rocket propellant and metal moving at Mach 4 carried destructive force–enough to frighten his adversary.

As he considered how many of the sixty-four missiles to use against the stronghold and how many to preserve for control of the sky, his operations officer's voice refocused his thoughts on a new obstacle.

"Patriot missile radar, bearing zero-three-five."

Wong called up a map.

"That's Nanshang Island," he said. "Philippine-occupied. Sixty miles north of the Second Thomas Shoal."

"I concur with Nanshang Island," the operations officer said. "More Patriot missile radars! One is coming from Thitu. The other is coming from the Philippine mainland–from the southern tip of Palawan Island!"

"Can you estimate how many individual systems are energized?"

"Each site is energizing only one system."

"Damn!" Wong said. "They have Patriot missile batteries, but they're not turning all their systems on. They want us to guess how many and to be frightened. It's a warning."

He counted five railgun shells dodged before the expected bad news came. Unwilling to race face-first into an unknown amount of long-range surface-to-air missiles, the bombers and their fighter escorts were turning back to their air bases in the Guangzhou Military Region.

Worse, the Philippine jet fighters took advantage of the retreat and made sharp turns towards his task force, making his anti-air missiles precious for their primary purpose of defending his sky.

Wanting to blame his aviator colleagues for cowardice, he instead accepted the wisdom of their retreat. Philippine military forces had made a statement across a network of landmasses, and his countrymen needed to assess the risk.

But understanding his predicament failed to improve it.

In a moment of doubt, he considered giving up and running, but he considered himself committed. Forty miles from the railguns, he decided to drive forward and see his mission to its end.

CHAPTER 16

Glaring at Lieutenant Commander Flores had become an annoying necessity. Jake kept half an eye on him, wanting the look of terror on the man's face to vanish.

But it remained, and the officer's demeanor conveyed an isolating edginess. The former French Navy sailor who served as Jake's quartermaster, monitoring the *Wraith's* position under exacting scrutiny, had slid to the opposite side of the navigation table from Flores.

Jake smelled the Philippine leader's fear but hoped that his spine would stiffen during real action. The test of his crew's mettle was barreling down upon him in the form of a purposeful and deadly task force.

Staring at the tactical display beside his foldout captain's chair, he slid a headset over his ear for a private conversation with Renard. He lifted his chin.

"Henri!"

"Yes, Jake?"

"Raise the communication buoy."

With his link to the Frenchman established, he welcomed his mentor's thoughts.

"I have five anti-submarine surface combatants heading my way, plus helicopters and a *Shang* submarine."

"Correct," Renard said. "You almost sound concerned."

"My biggest concern is the *Shang*. That thing is dangerously quiet and has nuclear speed and endurance. But it needs to move fast to stay ahead of the surface ships. That will make it loud enough to hear."

"Of course," Renard said. "You have the tactical advantage of positioning. My greater concern for you is the helicopters."

"It depends how close they get to me."

"Would you like me to rid you of them now?"

"Is that possible? I thought the destroyer was jamming our railgun rounds. Shooting at helicopters without guidance is like swatting a fly with a pencil."

The display showed the closest helicopter patrolling ten miles ahead of the line abreast of Chinese ships, ten miles from the *Wraith*. Jake felt safe at that distance, but not much closer.

"There's a surprise in store for any of our Chinese adversaries who approach within line of sight of the module's planar array," Renard said. "In that event, we won't need GPS satellite signals to guide rounds, but instead we can use the module's closer and stronger power source."

"You thought about that ahead of time?" Jake asked. "You considered jamming and made the rounds guidable by both GPS and local power? I don't remember that in the tech manual."

"It was an advanced, minimally tested feature I chose not to publish. But I have faith in it."

"Field testing will tell," Jake said.

"It makes neutralizing helicopters possible if they climb high enough to be exposed to our planar array. They need to climb to reposition between their searches with their dipping sonar systems."

"Fine. If you get the chance, do me the favor. It's going to get hectic out here, and I don't need to accidentally end up underneath a helicopter."

"Of course," Renard said. "Now what of the surface combatants? The corvettes lack the firepower to threaten the railgun module, but the other three ships pose real risks, especially if they can position themselves to target the weakness where the Eagle Strike weapons penetrated the outer layer of armor."

"You can handle the frigates, right?" Jake asked. "If they want to use their cannons, they'll get close enough for you to guide rounds into them. I'll shoot torpedoes at them if I can, but they'll probably remain out of range while I'm dealing with the destroyer."

"Correct," Renard said. "Which places you in a quandary. You need to reposition yourself to protect the exposure in our armor from the destroyer, but doing so would sacrifice your ambush position for the *Shang* submarine. You'll have to make noise and possibly detach your drones if you reposition."

"I can keep the drones if I'm careful," Jake said. "And I'm not here to protect my own ass from a submarine. I'm here to protect a fortress. I'll get it done."

He freed his mind from the strain of his responsibilities and considered the larger picture.

"What about the air battle?" he asked. "There's still a bunch of missiles left in that task force."

"We've reached a stalemate," Renard said. "The destroyer's remaining missiles were damaged in their launch cells, leaving only the frigates' weapons as concerns."

"They're low on Eagle Strikes, right?"

"Low or even exhausted. No matter, they have so few left that the point defenses could defeat them. My concern is the anti-air missiles if used in surface-strike mode. That could become another saturation attack, and it's a grave exposure if such missiles targeted the gap in the armor."

"So what's stopping them from shooting at us?"

"When the Patriots turned back the bombers, our fighter jets were free to vector towards the task force. They're circling at low altitude outside of missile range, but they are forcing the frigates to preserve their arsenal."

Jake did quick math in his head.

"That sounds to me like the task force still has enough missiles to hold off the fighters and slam a dozen or two missiles into the module."

"But now that the Chinese are close enough to Palawan Island, they are in range of ground-attack Bronco aircraft. We are sending two squadrons towards them but keeping them out of missile range. We have also sent several dozen trainer and non-combatant aircraft into the sky. The Chinese air commander can't distinguish threat from decoy and is forced to retain his anti-air defense arsenal."

"I'm impressed, Pierre. My concern is–"

"Torpedo in the water!" Remy said.

Jake looked at the toad-shaped head of his sonar expert. Remy had been silent for hours, and the announcement without warning seemed surreal.

"Got to run," he said.

"Understood," Renard said. "Leave the line open as long as you can so that I can hear."

As Jake dropped the headset to the console, he asked his instinctive questions.

"Whose torpedo, where, and intended target? Give me all you got, Antoine."

Remy turned his head with deliberate calmness, lowering his earpiece to his neck.

"It's far away," he said. "Its signal strength is hardly above background noise. I barely hear it from drone one."

"Put a line of bearing in Subtics," Jake said.

"Done!" Remy said.

Jake's screen showed the torpedo sounds coming from the west, suggesting that an adversarial vessel had started to circle around the back of the Second Thomas Shoal.

"I lost it!" Remy said. "It must have passed through an acoustic layer. Its sound isn't reaching us anymore."

"Are you sure it was distant?"

"Positive, Jake. No cause for alarm."

Lieutenant Commander Flores moved below Jake, his fingers trembling.

"What are you going to do?" he asked.

"Nothing. Calm down."

"What do you mean, nothing? There's a torpedo out there!"

Jake leaned forward.

"This doesn't change my tactics. For all I know, that could be a frigate or helicopter dropping a weapon on a ghost, or God forbid, on the *Rankin*. But it doesn't affect me. I'm going to reposition to the south to protect the module from gunfire at its damaged armor."

"What if it's the *Shang* shooting at the *Rankin*?"

"Then I pity our Australian friends," Jake said.

"You have to do something!"

The man's instability crossed the line. Jake decided to remove the potential disruption, and he formulated a lie to distract him.

"Yes, actually," he said. "I see your point. I'll need to talk to Claude about my plans before I strain the battery. I want to make sure we have enough power remaining for what I plan to do."

"And what's that? What do you plan to do?"

"If you'll give me a minute, I'll let you know. But let me discuss the maneuver with Claude first."

Jake ignored Flores' nervous hand wringing and hailed LaFontaine on a sound-powered phone. With the Philippine officer on the edge of sanity, he risked switching to a foreign language.

"Claude," he said in French. "Listen carefully. Send the corpsman with sedatives and two men with small arms to the control room. I want our guest crew's senior officer taken to the wardroom, sedated, and held under guard."

"You're joking," LaFontaine said.

"No. He's about to lose control."

"That will create an uncomfortable scene. The Philippine crewmen may not like it. You need to be delicate."

Jake considered his engineer's advice.

"Good point," he said. "Slight change of plans. Send the three men to the wardroom instead. Then have one of them leave his arms with the corpsman, head to the control room, and invite the senior officer to the engineering spaces. He'll say that you need his help in engineering. But, of course, divert him to the wardroom."

"Will he believe such a silly ruse?"

"He might. If not, I'll drag him to the wardroom myself. I'll set up the trick by mentioning that you're having trouble analyzing something back there."

LaFontaine sounded indignant.

"What might I have trouble analyzing? I've been operating this technology for more than twenty years!"

"Just go with it, for God's sake."

"Fine, Jake. Give it five minutes."

"Make it three."

Jake jammed the phone back into its cradle.

"What did he say?" Flores asked.

"He's not sure if the battery has enough power left in it for what I'm planning."

"What are you planning?"

"Excellent question," Jake said. "Let's review it at the navigation plot. Henri, join us."

The Frenchman nodded, stood, and walked to the chart. Jake stepped down from the conning platform and huddled beside him.

"We need to reposition ourselves," he said.

"I was afraid you'd say that," Henri said. "If you mean to protect the damaged side of the module, we need to make haste."

"You're not going to risk making noise by moving now, are you?" Flores asked.

Henri glared at the officer and opened his mouth to launch a counterargument, but Jake snapped a rapid order under his breath in French while kicking his mechanic's leg.

"Shut up."

The Frenchman cleared his throat.

"Good point, Commander Flores," Jake said. "In fact, what I meant was that we could use the prevailing currents to achieve our goals without so much as making a peep. Don't you think that's an excellent idea?"

The Philippine officer's glistening forehead reflected the room's red light. He appeared captured in thought, pondering Jake's absurd suggestion as a possibility. His face scrunched in disbelief but then relaxed in foolish hope.

"I think it's possible," he said.

"Of course," Jake said. "In fact, I'd like you to pull up the ocean currents on the chart and verify the plan for me. I'd hate to screw this up because I miscalculated."

"Okay," Flores said.

While the spooked officer fumbled with the chart's controls, Jake lowered his head and voice and continued his chat in

Henri's native language.

"I think he's in shock," he said.

"I can see that," Henri said. "Not that either of us are doctors, but we need to make a rapid diagnosis and take action."

"It's already in progress," Jake said. "Just wait."

"We don't have forever. That torpedo out there may mean nothing, but it could mean that hell is about to rain down on us."

"You sound as nervous as he does."

"You know me better than that."

"Then shut up. I think we're making him more nervous by running our mouths in a language he doesn't understand."

As the Frenchman grunted, Flores looked up from the screen.

"The currents won't help us," he said. "They're going in the wrong direction.

Jake straightened his back and welcomed the relief as one of LaFontaine's engineering technicians entered from the aft door.

"Jake," he said. "Claude wants help with some battery calculations in the engine room."

"I need to stay here," Jake said. "But Commander Flores should be able to help."

Flores offered Jake a blank face.

"Go ahead, Commander Flores. Claude needs you."

"Okay, Jake."

As the officer lumbered away behind the technician, Jake closed the door behind him and returned to Henri. He tapped his finger on the chart on a position protecting the stronghold's broken exposure.

"Get with Durand and figure out a movement plan to get us here," Jake said.

"To better protect the module's damaged flank."

"Right. But I want to move the drones, too, so that we can still listen for the *Shang*. So it will be a series of walking and drifting, for the *Wraith* and the drones, to listen for the *Shang*. Get me a plan in three minutes."

"I will see it done, Jake."

Seconds later, Remy's voice filled the compartment.

"I've regained the torpedo! Terminal homing!"

Jake's heart sank as he accepted that the Australian commander and crew he just befriended would die. He returned to the conning platform, donned the headset, and hailed Renard.

"Are you getting this?" he asked.

"All of it, sadly," the Frenchman said. "I told Cahill to stay out of this. Damn him!"

"I know, Pierre. It's not your fault."

For a rare moment, Renard had nothing to say. In the silence, Jake watched the tactical scene unfold. The torpedo's trajectory, as best Remy could approximate it with guesses of its speed and distance from the *Wraith*, originated from an invisible source and sought an invisible target.

"Pierre?" he asked.

"Yes?"

"That torpedo couldn't have come from a surface ship, not based upon its track."

"Agreed. And there are no helicopters in the vicinity, either."

"Well, shit. If Cahill gets himself killed, let it be for a good reason. That's a submarine-versus-submarine exchange. Now I know where to search for the *Shang*. I can use active sonar from my drone and nail the son of a bitch."

"Indeed, my friend! Please, be careful and remember that your primary goal is defending the railgun module. But by all means, avenge our Australian colleagues."

"The torpedo has acquired countermeasures!" Remy said.

"Our colleagues may have a prayer if the countermeasures work," Renard said.

"Don't hold your breath," Jake said.

"I was trying to be optimistic."

"The torpedo has penetrated the countermeasures and has reentered terminal homing!" Remy said.

"It's over, Pierre," Jake said.

Another rare moment of silence from Renard.

"Torpedo is range-gating!" Remy said.

Jake counted seconds in his head, expecting his new friends to die before he reached double digits.

"Explosion on the bearing of the torpedo!" Remy said.

Awaiting reports of twisting metal and crumpling compartments, Jake seethed and indulged in a moment of frustration with a scream.

"Fuck!"

"Easy, Jake," Remy said.

"Look, man, I'm sorry," Jake said. "I'm pissed off! I'm going to tear that fucking *Shang* in half!"

"No, Jake," Remy said. "I meant that it wasn't a kill shot. It was a small explosion. I didn't hear signs of a hull breach, either."

"Maybe you just missed it."

"I never miss anything, not when it's this important. Wait!" Remy smiled while he pressed the earpiece into his head.

"What's going on in that twisted head of yours?" Jake asked.

"I figured out what happened, and you're going to like it."

"Just spit it out, man!" Jake said.

"The *Rankin* wasn't the target. It was the shooter."

"How? How can you know that?"

With a businesslike demeanor, Remy turned his head back towards his monitor. The gesture struck Jake as insubordinate until he digested his sonar expert's final statement.

"I hear limpets."

CHAPTER 17

"Cahill just gift-wrapped the *Shang* for you," Jake said.

"You can't imagine my relief," Renard said. "I fault myself for underestimating him, but in my defense, I've never seen him in action. I shan't make this mistake again."

"He was just smart, Pierre. Nothing heroic. He made a good guess of where the *Shang* would be to protect the surface ships, and he got there and waited. I shouldn't have doubted him either."

"So be it. He's succeeded. Now we must capitalize on it."

"After the crew of the *Shang* realizes they're still alive and put on clean underwear, they're going to surface and send divers over the side to pry off the limpets. If I were them, I'd make sure to do that ASAP before getting any closer to the railguns."

"Perhaps."

Jake studied his display, considered the height of the railgun module's radar arrays, and ball-parked the distance-to-horizon calculation.

"The *Shang* is still over the railgun module's horizon," he said. "But when it surfaces, you'll have it trapped. It can't send divers over the side and move fast at the same time. You can hit it with good old-fashioned aiming and shooting. One round should be enough to keep it pinned on the surface, but I'd put in four or five for good measure."

"If the opportunity arises, of course. But it's quite possible that the *Shang* surprises you with its reaction. Recall why you created the limpet weapon in the first place."

Jake had conceived of the weapon as a way to force a submarine to surface and surrender. But a forced surfacing required a nearby platform capable of exploiting the limpets' noises with a sonar system and a threatening torpedo.

"Shit, Pierre. The crew of the *Shang* doesn't know that we have two submarines. They think the *Rankin* is the *Wraith*. They think I shot them with a limpet, and they think they're running away from me."

"Don't give them time to think about it. If they gather themselves, they may recognize the limpet weapon as being part of a two-submarine tactic. I recommend that you take matters into your own hands immediately."

"Yeah. Right."

Jake raised his chin to Remy.

"Antoine!"

"Yes?"

"Do you have the *Shang* on both drones and on hull sensors?"

"Yes!"

"Do you have its course and speed nailed down yet?"

"With limpets, it's academic. Gift-wrapped, as you said. You can fire when ready."

"Very well, Antoine," Jake said. "Assign the torpedo in tube one to the *Shang*."

While Remy tapped buttons, Jake announced his attentions to the control room.

"Attention everyone!" he said. "I'm going to shoot a slow-kill weapon at the *Shang*. Immediately after shooting, I'm turning our ship and drones south to defend the module."

Twisting in his seat, Henri shot Jake a disparaging look.

"You could release the drones now," he said. "Our adversaries may hear them while you move them."

"That's fine," Jake said. "That's why I position them far away from our ship."

"Releasing them would allow you to reload the tubes."

"I know. But I'm going to hold them until I'm sure that the *Shang* is out of the picture. Stick with your plan of moving the drones with our ship. Keep them in a constant relative position to us, walking and drifting, just like we reviewed."

Jake hesitated for a moment of unspoken communication with Henri. After a decade of companionship, he recognized the Frenchman's body language and could distinguish theoretical questioning from blatant disagreement.

The single episode of blatant disagreement–the time when deferring to his colleague's judgment had saved their submarine near an isolated Taiwanese island–emblazoned in his memory, Jake needed less than a second to identify Henri's reluctant but supportive acceptance with keeping the drones.

"Tube one is ready, assigned to the *Shang*," Remy said.

"Are you ready with tube one, Henri?" Jake asked.

"Ready!"

"Shoot tube one!"

His ears popped as the flushing whine of the torpedo launch filled the *Wraith*.

"Tube one, normal launch," Henri said. "Wire guidance engaged."

"Very well," Jake said. "Let's get moving. All ahead two-thirds."

"The engine room acknowledges ahead two-thirds," Henri said.

Jake watched digits on a speed gauge tick through five knots, and when the *Wraith* reached the velocity for steerageway, he turned.

"Left fifteen-degrees rudder," he said. "Steer course one-nine-zero."

Its conning tower creating drag above the vessel's cylindrical hull, the submarine rolled into the turn, unlike surface ships whose momentum tilted their superstructures outward during maneuvers. The deck tilted left below Jake's soft-soled shoes.

"Lieutenant Santos!" Jake said.

The seated Philippine officer looked over his shoulder.

"Approach the conn," Jake said.

The young officer stood and walked in front of the polished railing. Jake leaned forward.

"You know you're officially the senior officer aboard this vessel now, right?"

A mix of bravado and respect for danger placed a glint in the man's eyes and hardened his features. His jaws looked ready to snap his teeth, and Jake liked the man's balance of fear and self-control.

"I understand," he said.

Jake smiled and hoped to establish a quick rapport.

"You remind me of myself when I was in the service," he said. "You look scared, but the right amount of scared."

"My men need to see someone in a Philippine uniform keeping the right perspective."

"That statement alone is enough for me to know that you can handle this. Flores wasn't handling it. I have him sedated and under guard in the wardroom."

"I assumed you did something like that," Santos said. "I thought you handled it well. I've been concerned about him since we began our training."

"Really?"

"We all have. He's known for being a capable mariner, but every training scenario we went through that put us in tight spaces made him uneasy. I suspect he may be claustrophobic."

"Whatever it is, he's not cut out for this. Regardless, you're the man now. Are you ready to manage the tactical picture for me?"

"What about the drones? I'm managing one of them for Durand."

"I'm going to cut one soon. I need a second pair of eyes monitoring my quartermaster, watching the movements of hostile assets, and recommending adjustments to the torpedoes I shoot. Are you the man for the job?"

"Heck, yes! I can handle it."

"Great. Hold on."

Jake looked at Remy.

"Antoine, can you track the *Shang* without drone two?"

"With those limpets on it, I could track it by sticking my ear against our hull."

"Very well," Jake said. "Attention everyone! I'm stationing Lieutenant Santos as the tactical coordinator."

"Noted in the deck log," Henri said.

"Lieutenant Santos," Jake said, "you have thirty seconds to give me a recommendation about what to do with drone two before I release it."

"Yes, Jake!"

The officer turned to the navigation chart and studied the moving chess pieces.

"Set it in decoy mode?" he asked.

"That's a good start. Make it broadcast noises that mimic our submarine to fool our adversaries. But what course, what speed, what volume level?"

The youngster leaned over the chart and walked dividers between varied points, playing an enthusiastic what-if game.

"Northwest," he said. "Maximum speed, maximum volume. That will make it appear like it's a submarine attempting to get between the eastern frigate and eastern corvette. It's going to run out of battery fast, but it should get there in time to create a distraction."

"Perfect," Jake said. "Durand, send drone two on course three-four-zero, maximum speed. Shift it to decoy mode, maximum power."

The former French sailor tapped buttons, working through control menus with impressive speed.

"Drone two is on course three-four-zero at ten knots. It's in decoy mode, broadcasting at maximum power."

"Very well," Jake said. "Release drone two. Henri, reload tube six with a slow-kill weapon."

On his way to Jake, Henri offered a congratulatory smile to Santos, who beamed with pride.

"Are you sure you want a slow-kill weapon in tube six?" the Frenchman asked. "You're proving the weapon against the *Shang*, and you'll have your proof of its design in less than three minutes. Shouldn't you use a conventional torpedo for the surface targets?"

"I see no need for needless killing."

Henri's look straddled the line between questioning and defiance, but Jake held his ground, and the Frenchman returned to his station to carry out the order.

"Reload tube six with a slow-kill weapon, aye, sir," he said.

Remy called out that the *Shang* turned west in an attempt to escape the *Wraith's* torpedo. Countermeasures threatened to confuse the weapon.

"Guide our torpedo through the countermeasures," Jake said. "Drive it right through. Ignore false noises."

"Our torpedo is through the countermeasure field," Remy said. "Fifty seconds to detonation."

Jake watched his display and noticed that the data had gone stale. While the *Wraith* moved, it dragged the communications buoy underwater and severed the data link. But he had the front row seat to the intersection of his torpedo with the *Shang*.

As their icons merged, Remy announced pending victory.

"Our torpedo is range-gating," he said. "Detonation!"

"Count the warheads," Jake said. "Make sure you hear them attach."

"At least three already!" Remy said.

"It doesn't take many for this to work," Jake said.

"I'm losing count," Remy said. "At least twelve have attached to the *Shang's* hull. One of them is surely to be from the first group. Submunition detonation is imminent."

Seconds ticked away in Jake's head as he awaited the results of his brainchild's first field test. Limpets were drifting upward and magnetically clamping to his victim. But instead of wailing electronic tracking frequencies, these parasites carried small explosives.

"Detonations!" Remy said. "Four submunitions!"

Four six-inch holes punctured the *Shang*. In two minutes, any submunition that had found its way to its hull from the second group would explode, followed by the third and then final group of six small warheads.

"If it's in their engine room, that's enough damage," Jake said. "If it's someplace else, they may need to see a couple more explode before they realize they need to surface."

"High-pressure air!" Remy said. "Hull popping! The *Shang* is emergency blowing."

"Yes!" Jake said.

"Backhaul tube one," he said. "Reload tube one with a slow-kill weapon."

He met Henri's glare from across the room. The Frenchman's face portrayed his disagreement and his preference to have a full-sized heavyweight warhead readied for the surface ships. After a silent moment, his expression changed to reveal his deference to Jake's judgment.

"Reloading tube one with a slow-kill weapon," Henri said.

"Lieutenant Santos," Jake said. "Recommend the final deployment of drone one in decoy mode."

"Half speed, maximum power, course two-eight-zero," Santos said. "Half speed is preferred since we want the decoy to remain between us and the nearest corvette."

"Right again," Jake said. "Durand, send drone one on course two-eight-zero, half speed. Shift it to decoy mode, maximum power."

The young Frenchman tapped buttons with practiced speed.

"Drone one is on course two-eight-zero at five knots. It's in decoy mode, broadcasting at maximum power."

"Very well," Jake said. "Release drone one. Henri, reload tube five with a slow-kill weapon."

"I've ordered tube five reloaded with a slow-kill weapon. You have only one slow-kill weapon remaining in the racks after tube five is loaded," Henri said.

Jake suspected that chaos reigned on the surface. A Chinese submarine had blown to safety, and, after what he considered a fair chance to abandon ship, more exploding submunitions would assure the *Shang's* final descent.

Two drones were emanating sounds of a *Scorpène*-class submarine, deceiving both surface vessels and helicopters. Philippine gun boats were close enough to harass incoming combatants, and railgun rounds became increasingly accurate as the battle approached its crescendo.

Though he sensed his enemy's confusion, he desired to confirm his opinion and find a way to act upon it. The surface combatants remained outside his hearing, and he wanted a snapshot of their activity.

"All stop," he said.

As the *Wraith* drifted, Remy startled him.

"Active sonar!"

"Whose? There's nothing out there?"

"Helicopter! Bearing three-five-five!"

"Shit! Signal strength?"

"Moderate, but I don't like it," Remy said. "It's close enough for our hull to give a return."

Expecting no mercy like he had shown his enemy, Jake's thoughts turned to death–his. Realizing that detection by a helicopter equated to helplessness, he let awareness of his mortality paralyze him.

"Jake!" Henri said.

"What?"

"I just asked you what we should do."

"Sorry. I didn't hear you. All ahead one third. Rig the ship for ultra-quiet. Everyone who's not keeping the ship operating goes straight to their racks. Let's not give the helicopter transient noises."

"I will see to it," Henri said. "Is there anything else we should do? We don't have a helicopter evasion plan."

"That's because there is no such thing, except maybe for asking for help from above."

Henri offered a rare quizzical expression.

"Do you mean for us to pray?"

For a moment, Jake wished he had someone to pray to. He imagined it would bring an otherwise elusive peace. If there existed a recipient of human prayers, he hoped that such a power would deliver him from the helicopter.

"I don't suppose it could hurt," Jake said. "But that's not what I meant."

"Then what?"

"Prepare a message in a one-way transmission buoy for Pierre. Give him our coordinates and ask for gunfire support, whether he can hit the helicopter or not. He needs to at least harass it to get it off our backs."

"I understand," Henri said. "Help from above. I'm preparing

the buoy now."

"God knows how long we have," Jake said. "Get it launched ASAP."

CHAPTER 18

"Loud splash in the water, bearing zero-two-five."

"Splash? Like a railgun shell?" Jake asked.

"No, not as clean," Remy said. "I don't know how to describe it, but it's a lot more chaotic. And gentler."

"Gentler? Like a crashing feather? Just tell me what the heck you think it is."

"I think it was a crashing helicopter. It didn't hit too hard because it was probably fighting on the way down."

"That would be good news," Jake said. "But wouldn't you hear the shell hit the helicopter first?"

"Not if it was at high enough altitude. I also hear buckling metal now on the bearing of the splash, but it's light metal. Not a lot of mass. It's a sinking helicopter."

Jake exhaled and tried to turn his attention towards surface combatants, but Remy made another announcement.

"The final group of submunitions just exploded on the *Shang*," he said. "We'll need to review the audio playback for final judgment, but I count that seventeen of twenty-four submunitions attached and exploded."

"Excellent!" Jake said. "Is the *Shang* sinking yet?"

"Not yet, but it's only a matter of time for a ship with so few compartments."

"Then that's it for the *Shang*, and the helicopters would need brass balls to chase us down now," Jake said. "It's us versus five surface combatants, and we know where they're going."

"We'll need to accelerate to get between the railguns and the task force before it arrives," Santos said. "We need to get there in under twelve minutes."

"Very well, Lieutenant Santos. Henri, all ahead two-thirds."

Jake stepped down from the conning platform and bent over the navigation chart.

"Draw a red arc twenty miles from the edge of the railgun module," he said.

Santos obeyed, and the curve appeared.

"Now draw a line from the center of the module out on a bearing of three-five-five."

As the line cut across the arc, Jake tapped the intersection.

"This is the farthest away that I expect the destroyer to start shooting," Jake said. "Now draw an arc ten miles from the edge of the module."

"Done."

"That's where the module's radar will have a line of sight to guide rounds and protect us," Jake said. "I'll assume that's our safe zone where our enemy won't go."

"This looks favorable, Jake," Santos said. "We can be in the safe zone while our torpedoes reach the target."

"Barely, and we need perfect targeting with perfect timing. We'll need to have our tactical data feed."

"We can do that once we reach our loiter position."

"You're getting the hang of this," Jake said. "Our tubes will also be reloaded by then. When you're commanding your own submarine someday, you'll have to keep in mind how long and how loud torpedo loading is. On this class of submarine, I have an automated torpedo room. You may not, and it adds variance, unpredictability, and noise risk."

"I was promoted to lieutenant only a year ago. I'm only supposed to be the executive officer of our first submarine."

"I think you just got bumped to the head of the line for command, at least if my recommendation carries any weight."

Jake walked back to the conning platform and flopped onto his foldout chair.

"Surface explosions!" Remy said. "Missiles have hit a target behind us."

"The *Pilar*?" Jake asked.

"I'm afraid so."

"How bad? How many?"

"Two explosions. The *Pilar* has stopped its screws and is drifting, probably to avoid fanning the flames."

"Most of them may have survived."

Jake clasped his hands, pressed his elbows into his thighs, and cleared his mind. Henri's pant legs crossed in front of him.

"What can I do for you?"

"I thought I would take advantage of a quiet moment to render my candid opinion."

"I thought you were always candid with me."

"I've made you change your mind once, and that's only because I was one hundred percent certain that following your advice was going to end my life. But in this case, I don't have as strong a position."

"So you didn't defy me in front of the crew."

Henri leaned his buttocks against the polished rail.

"Correct," he said.

"Thanks."

"But I still think you're wrong."

"About the slow-kill weapons?"

"Yes, of course. Understand that I have the utmost respect for your abilities. I've never said this before, and I may never again, but I think you're even more gifted than Pierre in commanding a submarine."

"Can I stop you there? I'd like to savor the moment before you say 'however'."

Henri crossed his arms and legs.

"However, you're taking your experiment or your statement or whatever you wish to call it regarding your slow-kill weapon to an extreme. You've just enjoyed a resounding success against the *Shang*. Why don't you arm us with the heavyweight torpedoes that are guaranteed to accomplish our mission?"

"Slow-kill weapons will accomplish the mission, even on surface vessels. That's why they have a surface mode where all twenty-four submunitions explode without delay. I know it's a novel idea, but I don't see why I can't sink a warship without killing everyone on it."

"That's my concern. I fear that you'll be offering second chances where second chances may prove fatal–to us."

"You've trusted me in all situations, and, except for the one time I deferred to you, my plans have always brought us out alive, even if we had to let one of our ships blow up to get it done."

"I guess you're right. I know you're right. I just needed to express my concern."

"It's fine. You needed to speak your mind."

"As usual, the burden of decision rests with you. I don't envy the isolation of leadership, but while it's your burden to bear, you have my support."

As the Frenchman returned to his station, Jake noticed that the *Wraith* was positioned to coast to its loiter point.

"All stop!" he said.

The submarine drifted, reducing the mild but noticeable vibration of fluid flowing over its hull. The lessened self-noise and continuous closing in of the task force created an effect Jake hoped to witness.

"The noise floor has fallen," Remy said. "I can hear to greater distances. I'm now tracking high-speed cavitating screws. Cleanly cut blades. Precision machinery for warships."

"Multiple contacts?" Jake asked.

"At least two. I need bearing separation to be sure, but I think a third ship is within hearing range but being masked by the others."

"I'm about to give you the luxury of a radar-fed tactical data link. Get ready for spoon feeding."

The speed gauge showed two knots and slowing.

"Henri, raise the communication buoy."

"It's raised," Henri said. "But I'm not getting anything."

"Antoine, give me a bearing to our communications ship."

"Bearing zero-eight-one, but its signal strength has weakened as we drove away from it."

"Henri, aim our radio to zero-eight-one, narrowest beam."

"I've got the link," Henri said. "Update is complete."

As icons vanished and reappeared at their updated positions, Jake felt relief that the two remaining helicopters had moved behind the combatants.

He credited the Chinese task force commander with realizing

that his airborne submarine hunters could approach no closer to the module without becoming railgun fodder each time they repositioned their dipping sonar systems. They could, however, protect his flanks while the surface vessels looked forward, continuing to blast their sonar energy into the water.

He slid on his headphone.

"Pierre?" he asked.

"I'm here, Jake. What's going on?"

"It's quiet from my end. You have my coordinates?"

"Yes."

"What's happening up there?"

"The *Pilar* took two Eagle Strikes in its port side, one in the engine room, one amidships in the berthing areas. Fires are out of control, but teams are fighting them. The *Alcatraz* has sustained no further damage since we last spoke, but the fires have spread beyond control, and it has been declared a lost cause. It is being abandoned."

"Shit."

"Our gunboats are challenging the task force, but they've been held off. The only good news is that I've kept the helicopters away from you, even with just one railgun."

"I owe you a beer for getting one off my back."

"My pleasure keeping you alive."

"The second gun is still down? You said the damage to the module had dislodged an electrical connection."

"Apparently the field repairs are more challenging than anticipated. Nevertheless, I will hope for the second gun to come back online soon. We may need it. The Chinese have just developed a tactic that concerns me."

Jake noticed the tightening in the grouping of the incoming warships. The destroyer had slowed, allowing its escorts to form a square around it.

"What are they doing?" he asked.

"They're taking station on the destroyer," Renard said. "I've also noticed them experimenting with close-in weapon systems, shooting down railgun shells as they dodge them."

"They're going to form a grouping so that they can protect themselves together. They'll be close enough so that every ship's close-in weapon system will get a crack at every incoming round. That multiplies their defenses by five against each round, in addition to the jamming."

"That's my concern."

"It also means that my torpedoes are going to hit random targets, unless I get gnat's ass accurate guidance."

"You would be wise to allow the torpedoes to do as they will, as opposed to exposing your communications buoy to their radar searches."

"No kidding. That's how it's going down. I'll take care of it now. Hold on, Pierre."

He checked the display and drew his conclusion.

"Lieutenant Santos," he said. "If I shoot a torpedo now at minimal speed, will it have enough endurance to reach the ships of the task force on their present course and speed?"

Where Jake would have used dividers, the younger man impressed him with his dexterity manipulating the capacitive touch screen. A green line sprang from the crosshairs of the *Wraith*, the proximity of its timed tick marks tightening where the proposed torpedo's trot would accelerate into a terminal sprint.

"It would reach, Jake. It would have approximately twelve percent fuel remaining to allow a little extra in case the targets change course or if they hear it coming and try to evade."

"It's going to be a silent run until the last minute," Jake said. "So they won't hear it. More specifically, they won't hear them. I'm firing all my loaded torpedoes."

"All?" Santos asked. "Including the heavyweight?"

"My humanitarian sentiment is wearing thin."

"Should I get all tubes ready to launch against the destroyer?"

"Five of the six," Jake said. "Which one will I hold back?"

"The Exocet in tube four."

"Correct, make all other tubes ready against the destroyer, slowest search speed. Inform me when I can launch."

Santos crouched at a control panel beside Durand, and the duo's fingers flew across touchscreens as they readied the weapons.

"Tubes one, two, three, five, and six are ready," Santos said. "All are targeted at the destroyer."

"Are you ready to shoot, Henri?"

"Ready!"

"Shoot tube one!" Jake said.

His ears popped, and he awaited verification that the weapon cleared the *Wraith's* bow under his control.

"Tube one, normal launch," Henri said. "Wire guidance engaged."

"Cut the wire to tube one. Backhaul tube one and reload with a heavyweight torpedo."

"The wire is cut, the tube is draining in preparation for loading with a heavyweight torpedo," Henri said.

"Shoot tube two!" Jake said.

Four more times the pneumatic system whined, and four more time his ears popped. A salvo marched from his ship towards his intended victim and its protective posse.

"Backhaul tube four and reload with a slow-kill weapon."

Henri gave the disapproving glare.

"The slow-kill is in case I feel nice again. Five heavyweights in the other tubes should be enough for all destructive purposes."

"The loading system is backlogged while catching up with the other tubes. I expect to have tube four backhauled of the Exocet and loaded with your last slow-kill weapon in twelve minutes."

"Very well, Henri. Lieutenant Santos, approach the conn."

"Yes, Jake?"

"Quiz time for the future submarine commander. Why didn't I shoot the Exocet?"

"It would be a wasted weapon."

"So what? It would do more good flying at the destroyer than sitting in my torpedo room. It would force the task force to expend an anti-air missile on it, since they'd be crazy to let it test their point defenses. So why did I hold it back? Remember that you're on a submarine and not a surface ship."

"I think I understand," he said. "It would reveal our position with the exhaust plume visually, and it would expose us to radar."

"Correct. Like a tracer bullet working backwards. Now why didn't I just eject it? It would save me time in reloading if I did so."

The young officer frowned with thought.

"I really don't know. I hadn't considered that. Ejecting weapons isn't something we do in the surface fleet, unless the weapon has malfunctioned and become a threat to the host ship."

"It was a trick question. The correct answer is that it depends. When you're commanding your own ship without regard to cost, you might have ejected it for the speed of reloading the tube. Keep that in mind for reference. You'll probably never have to do it, but if seconds count for a reload, it's a hastening technique. As for me, I'm a mercenary and have to think in terms of cost. Since I believe I have enough time to reload all my tubes, I kept my million-dollar missile."

"I understand."

"What about the other five tubes. Why did I cut the wires and backhaul them? Why not keep the wires and guide them in?"

"I'm not sure you care which targets you hit. They're all grouping together and each one is a threat to us."

"True, but I want to hit the destroyer."

"I think, if I understand sonar system accuracy, you can't distinguish one ship from another from sonar alone, if they are as close together as we expect them to be."

"Correct. It's going to be chaos. It's possible to steer torpedoes after the first detonation and the ships start running and separating, but you could pull a torpedo off a legitimate target and send it into oblivion by accident. May as well let the torpedoes determine their own fates."

The student nodded.

"But there's no harm in keeping wires attached, is there?" Jake asked. "So why did I cut them?"

"To reload faster."

"Not just faster, but to make all my reloading noises now while the targets are still too far away to hear. Speaking of which, they're getting close enough to sniff our radio."

Jake slid the headset over his ear.

"Pierre?"

"Still here. I see the torpedoes from your Subtics system, but I'm afraid this is where the luxury of our communications ends. The task force approaches. You need to lower your buoy and go dark."

"Yeah, it's time, Pierre. Wish me luck."

"I would, except that you don't need it. I trust that you are still charmed and that you will protect all my investments, including yourself."

CHAPTER 19

"What's going on out there, Antoine?"

"It's becoming terribly repetitive," Remy said. "Every ten seconds, I hear close-in weapon systems firing. They sound like chainsaws coming in rapid bursts from multiple ships. Then I hear a railgun shell hit the water, unless it's a hit."

"There's only been four damned hits in the last five minutes! On this bow-on aspect, you'd hope that a hit would cut through one of these ships lengthwise and wreak havoc, but so far, nothing has slowed them down."

Jake looked to the display and counted three minutes before his first torpedo would reach its target. The warships had deviated from his expectation of their movement, but they would remain within the wide acoustic cones of his weapons' seekers.

"Hit!" Remy said.

"Which ship?"

"Either the frigate or the corvette on the right. It's impossible to tell which one."

"Let's hope it means something," Jake said.

Remy's body curled forward with intense listening.

"The screw of the frigate to the right is slowing. It's losing speed. The last shell must have damaged its propulsion train."

"It probably took out a diesel," Jake said. "Good."

Henri looked up from his console.

"All tubes are reloaded," he said.

"Very well, Henri. Antoine, how long until my first weapon detonates?"

"Approximately ninety seconds."

"Very well, Antoine. Lieutenant Santos, ready tubes one and two for the destroyer. Durand, help him."

Hands flew across vertical touchscreens of the Subtics tactical system.

"Tubes one and two are ready," Santos said. "Targeted at the destroyer."

"I'll wait until our first salvo detonates before firing," Jake said. "I want to see where our victims run before shooting. Remy, when the chaos starts, do whatever you can to keep track of that destroyer. Don't lose it in the mess."

"I'll do what I can. I'm good, but the laws of physics still apply."

"You know what I mean," Jake said. "How long until my first weapon goes active?"

"Twenty seconds."

Jake rose from his foldout chair and braced himself against the polished rail.

"Get ready, everyone. Hell is about to break loose."

Hell burst forth with a deceiving whimper.

"Our first weapon has detonated. Submunitions are deploying," Remy said. "Many of them are attaching. I've lost count."

"Very well, Antoine."

"Explosions! Rippling across the hull of the target!"

"Can you tell which one?"

"No, not yet. But the second weapon is range-gating on its target, and the third is entering terminal homing."

"Henri!" Jake said.

"Yes?"

"You were wondering about the benefits of slow-kill weapons against surface targets?"

"Not in so many words."

"Our second weapon has detonated!" Remy said. "Submunitions are attaching!"

"Very well, Antoine," Jake said.

"You were saying?" Henri asked.

"I think we just stumbled upon a hidden benefit of the slow-kill weapon. The damage is invisible above the waterline. The other ships don't know to run yet. Heck, even the ships that have been hit don't know why they're flooding."

"They'll figure it out," Henri said.

"Eventually," Jake said.

"Ripple explosions from the second target!" Remy said. "Our third weapon has detonated! Submunitions are attaching! Targets are zigging. They're turning in different directions."

Jake studied the scene on the navigation table. Acoustic lines of bearing fanned out as the smaller ships turned, but the destroyer appeared to stay on course, barreling down on the *Wraith*.

"Why isn't the destroyer changing course?" he asked.

"I have no idea," Remy said. "I don't think we hit it."

"What do you mean, 'you think'? How do you not know?"

"Hold on! Our heavyweight torpedo just exploded. I believe it hit the damaged frigate that was already slowed. That's a confirmed kill. The keel is cracked."

A mixture of relief and repulsion filled Jake. He had reduced the number of lethal weapon platforms that hunted him from five to four, but he had condemned one hundred and sixty souls to death by drowning, burning, shock blast, head wounds, lacerations, internal hemorrhaging, and vaporization.

The few Chinese sailors who might survive the devastation would endure permanent physical and psychological scars. He swallowed the guilt and slid it to the backburner of his conscience, along with hundreds of prior victims, for future processing.

"Very well, Antoine. The northern frigate is sunk. What about the rest? What weapons hit which ships, and why the hell is that destroyer acting like Satan himself is willing it forward?"

"The ships have deployed decoys. They've launched countermeasures. They're churning wakes all over the place. Their sonar systems are blaring at maximum power. Helicopter dipping sonars are transmitting. Philippine gunboats are still circling and trying to harass them. It's complete chaos!"

"Are you tracking the destroyer?"

"No. Give me a second to find it. You should have brought a second sonar expert if you wanted to hear every note of this symphony!"

Jake stepped across the tiny room and crouched beside Remy. He grabbed a spare headset and pressed one of its muffs against his ear.

"You track the destroyer," he said. "Get me a targeting solution to break it in half. I'll listen for the other shit out there."

"I'm afraid you're not good enough to listen for the other shit out there, as you call it."

"Trust me."

"On all other matters, yes. On this, not so much."

"Just find me that destroyer."

"I see that I have no choice."

The sonar expert shrugged, pressed his muffs against his head, and curled forward.

"I have it," he said.

He tapped his screen and assigned an acoustic line of bearing to the clean frequency of the destroyer's screws.

"The solution is ready," he said.

Jake turned to Durand.

"Assign tubes one and two to the destroyer."

"Tubes one and two are assigned," Durand said.

"Henri, are you ready to shoot tubes one and two?"

"Ready!"

"Shoot tube one!"

Whining and ear popping preceding Henri's confirmation that he controlled the unleashed weapon.

"Shoot tube two!" Jake said.

After confirmation of the second weapon's control, it joined the first in racing towards the destroyer, but Jake wanted more.

"Durand, assign tube three to a phantom target twenty degrees to the left of the destroyer, same distance, course, and speed as the destroyer."

The young sailor looked at Jake for a quizzical moment, but then he processed the command and tapped keys.

"Tube three is assigned to a phantom target twenty degrees left of the destroyer, same distance, course, and speed."

Jake looked to Henri.

"You ready?"

"Ready!"

"Shoot tube three!"

His ears popped, and he yawned once again to relieve the pressure. A glance at Durand showed a young face, eager to comply.

"Now do it for tube four," Jake said. "Except this time, do it twenty degrees to the right."

"Tube four is assigned to a phantom target twenty degrees right of the destroyer, same distance, course, and speed."

With the fourth weapon seeking the boxed-in destroyer that sprinted into his oncoming weapons, Jake considered his mission to be minutes from completion. But with his hand pressing the sounds of the ocean against his ear, he discerned something that sent his adrenal glands into overdrive.

He looked at Remy, whose body curled in consuming focus, and he knew better than to interrupt him. To confirm his fears without his sonar guru's help, he listened to a cacophony of rhythmic, whining shrillness.

In his gut, he knew what was coming before Remy's back straightened to declare the truth in stone.

"Torpedoes in the water!" he said. "Multiple high-speed screws. Too many to count."

Jake couldn't remember an equaled look of terror in the guru's face. He leapt from his seat and yelled as he darted to the conning platform.

"All ahead flank, cavitate! Maintain course one-nine-zero. I'm evading to the south. Lieutenant Santos, mark datum! Make sure we know exactly where we are right now!"

"Datum is marked," Santos said. "Should we launch countermeasures?"

"No, it's way too soon," Jake said.

The *Wraith's* acceleration shook its circular ribs.

"Henri, flood the communications buoy and then cut it. We don't need it us slowing us down."

Henri acknowledged the order and turned to his panel to carry it out.

"Antoine, can you track all the torpedoes?" Jake asked.

"Not a chance!"

"Can you rule out the ones that are drawing wide and track the rest?"

"No! There are too many! Every ship in that task force just unloaded its arsenal!"

"Okay," Jake said. "We don't need your listening expertise anymore. Anything that can kill us is loud enough to see visually on Subtics, right?"

"Well, yes?"

"Subtics has a mode where it can auto-identify targets based upon a signal-to-noise ratio threshold, right?"

"It's a dangerous mode!" Remy said. "It creates too many false targets."

"So what? Do it. Then you, Durand, and Santos go through and sift out the false targets. Got it?"

"This is something we've never practiced!"

"You have a better idea?"

"No," Remy said.

"Don't worry about screwing it up. There's nothing you can do pressing buttons on the tactical system to make this any worse."

"Got it, Jake. I will try. Let's go, guys!"

Below Jake, the navigation chart became a portending of inescapable doom. Forty-one flashing red inverted triangles appeared near the locus of fleeing warships. Automated subscripted numbers allowed him to count them.

"Forty-one, Antoine? That's impossible. That's more than they have."

"I warned you about false targets."

"Start by listening to the most dangerous ones and rule them in or out as real weapons. I'm going to gray out the ones that are drawing away, whether they're real or false."

Jake darted to the navigation display and tapped the red triangle with the subscripted number of forty-one, invoking a list of data by it. On the row depicting the range from the *Wraith*, three dashes indicated a critical gap in his knowledge. The speed row showed an educated guess of fifty-five knots, and the bearing to the torpedo read three-five-zero.

All the torpedoes would show bearings near the northwest, the direction of their launch platforms, and all would be moving at fifty-five knots. As he tracked them over time, he would make estimates of range and determine which ones vectored away and which ones came for him.

If the shooters knew his location and had aimed at him, he was dead. He hoped they had instead taken a blind buckshot approach. As seconds ticked away, the bearing lines to torpedo forty-one showed the weapon drifting right, vectoring behind him.

He exhaled as he grayed it out and focused on the other forty instruments of destruction. Checking the weapon beside it, he noticed that it also pointed aft of his stern. After he turned it gray, he checked and grayed a third.

"Antoine," he said, "I think these are all shot in a nearly parallel formation, either that or slightly fanned out."

"They didn't start in a perfect line abreast. So they can't be perfectly parallel. It's more likely they are fanning out slightly. That's how I would attack us if I were them."

"That's good," Jake said. "We have a chance."

Returning his gaze to the navigation display, he realized that relying on speed, maneuvering, and countermeasures to escape the torpedoes would end his life. Survival required something unusual to reveal itself to him.

It did.

The Second Thomas Shoal provided storm protection to local fishermen. As he admired its long, teardrop shape, he noticed that it tapered to a southern tip. And though the shallow western shoals were impassable, he saw haven on the eastern side, where the *Sierra Madre* had passed decades ago before beaching at the northwest tip of a sunken lagoon.

"We make for the other side of the shoal," he said.

He walked dividers across the chart and calculated.

"We're three and a half miles from the southern edge," he said. "We're making twenty-six knots. I need eight minutes and twenty seconds to turn the corner. Are we going to be alive that long, Antoine?"

"I'm still analyzing the most dangerous torpedoes."

"Very well. Keep analyzing. I'll make my own assumptions."

He walked dividers again, muttering conservative suppositions to himself.

"Bump torpedo speed up to sixty-five knots. Assume they were shot from eight miles away. Assume that I'm not opening any appreciable distance while evading."

"How long do we have?" Henri asked.

"Seven minutes and twenty seconds. We need to either buy ourselves a minute, or we need to hope that I'm being a minute too conservative."

"Will countermeasures help?"

"At the right time, they might, but not yet," Jake said. "Not until we verify that at least one of these torpedoes has an intercept course for us. Let's keep running and reassess."

He reached for a sound-powered phone, twisted its dial to the engine room, and whipped the ringer handle. He lifted the phone to his cheek.

"Engineering," LaFontaine said.

"Claude, what's holding us back? Can you squeeze anything else out of our propulsion plant?"

"I don't know this ship as well as the *Specter*. I wouldn't dare push its limits beyond design."

"I know that! Tell me what you see holding us back. Battery cell temperature, shaft torque, lube oil temperature. What limit are you up against? Even a quarter knot could make a difference!"

"Shaft torque. It's twisted one and a quarter turns from the reduction gear to the stern bearing. That's the design limit, and if I push it harder, our shaft could snap."

"Shit. That's a real limit."

"I promise you, I understand the urgency. If there were another quarter knot to spare without risk of complete propulsion collapse, I would give it to you."

"I know, but I had to ask. What about our battery? Is it going to hold?"

"Yes, you have twenty-two minutes until cell inversion."

"Very well. Just keep it running back there."

As he stowed the phone in its cradle, Henri stopped beside him and whispered.

"Should we prepare to abandon ship?"

Given his history, Jake had forced his staff to rehearse the procedure for driving to the surface and escaping out the hatches with lifeboats and small arms. He knew they could find their way off the *Wraith* within ninety seconds of giving the order.

"Wait," he said. "Call me crazy, but I've actually got a feeling that we'll be driving the *Wraith* home."

CHAPTER 20

Three minutes into his evasion from the torpedo swarm, Jake recalculated geometries for the fifth time. Five phantoms and thirty-two inaccurate torpedoes had slipped into his recent nightmares, but four high-speed hunters appeared to have caught the *Wraith's* scent.

Relieved, he realized that Otto fuel-powered propellers thrust the incoming agents of death towards him at fifty-eight knots. Given the extra breathing room versus his original assumption of sixty-five knots, he planned to reach the shoal's southern tip seconds before all of the weapons.

Except one. Maybe.

"How does it look?" Henri asked.

"Come look," Jake said.

"I grayed out this huge grouping on the right since they're drawing behind us. Same for this smaller group on the left that's drawing far enough ahead of us. Remy removed the false torpedoes."

"I see two on intercept courses."

"Correct. Those two are on intercept courses, and this one might pick us up when its seeker goes active. In fact, it might already hear us passively. But it's less of a concern than those two."

"And this one–ahead of us to the south?"

Jake looked at Henri.

"That one scares me the most. Its seeker's going to go active in front of us. If it looks back over its shoulder far enough, it's going to turn ninety degrees and come punch us in the face."

"Sprinting into a torpedo is quite the opposite of prudent behavior, Jake."

"You'd rather turn back into the other three?"

"Of course not. We're damned either way. So what will you do if the lead weapon acquires us and turns?"

"Right now, I just hope that it doesn't. Because if it does, it's up to countermeasures, luck, and prayer."

"You would consider prayer?"

"It's a figure of speech."

"Not really."

"I meant whatever it takes."

"That's not how prayer works."

"I don't need a philosophy lesson now."

Jake heard Remy stirring behind him.

"Active seekers! The torpedo seekers are starting to awake!"

"Very well, Antoine. What about the primary four?"

"Not yet. Soon. Yes! The first is active. Now the next."

"Tell me if any of the four change course after they go active, especially the one in front."

Tapping the map, Jake zoomed in on the shoals' southern tip.

"Shall I prepare to abandon ship?" Henri asked.

"No. We're half a mile from the turn. We can make it."

"You mean, if the lead weapon doesn't see us."

"We're on a good aspect. We're almost bow on. It will minimize our sonar cross section."

"Does that really matter?"

"A little. I'm trying to wish ourselves small."

Jake turned and leaned over Remy's shoulder.

"What's going on with that lead weapon?"

"I think it's active."

"You don't know? That's good. That means its active seeker transmission isn't reaching us."

"Right. Count your blessings. We're also positioning ourselves behind it. I think we're okay."

"Good. That leaves only the three in a tail chase."

"You need to turn soon," Remy said.

Jake turned and stooped over the chart as Henri returned to his control panel. The *Wraith's* inertial navigation system placed the submarine a stone's throw from the shoal. Allowing for the vessel's advance and transfer, the display showed the tactical system's calculated recommendation of the turn's timing.

"Left full rudder!" Jake said. "Steer course zero-one-zero."

As the *Wraith* rolled through the extreme about-face, he held the navigation table and monitored his position through the turn. The ship hugged the shallow rock.

"Get ready for gaseous countermeasures," he said.

Keeping one hand on the rudder's joystick, Henri stood and reached for a button.

"Ready."

When the crosshair rounded the shoal, Jake recognized his opportunity to leave a blinding wall of bubbles behind him.

"Deploy gaseous countermeasures!"

Explosive gas hammered the hull as launchers spat compressed gas canisters into the sea. Jake tapped the display to mark the location for reference.

For a moment of ignorant bliss, effervescent water separated the *Wraith* from torpedo seekers.

"Do you hear anything?" Jake asked.

"Just our countermeasures and a lot of our own flow noise," Remy said. "A full-speed turn with full rudder makes hearing anything almost impossible."

"Keep listening."

Henri released the joystick to set the rudder amidships.

"Steady on course zero-one-zero," he said.

"Very well."

"That's it, then," Henri said. "If we've left the torpedoes on the other side of the countermeasures and shoals, we survive. If a weapon passes through, however..."

Nobody cared to finish his sentence.

Time slipped forward in tortured agony as Jake caught himself seeking a conversation with a dubious deity about his survival. He made note that, if he survived, he would engage Henri in the philosophical discussion he had cut short moments earlier.

Glaring at Remy as he curled and then stiffened, his heart sank. In that moment, he understood the adage about there being no atheists in foxholes.

His face ashen, Remy was a talking corpse.

"Active torpedo seeker, bearing one-nine-zero."

Jake swore under his breath.

"Fuck."

"What do we do?" Henri asked.

Jake dropped his head between his shoulder blades and stared at the floor while announcing his defeat.

"Prepare to abandon ship."

Sixty seconds later, the control room had emptied of all but four men. Jake stood at the charting table beside Henri and Lieutenant Santos while Remy stayed at his sonar console.

"I suppose Claude stuck around the engine room."

The response came from a loudspeaker.

"Of course," LaFontaine said. "I will see to it that this engine room continues running as long as you are aboard."

"What about you, Lieutenant Santos? You could join the men by the exits."

The young officer looked at Jake with defiance.

"No, I can't. Whatever fate you're facing, I'm facing it with you."

"So be it," Jake said. "Antoine, do you have an updated solution to that torpedo?"

"The countermeasures bought us thirty seconds. It's going to reach us in two minutes."

"Santos," Jake said. "Where can we cross the shoals into the lagoon? The *Sierra Madre* did it seventeen years ago. We can do it, too."

"It was farther north," Santos said.

"Antoine," Jake said, "if I deploy countermeasures, I can buy fifteen to thirty seconds per batch."

"That's only going to delay the inevitable, Jake. It's over."

"I agree," Santos said. "The *Sierra Madre's* crossover point was too far away."

"Damn. I was afraid of that. Can we cross anywhere else? Keep in mind that our draft is twenty feet when surfaced."

"There's nothing deep enough, at least nothing we can reach in time."

In desperation, Jake scanned the chart for inspiration. Nothing came to mind other than abandoning the ship he had stolen. Surfacing the *Wraith* would make him a target for Chinese guns and missiles, but he preferred facing those speculative dangers over a torpedo rupturing his hull.

"Henri," he said. "We need to surface."

"Are you sure?"

"It's time. And since we're shallow, drive us up and use our high-pressure air banks to blow our ballast tanks dry."

"I shall see to it."

As the deck angled upward, Jake walked to the conning platform and raised the periscope.

"Raise the radio mast, Henri."

Seconds later, the tactical scene merged data from the Philippine control center with that of the *Wraith's* organic Subtics system.

Grayed out, the surviving frigate and corvettes appeared as lifeless icons, special notes beside them proclaiming that each ship had fallen dead in the water and had surrendered. Jake deduced that the railgun had inflicted the requisite damage on their engines.

Had his mortal terror allowed it, he would have felt a vengeful pleasure in seeing the gray icon of the destroyer. The note beside it indicated that a torpedo from the *Wraith* had snapped its keel. However, it had met its demise within cannon range of the railgun module, and he worried about his mission and the stronghold's survival.

A familiar voice on a loudspeaker offered him insight.

"Jake! Jake!" Renard said.

"I'm here, Pierre. Getting ready to abandon ship. I've got about ninety seconds. Did I at least protect the module?

"Yes. Mostly. The destroyer landed a dozen shells before your torpedo hit. The armor on the southeast corner collapsed, but you spared the expensive inner equipment."

"Well, that's good to hear. Sorry I couldn't spare your submarine, though. I'm about to give it back to the ocean."

"I see your predicament on the tactical feed," Renard said. "Your escape plan was brilliant, evading thirty-five of thirty-six torpedoes."

"Let's finish this talk later. I need to go swimming."

"Before you do that, try extending your run a bit with more countermeasures."

"Sure. Why not? It can't hurt. Henri, go ahead and launch another pair of compressed gas countermeasures."

As the popping thuds echoed through the *Wraith's* ribs, Jake called out to Pierre.

"I really need to go now," he said.

"Do you? Look again. Do you see the *Alcatraz*?"

He had ignored the gray icon of the burning hulk, which had moved within three miles of his submarine.

"What are you doing?" Jake asked.

"The *Alcatraz* is a lost cause, but it still has propulsion. When I saw the task force shoot its torpedo arsenal at you, I figured you might need the help."

"Help? Explain."

"Consider it a gift for a tactic that we've used before."

Jake scanned his memory banks for abnormal tactics he'd used over ten years of extreme submarining.

"You want me to do what we did with the *Bainbridge*?"

"Yes, but the inverse. Sacrifice the surface ship. Save yourself—and my investment."

"Are there still people aboard the *Alcatraz*?"

"The throttles are pinned open, and the captain is the last man aboard piloting the ship. A helicopter is hovering above the bridge with a hoist for him."

"When will he jump?"

"Right after his bow passes yours."

"Then I don't need to do anything but launch another set of countermeasures, head topside, and wait, do I?"

"For your safety and that of the crew, I recommend that you send everyone overboard. Helicopters and gunboats will retrieve you."

"The torpedo has circled back and has passed through our countermeasures," Remy said. "I estimate sixty seconds until impact."

"Henri, deploy another pair of gaseous countermeasures."

The hull thudded with the deployment.

"Now launch our noisemaker countermeasure from the three-inch launcher."

Henri pressed a button.

"The noisemaker is launched."

"The torpedo has ignored the gaseous countermeasures," Remy said. "It doesn't appear to acknowledge our noisemaker either. No change to torpedo behavior."

"It's over guys! Claude, do you hear me?"

"Yes, Jake," LaFontaine said.

"Get off this ship! Everyone goes overboard! Now!"

Sultry air became a moist artificial wind across Jake's cheeks as he stood on the *Wraith's* bow. Fires dotted the night, orienting him in the moonlit darkness.

Residual oil from the burning landing craft *Sierra Madre* cast dim light on the railgun module, but distance prevented him from seeing the damage with his naked eyes.

To the north, the *Gregorio del Pilar* appeared as two fires under a canopy of black clouds that blocked starlight. Further west, three clusters of small fires, barely visible on the horizon, showed the resting place of the three surrendered Chinese ships.

A mile away, the green running light of a gunboat offered his crew refuge from the sea through which they swam, and elevated white lights undulating with rotating rhythm pinpointed a waiting helicopter.

Dead ahead, blazing so brightly that its fires reflected off the submarine's bow wake, the sprinting *Alcatraz* offered its dying mass as a sacrifice to the *Wraith*.

Backlighting flames casting shadows, the Philippine frigate's bridge became deep blackness. He stared at its ominous opaqueness, offered its invisible captain a salute, and followed his crew into the salty water.

Kicking through the fluid, he strained his extremities to distance himself from the pending explosion. Wanting to stop and look, he exercised judgment and continued to kick, as he had ordered his men to do.

The explosion sounded like Armageddon through the water and the air, and then a surface wave caught him. Atop its crest, he continued kicking, unsure what debris may fly in his direction.

When exhaustion and impatience overcame him, he flipped onto his back.

The fires of the *Alcatraz* angled upward as the frigate's severed halves twisted into the water. Jake strained his eyes for the *Wraith* but saw nothing. He trusted that the *Alcatraz'* martyrdom implied the submarine's survival.

The former Malaysian vessel seemed charmed, like his own adopted child, and he wanted to see it again.

The white light of a helicopter dipped towards the horizon, shot across the sky, and disappeared. Jake surmised that its occupants sought the runaway *Wraith* to board it, duck inside it, and shut its throttles before it either ran aground or started destroying its battery cells.

The blinking light on his life jacket assured him of being found, but the rescue effort tested his patience, and fear of sharks compelled him to swim towards the shoal.

Unsure if his imagination tormented him or if the dorsal fin were real, he returned to normal breathing when the helicopter winch pulled him from the water.

As his height of eye ascended, he caught a glimpse of the *Wraith*. It had coasted to a stationary resting place in calm waters, and it appeared at peace.

He wiped a tear from his cheek before the deck crew hauled him into the aircraft's cabin, and he blamed the wind for whipping the moisture from his eye.

CHAPTER 21

A surreal calm enveloped the command center.

Renard inhaled a long drag from his Marlboro, exhaled smoke, and adjusted his headset.

"It's a pleasant surprise to hear from you Commander Cahill," he said. "I see by your data feed that you found your way to a friendly ship with encrypted communications equipment."

"Indeed I did, mate. I don't expect to be talking long. Just thought I'd let you know that we're okay out here and grab meself a tactical update. I'm running through the data and showing it to me boys like a movie. It tells a great story–all except what happened at the end. What's the verdict for Jake?"

"He's fine. I used a little creativity. The *Alcatraz* was abandoned and burning. So I decided to exchange it for the *Wraith*."

"Clever, mate! Is everyone from the *Wraith* okay?"

"I think so, but I need to verify. You'll need to excuse me. You should go dark anyway."

"Right, mate. See you tomorrow night. Back at the covered wharf, right?"

"Correct. I'll buy the beer."

Renard switched frequencies and hailed his submarine. Nobody answered, and he tried again.

"Sorry, Pierre," Remy said in French. "I was trying to change into dry clothes."

"No need to apologize. Are you still alone?"

"They dropped me off first so that I could stop the shaft. Me, of all people!"

"You must have been the first person the rescue helicopter crew found who admitted to being capable of shutting down the plant."

"I was the first person they found at all! Claude has always made sure that I know the right buttons to press to shut down his precious propulsion plant. So I volunteered, and when I got here, I shut it down."

"Well done, Antoine. But who else is with you?"

"It's just me! I'm alone, but I did have a companion on my helicopter ride. The captain of the *Alcatraz* was with me on the flight."

Renard inhaled soothing nicotine.

"But he's not with you now?"

"No. He stayed on the helicopter. I don't think he wanted to join me on the *Wraith*. His English wasn't very good. Or maybe he just didn't want to talk. We could see the floating halves of his ship burning below us as we flew."

"It's traumatic losing one's ship," Renard said. "The initial reports count sixty-eight of his men lost."

"I'm sorry to hear that, Pierre. A lot of people died this night. Too many for my tastes."

"Eighty-nine souls at last count," he said, "and most of them from the frigates. God knows how many Chinese perished, too."

"This is all terrible," Remy said. "I sometimes wonder if I'm in the right job."

"What else would you possibly do? You're the best sonar technician in the world."

"After tonight, I should consider retiring."

"Unthinkable! I will always call on you when I need sonar expertise, and as long as I am breathing, I intend to continue deploying my submarines."

He enjoyed hearing himself referring to the ownership of multiple submarines.

"Can I go now, Pierre? I'm still dripping seawater on the deck plates. I would like to change into something dry."

"Yes, of course, my friend. A crew to navigate the *Wraith* back home will soon join you."

In the silence, Renard scanned the center. Adrenaline drained from each man's frame, and weary bodies had curled forward in chairs during the tedious rescue effort. The ventilation system strained to extract cigarette smoke and body odor from the room.

Navarro stood next to Admiral Torres, his speech moving with rare lethargy. The chief represented the exhaustion of his entire military. His words remained beyond Renard's hearing, but the Frenchman knew their subject matter–tend to the wounded and bring everyone home.

Renard thought ahead to Navarro's next conversation–after having fended off the Chinese tiger, what to do next?

As the conversation between the chief and the admiral lost steam, Renard stood and reached for the ceiling. His vision became dizzy with blood draining through him, but he noticed Navarro gesturing him to come by.

He doused his cigarette in an overfilled tray and then walked to the stairs. After a sharp turn, he stood beside the Philippine leaders. The stench of nicotine and nervous sweat repulsed him, but he stifled his gag reflex, and he suspected that they found his dirty scent equally revolting.

"Gentlemen," he said, "we may be victorious, but we are hardly outside the fog of war. We need to keep our wits about us as we take our next steps."

"We have retrieved your entire crew," Torres said. "The last man is aboard our gunboat."

"I appreciate the efforts of your sailors. Their urgency and efficiency in saving my men from sharks is almost as impressive as their valor and skill in combat."

"The storm is over," Torres said. "All our people are being tended to. My concern now is the Chinese survivors."

"That is a matter of policy," Renard said. "Have you discussed the message that you wish to send to China and to the entire world, for that matter?"

"Yes," Navarro said. "We are not animals. We have agreed to detain and to render medical assistance to their survivors, but I fear they will scuttle their ships before allowing them to fall into our possession."

"You may count on that," Renard said. "They will not let you have them. However, for your propaganda needs, I recommend gathering as much night vision video as possible of you rescuing your adversary from their sinking ships."

"That's an excellent idea," Torres said. "But I am running out of helicopters."

"Will you allow me a telephone call, then?" Renard asked.

He climbed stairs to the observation room and called Olivia McDonald. Her groggy, throaty voice overlaying the whining tones of jet engines suggested that he had awoken her while in flight.

"Don't tell me you slept through that," he said.

"Not a wink, but I passed out immediately after the *Alcatraz* exploded. I was impressed by that move, but I suppose I should have expected it from you."

"You didn't want to wait to hear that Jake was safe?"

"He's a great swimmer, and I would put money on him versus any shark that would mess with him."

"He is indeed fine. I haven't spoken with him yet, but every man is accounted for from my ship."

"Congratulations, Pierre. You must be on top of the world."

Somehow, he suspected she was ready to bring him down.

"For the moment."

"What can I do for you?"

"Can you dedicate a satellite to capturing the Philippine rescue effort of the Chinese surface combatants?"

"It's already happening. Navarro made a good call extending the olive branch."

"I might have known. Will you be willing to share the video for his management of international sentiment?"

"Of course, Pierre. I wouldn't dream of keeping such exquisite footage to myself. May I go back to sleep now?"

"Accept my apologies for having doubted your support."

"Accepted. Oh, and one more thing, Pierre."

"Yes?"

"In three days, I want you and Jake in my office for a debriefing of this entire affair. We need to discuss your future."

The line went dead, and he returned to the Philippine leaders.

"You are assured of video footage from the United States. Of course, I recommend that you gather your own footage as well, when possible."

"I have seen to it," Navarro said. "I am allocating air force assets to assist."

"Excellent."

"Now, as I remember your plan for the post-deployment phase of the railgun module," Navarro said, "you suggested retaking Mischief Reef next. Does the absence of one railgun or the loss of our frigates and half our gun boats alter that plan?"

"Not at all," Renard said. "In fact, your defeat of the Chinese task force simplifies it. The challenge is learning how to appear gracious in the international spotlight while forcefully retaking that which was and is rightfully yours."

"I have an update," Torres said. "The fires on the *Pilar* are under control. The ship is seaworthy, and its main gun is functional. It's available for assisting with taking Mischief Reef."

"Are the marines still aboard?" Renard asked. "I mean–are they capable of their duties."

"Yes, the entire platoon survived."

Renard looked at Navarro.

"Then I recommend sending the *Pilar* to Mischief Reef and having a boarding party standing by while the president's staff instructs the Chinese ambassador to arrange for a peaceful transfer of the reef's personnel back to proper Chinese soil. Continue to send your transport ship of marines to the reef as a backup landing force."

"Such success and position of strength is new ground for us," Navarro said. "Literally and figuratively."

"Your immediate goal is to simply occupy the reef. Once that is done, you shall reposition your Patriot missiles from Nanshang Island to Mischief Reef for better protection of the railgun module. Once you've repaired the second gun and replenished the module's magazine, your zone of protection from the Second Thomas Shoal to Thitu will be formidable."

"Mischief Reef is an obvious and immediate next step. But can I expand my fishing areas? With the Chinese showing their willingness to deploy a submarine into the area, is my fishing fleet at risk if I send it in?"

"Within the protective radius, your risk is minimal for the fishing fleet," Renard said. "I don't expect that Chinese submarines would harass them, and the railguns and Patriot missiles will deter surface ships and aircraft. I recommend announcing this morning that your fishing fleet has new havens at their immediate disposal."

The nation's de facto leader appeared as tired as the Frenchman felt in his aging bones, but his enthusiasm inspired his continued probing.

"Turning back a Chinese task force, controlling fishing areas, retaking Mischief Reef, and creating a protective zone are enough reasons for me to declare this undertaking a success," Navarro said. "But I seek the greatest economic benefit. Now that we're here, on the other side of the confrontation, tell me what stands between me and the oil?"

"Submarines," Renard said. "Your adversary has shown a willingness to deploy its finest undersea assets to oppose you. They obviously see the value in the sea space that you just wrested from them, and they will come again to challenge your oil platform."

"The test data shows that the platform can withstand a torpedo. Based upon its design, my experts agree, but that's just a single torpedo. How it tolerates multiple torpedoes is a matter of speculation I wish to keep untested."

"And so you shall. I believe you'll be best served by a two-part protection plan, beginning with a submarine and followed by helicopter support, when they become available."

The small man's eyes gleamed under his bald scalp.

"What's the timeframe? I would obviously like to deploy the platform as soon as possible, but the helicopters have yet to arrive."

"Your anti-submarine helicopters should arrive in six weeks," Renard said. "I've hired operators to fly them and train your aviators. You will soon have your own detachment stationed on the oil platform, able to constantly search the waters around it for hostile submarines. This, of course, supported by merchant shipping with sonar systems surrounding the platform."

"Deterrence is a powerful force."

"Indeed it is. A man would be crazy to test a submarine's torpedoes against the platform while exposing himself to an immediate response by helicopter."

"And what to do until the helicopters arrive? You mentioned a two-part plan."

"I have a submarine I will dedicate to the cause–free of charge. I owe you for the delay of the helicopters, and it's the least I can do. Production issues with my suppliers may be out of my control, but I still hold myself responsible to provide you the protection I promised."

"Immediately? The platform is making no money while it floats next to my shoreline."

Renard lit up a fresh cigarette.

"Sorry. No. I may be magnanimous, but I am no saint. I will need four days to deploy your protection."

"Four? The *Wraith* is already on station. Why the delay?"

"Because I won't be using the *Wraith*. I'll be using the *Specter*. It will be arriving aboard its transport ship in two days. Then I'll allow half a day for transferring weapons from the *Wraith* to the *Specter*, and then the *Specter* will deploy to protect your drilling platform.

"Compared to a six-week delay, I can hardly complain about four days. But why the *Specter* instead of the *Wraith*?"

"Once the *Specter* is offloaded, I'm going to load the *Wraith* onto the transport ship and take it to the *Specter's* construction yard in Taiwan. The *Wraith* lacks a MESMA air-independent propulsion system, and I intend to fix that."

"MESMA?"

"It allows a submarine to spend weeks underwater without snorkeling, even while making appreciable headway, and I want my entire fleet to have that advantage. I had my Taiwanese partners build the *Specter* with it. They are quite capable of cutting the *Wraith's* hull and inserting a MESMA section."

Sagging skin at the corner of Navarro's eyes betrayed his fatigue as he offered a rare smile.

"I should have an agreement within hours to retake Mischief Reef," he said. "I can expand our fishing areas to fertile seas in the morning, and I can deploy an oil platform in four days. Despite losing a frigate, two gunboats, and a rusting beached hulk, I consider this a monumental evening."

The Frenchman blew smoke into the ventilation system.

"I earn my clients by repeat business and word of mouth," he said. "It has been my pleasure, and I trust that you'll keep me in mind for your future needs and those of your allies."

CHAPTER 22

The next night, Jake watched the stopwatch on his phone tick off the final minute of the sixty that had elapsed since taking his Naltrexone pill.

"Time!" he said.

"Here's your coldie, mate!"

The Australian slid him a pint, and he chugged it until the sting in his throat forced him to slam the quarter-full glass onto the table.

"This pill Pierre's making me take has no effect," he said. "I still love beer."

"Give it a few months," Renard said. "There's no need for alarm. Your love of beer will remain intact. It's the craving that will subside."

"Well, for now, you'll excuse me if I pickle myself as fast as I can."

The same foursome sat around the same table where they had met prior to the railgun module's deployment. However, Jake noticed a refreshing levity, even from the chief of staff.

"I think I'll have another," Navarro said.

"You earned it, my friend," Renard said.

The Frenchman levied a perfect pour with a foamy head.

"Nicely done, mate!"

Cahill's smile ebbed and he looked into his beer. Jake knew what troubled him.

"Are you sure you don't want to fight it?" he asked.

"Nah, it's okay, mate. I've been through it a thousand times in me head. I'm done with the navy."

Upon his arrival at the covered pier, Cahill had shared the news that his admiralty had relieved him of command for interfering in a bilateral engagement between the Philippines and China. He had been ordered to observe and share information with the Philippine forces, but engaging the *Shang*, even with a limpet weapon, had violated his orders.

"I'd fight it out of principle," Jake said.

"There's nothing to fight for, really. I've angered too many people to expect any future promotions, and if I get me ship back, everything's downhill from yesterday as far as adventure goes."

"So that's it? You quit?"

"Technically, I've been fired."

"So what are you going to do?"

"No idea, mate. Go home and take this uniform off. Find me a sheila and settle down. I'm sure there's some sort of work I could do. I haven't given it much thought yet."

"No kidding. This is bullshit and it's happening so fast," Jake said. "You were commanding a submarine in combat last night."

He finished his beer, poured himself another, and gulped.

"Combat," Cahill said. "It feels like I went through it all in someone else's body. I think I was scared when all those ships passed by me with their sonars blaring, but I don't remember feeling anything."

"That's how it is, man," Jake said. "It's weird like that. But what happened? How'd you tag that *Shang*?"

"It's as easy as you might guess. I just pushed ahead, waited, and listened. It was moving too fast to miss. I figured you could use the help, what with everything that was going on."

"You took advantage of an opportunity and may have saved my life. I can't believe the Royal Australian Navy doesn't get it."

"You have to see it from their perspective. I took Her Majesty's Australian Ship and a crew that's worth tens of millions of dollars in training investments, and I risked it all to help a mercenary take hostile action against an angry giant. Not exactly a recipe for making me a candidate for prime minister."

Finishing his second beer, Jake decided to slow his pace with the third. He poured with a savoring grace. As he slid the empty pitcher to the edge of the table, he noticed Renard in deep thought.

His mentor's face appeared hard, the lines of age more pronounced than he'd remembered. An unspoken vibe from the Frenchman tuned itself to Jake's empathetic frequency, and he knew to leave his friend undisturbed.

"After your service to our nation, I would hate to see you unemployed," Navarro said. "Admiral Torres could benefit from your services as an advisor. Our first submarine will be here soon, and we need technical and tactical experts to guide us. Of course, you'd need to be here frequently, but travel arrangements could be made to allow you to spend a significant time in Australia."

"Well, I'm flattered, mate, and I thank you. And I have no trouble traveling. I'd love to look into your offer. After last night, I'm feeling a real need for adventure."

"Then command my submarine!" Renard said.

Silence spread throughout the entire bar, its blend of French, Philippine, and Australian patrons entering a shared schism in the space-time-logic continuum.

Jake studied his mentor with burning eyes. As he absorbed the news, he suspected he had slipped into a dream.

"I have two submarines and only one Jake," Renard said. "I wanted to lead the *Specter* in defending the oil platform, but I've conceded that I'm too old. I need a man like you. No offense to Mister Navarro, but he can find consultants elsewhere. I, however, consider it a gift when I find a man of mettle whose vision aligns with mine and has the freedom to join me."

Having broken free of the tortuous path to his decision and the bondage of its secrecy, the Frenchman blushed with relief.

"Holy shit," Jake said.

"I hope you take no offense, Mister Navarro," Renard said.

"None taken. He would be underutilized as an advisor. I was merely trying to prevent his leaving the submarine field entirely."

"You know I appreciate the offer, Pierre. I really do. Words don't describe the honor of your confidence in me."

The Frenchman's response might have sounded like a plea from a weaker man, or it might have sounded like an order from an impatient man. But from Renard, it issued as destiny.

"Then say 'yes'."

The color in Cahill's face and the dilation of his pupils betrayed his exhilaration. The Australian had no chance, but he jockeyed for breathing room.

"How long do I have to decide?"

"The *Specter* deploys in two days. I'll give you until the lines are cast off."

Cahill sipped from his beer in a moment of silence that made Jake uncomfortable. He wanted to slap the answer out of him as the Australian lowered his glass.

"To be clear. You want me to command the *Specter*? It would be mine?"

"Initially," Renard said. "I would then task you in overseeing the addition of the MESMA plant to the *Wraith*. I'll want you to be as familiar with both ships as Jake is so that I can call on either of you to command either ship."

"And me crew?"

"Jake is fluent in French, and I'll keep pulling his crew from the French Navy. However, everyone in my fleet must be fluent in English, and I'll want cross-decking to assure knowledge transfer between teams. For your crew, I'll recruit from Anglophone navies."

"I know some blokes who would do this. There's even a few in this room who might join when their enlistments end."

"Excellent. I have no hesitation negotiating and paying for early terminations of enlistments with naval personnel departments"

"What about the *Wraith* being stolen? Aren't you worried about the Malaysians coming for it?"

"Possession is nine tenths of the law," Renard said. "And can you imagine a court of law that would have jurisdiction, much less attempt to enforce it? Piracy is our crime, and since five nations cannot agree who owns the water where we committed it, I don't see a bureaucratic legal process reaching us. The sheer embarrassment of it will make the Malaysians hesitate to do anything but declare the ship a loss."

Cahill twisted and grabbed the new pitcher as the waiter

brought it.

"That means you're always on the run when you're deployed. You can't just pull into any port and grab a beer. There's going to be a Malaysian guy waiting in every port with a machine gun ready to either take back the ship or extract revenge."

"Perhaps. But in my navy, there are only calculated port calls of necessity. If you want to visit a port for fun, you do so under a false identity that I will provide, and you spend the money from your generous salary to fly there first class."

"Yeah, how much is the pay?"

"Exorbitant. Trust me. Doesn't Jake look filthy rich?"

Jake shrugged and nodded.

"What about missions? What's coming next? If I do this, it's for the excitement. I'm afraid you've got me addicted to it."

"As always, I am pursuing several opportunities. However, I cannot share. I don't even share with Jake until a mission is a reality. But rest assured, I guarantee adventure."

"All right, then. Do I sign in blood?"

The smile cut across Renard's face.

"No need. Just say 'yes'."

Cahill shrugged.

"Yes."

Jake feared that jealousy might cloud the moment, but he surprised himself by springing from his chair and hugging his new partner.

Two days later, he glanced across the waiting room at Renard.

"Are your Taiwanese buddies this annoying?"

"They used to make me wait longer, until I saved their nation from extinction. Now I get direct access when desired."

"What's she doing?"

"She's showing us how important she is."

"You mean how important she thinks she is."

"No, she is actually as important as she thinks."

"Why?"

"Because we believe it. Otherwise, we would have left by

now."

A middle-aged lady in a dark suit behind a desk, flanked by an American flag and a CIA banner, lifted her nose.

"Miss McDonald will see you now."

As she led him and Renard through oaken doors into Olivia's plush office, Jake noticed that nobody had exited. He wondered if she had been engaged in a conference call, or if she had just made them wait in a textbook Asian power play.

Sexy with a curve-hugging suit, she stood and walked around her desk to greet him. As she embraced him, he sensed her coldness, the hug being a gesture of diplomacy more than an expression of caring between past lovers.

Her words sounded sterile.

"It's so good to see you, Jake. It's been too long."

Lines on her face showed age catching up with her, but in a world led by old men, she shone as a beacon of bright, young energy. As she kissed Renard's cheeks and then slinked back to her desk, her movement suggested that power and prestige had converted her innate confidence into arrogance.

He waited for her to sit before lowering himself into her leather guest chair.

"Thank you for coming, gentlemen."

Unsure who she had become, Jake clenched his jaw and deferred to his colleague's knowledge of decorum.

"It's our pleasure to be with you," Renard said. "We are most appreciative of your support in our latest endeavor in the Spratly Islands."

"You're too kind, Pierre. We helped each other. How were your travels?"

"Splendid. It's good to be back in the States."

"Yeah, me too," Jake said. "I'm just happy to be home. Well, almost home. We came here directly."

"How do you like my new corner office? It's a long way from my first open-air cube when I was just an analyst."

"It's impressive, especially for the CIA," Jake said. "It looks like you've hit the big time. What are you, second in line to replace the CIA director?"

"I'm well positioned within the director's executive staff," she said. "If Gerry wins the next election, as he should, it will assure me of all the clout I need to make it to the top."

Jake wanted to remind her that she didn't bring them there to gloat about her friend, the Secretary of Defense, being an early forerunner to win the next presidential election. But he stopped himself, questioning if the entire visit revolved around gloating.

"And a worthy candidate you are to lead your nation's intelligence interests," Renard said. "Tell me, what can I do to help further your cause?"

"Just keep doing what you're doing," she said. "I like the results when we team up, despite the complications we ran into in Argentina."

"We faced unfortunate circumstances together in Argentina," Renard said, "But the intelligence in the Spratlys was impeccable. You were masterful, and I can't thank you enough."

Her brow cast a shadow upon her eyes.

"No, you can't. So let's be honest. We need each other. Military efforts don't get resolved without knowing your enemy, your allies, and controlling the information–especially since the world is becoming aware of your mercenary submarine fleet."

"I agree," Renard said, "but you've been candid about controlling more than information. In fact, you've been quite candid about meaning to control me."

"Don't put words in my mouth."

"Veto power, you called it. The right to tell me that I cannot deploy my submarines where I wish. If that's not control, then perhaps my command of the English language is failing."

"I won't argue the semantics. Call it what you want."

Jake crossed his ankle over his thigh.

"She has veto power?"

"Miss McDonald has expanded the extent of her influence appreciably in the years that we've been privileged to know her. She is right. We need each other. That which I can accomplish with two submarines is beyond what I can support with my own intelligence community, broad as it is. Direct access to American intelligence is valuable, and I need it."

"So we agree," she said. "We're a team."

"I thought we always were a team," Jake said.

She smiled, and he thought he noticed a patronizing pity, as if she saw him as a child who misunderstood an obvious critical factor.

"Of course, Jake," she said. "We have always been a team. That will never change."

"We appreciate the assurance," Renard said. "As always, it's good to see you."

Jake sensed Renard stiffening his back moments before Olivia stood.

"I appreciate you stopping by, gentlemen. Let me walk you to the door."

Renard instructed Jake to remain silent until they reached their limousine.

"We flew to Langley and sat in her waiting room for two hours for that? Nobody said anything? It was all pleasantries and platitudes."

"Everything was said when we walked in the door. By doing so, you and I conceded that she is in charge. The rest was an informal script, even the part where I pretended to take offense at her veto power and her belittling of my feigned protestation."

"You're kidding. Do they teach that in rainmaker school?"

"If such a school existed, it would be required training."

They slid into the back of the limo, and it accelerated.

"That went so fast, I didn't get to ask her about the prisoners."

"I am privy to much of their fate," Renard said. "The Chinese survivors have been granted prisoner of war status. With the world looking on, they shall receive pristine treatment. Chinese medical teams have already been allowed access to them."

"What about the Malaysians?"

"They remain under guard aboard an anchored freighter."

"What's going to happen to them? The world thinks they're dead and that the *Razak* was lost at sea."

"I don't know. It's a matter for Navarro to navigate."

"You're not concerned?"

"I planned this endeavor knowing full well that they may all be returned to Malaysia and reveal that their submarine was stolen. But what do I care? The *Wraith* is mine, I'm customizing it to my liking, and I'm not giving it back."

As the chain link fence surrounding the private airport came into sight, Jake saw two Lear jets standing by on the tarmac.

"I guess we won't see each for a while."

"You're always welcome to visit," Renard said. "It doesn't have to be just when we're reshaping national boundaries."

"I need to get back to my family, first. Then I'll think about vacations."

"Understandable."

"I don't suppose you'll say what's coming next for us and when?"

Renard smiled at the floor and laughed through his nose.

"Have I ever?"

When the plane approached the Oakland County International Airport, Jake saw his blue Ford Fusion in the parking lot. The thought of his wife made him happier than he'd been in weeks.

After a smooth landing and a walk to the curb, he saw his wife driving the car. She parked, stepped out, and beamed with a wide smile as she ran to him.

Her embrace was like hugging a jackhammer. Bouncing with excitement, she slammed her head into his jaw, and he bit his tongue.

"Ouch!"

"Sorry, honey!"

"No, it's okay. Let's go home."

He drove, and as her excitement waned, he sensed her melancholy.

"What's wrong?"

"I was scared. All that war going on in China."

"It was the Philippines," Jake said, "although the Chinese were a big part of it. I've been reading about it. It looks like it was some intense combat."

She fell silent, and the gloom cloud drifted over her. He knew that she wanted to ask if he'd been involved, but she couldn't. Having to hold her concerns to herself grated her nerves, and she had learned over years of marriage to express herself through generalities.

"I get scared when you go to work."

"I know."

"I'm trying to start a conversation. You're supposed to say more than 'I know'."

"I know."

"*Erub!*"

"No swearing in Jesus's language."

Marriage to a Chaldean woman had taught him to recognize Aramaic swear words.

"Since when did you care about Jesus?"

"Well, I don't any more than when I left. But if you want to talk about something, I had an interesting conversation with Henri."

Her voice lightened.

"Go on."

"I had time one day and figured I'd ask him about his take on philosophy. You know, as part of my studies. He's pretty well versed in a few schools of thought."

"So, what'd he say?"

"He said that the primary duty of an adult is to be a contributing member of society while providing for one's dependents. Once that's taken care of, the next responsibility is seeking the truth about our fate in the universe."

"I agree. I like Henri."

"Me too."

Jake turned a corner and crossed into Farmington Hills, his

home town.

"He also said that avoiding such truth-seeking, whether by choice or force, is a failure as a human being."

"He's right. You never did any of that until you started talking to Bishop Francis back before he was a bishop. Since then you've been doing a good job."

"Thanks."

"Have you learned anything?"

He reflected upon the terror he had felt inside the *Wraith* and how it reminded him of his mortality. He started to understand that hopes of omnipotence were a fool's folly and that truth resided outside the limits of his personal power.

"Yeah, honey," he said. "You know how I've been reading about the evidence for intelligent design?"

"Yes."

"The evidence will never be perfect, but it's compelling."

"Really? So you believe in God?"

"I didn't say that. But I'm going to pursue the trail of evidence to its end for an intelligent creator. At the moment, though, I'm tending to favor the evidence for it more so than the evidence against."

"You're wishy-washy."

"No, I'm just working the process."

"Is that all you learned?"

"No. There's one thing I'm sure of."

He turned the car into his subdivision.

"Go on."

"Even though I somehow manage to get through every challenge I face, I'm only human. I'm not God, and no matter how many times I try to play God, I keep screwing it up."

"I'm glad you see that honey!"

"I do. And if there's a higher power helping me come home alive to you, I want to know what it is."

THE END

About the Author

After graduating from the Naval Academy in 1991, John Monteith served on a nuclear ballistic missile submarine and as a top-rated instructor of combat tactics at the U.S. Naval Submarine School. He now works as an engineer when not writing.

Join the Rogue Submarine fleet to get news, free audiobook promo codes, discounts, and your FREE Rogue Avenger bonus chapter!

Rogue Submarine Series:

ROGUE AVENGER (2005)
ROGUE BETRAYER (2007)
ROGUE CRUSADER (2010)
ROGUE DEFENDER (2013)
ROGUE ENFORCER (2014)
ROGUE FORTRESS (2015)
ROGUE GOLIATH (2015)
ROGUE HUNTER (2016)
ROGUE INVADER (2017)
ROGUE JUSTICE (2017)
ROGUE KINGDOM (2018)

Wraith Hunter Chronicles:

PROPHECY OF ASHES (2018)
PROPHECY OF BLOOD (2018)
PROPHECY OF CHAOS (2018)
PROPHECY OF DUST (2018)

John Monteith recommends his talented colleagues:

Graham Brown, author of The Gods of War.

Jeff Edwards, author of Steel Wind.

Thomas Mays, author of A Sword into Darkness.

Kevin Miller, author of Declared Hostile.

Ted Nulty, author of The Locker.

ROGUE FORTRESS

Copyright © 2015 by John R. Monteith

Stealth Books

www.stealthbooks.com

The tactics described in this book do not represent actual U.S. Navy or NATO tactics past or present. Also, many of the code words and some of the equipment have been altered to prevent unauthorized disclosure of classified material.

ISBN-13:978-1-939398-30-7
Published in the United States of America